Faithful unto Death

By Sarah Hawkswood

Servant of Death
Ordeal by Fire
Marked to Die
Hostage to Fortune
Vale of Tears
Faithful unto Death

a&b

Faithful unto Death

A Bradecote
and Catchpoll Mystery

SARAH HAWKSWOOD

Allison & Busby Limited
11 Wardour Mews
London W1F 8AN
allisonandbusby.com

First published in Great Britain by Allison & Busby in 2019.
This paperback edition published by Allison & Busby in 2020.

A CIP catalogue record for this book is available from
the British Library.

First Edition

ISBN 978-0-7490-2414-7

Typeset in 11/16 pt Adobe Garamond Pro by
Allison & Busby Ltd.

The paper used for this Allison & Busby publication
has been produced from trees that have been legally sourced
from well-managed and credibly certified forests.

Printed and bound by
CPI Group (UK) Ltd, Croydon, CR0 4YY

For H. J. B.

Chapter One

June 1144

Edwin relaxed. In the cool of the summer evening, he had enjoyed a tryst with his cousin from the next village. Haymaking would start on the morrow, and there would be no spare time for dalliance over the next days. The fallen branch by the edge of the coppice gave enough support for a man to have no cause for worry over his balance when obeying a demand of nature, and nature was certainly being quite vociferous. It was only then, with his braies about his knees, that he saw it, the greyish, pale shape half-concealed by a trail of ivy. A hand was a hand, be it never so dead, and the fingers blackening. He blasphemed, crossed himself, and put too much of his weight upon the branch, so that it creaked ominously. Edwin hauled up his braies, nature's call forgotten, and let curiosity overcome horror. He took the few steps cautiously, as though the dead flesh might suddenly move and grab at his ankles. His heart was thumping in his chest. He drew back a frond, and there lay the body of a man, birth-bare, the flesh beginning to discolour. The eyes at least were closed, and for that Edwin gave up thanks to heaven, but the corpse was ripening, even in this shaded summer woodland.

'God have mercy,' whispered Edwin, and crossed himself again. He was praying for the dead man, but not him alone. This was a man he had never seen before, and if nobody else could vouchsafe his name, there would be a penalty upon the Hundred. A man who died naturally would not be half-concealed in such a place. For a moment he wondered if he might lug the corpse to the Hundred boundary. He had little doubt that is what had happened before. Why otherwise would a man, neither from his village nor its neighbour, be found away from any track or pathway, and robbed of every stitch upon him? The smell, and the thought that the underside of the corpse might be even less pleasant, decided the peasant. He went, with swift footsteps, but a heavy heart, to find Godwin, the village reeve.

Godwin, reeve of Cotheridge, walked the four miles to Worcester at as fair a pace as he might in the early morning sunshine, and went first to his overlord, the Church. The Priory of St Mary held Cotheridge, and his dealings with Father Prior were frequent enough for him not to be overawed. He was also keen to have an ally, and one of greater standing, when he made his bow before the lord Sheriff, William de Beauchamp.

Father Prior's brows furrowed at the news, but he treated it calmly, with all the gravity one might expect from a cleric. He shook his head over the wickedness and agreed to come straight away before the lord Sheriff.

'I know that he is at the castle, for I spoke but yesterday with his lady, who had come to offer thanks for the recent recovery of their daughter from an ague. Assuredly, he must be told of this terrible find immediately.' With which the prior rose, and the pair, with Godwin one step respectfully in the rear, made their way the short distance to the castle and the seat of shrieval authority.

William de Beauchamp received the prior with courtesy and a hint of warmth, which left him when his eyes alighted upon the poor reeve, who wrung his hands as he delivered his tidings.

'And how far from the Hundred boundary?'

'No more than fifty paces, my lord, perhaps sixty, and the man was not fat, nor unusually tall. I have no doubt it was left so that the burden would fall upon our Hundred and—'

'Yes, yes. I am well aware of the "games" played with corpses,' interjected de Beauchamp, testily. Father Prior winced. 'At least if it has not been moved . . . since you found it . . . it may reveal something of use. I will send out my serjeant,' the lord Sheriff paused, and smiled to himself, 'and my lord Bradecote also. I will not have cold murder in my shire that goes ignored. Await them in the bailey.' He nodded dismissal. Godwin withdrew, but as the prior made to do likewise, de Beauchamp halted him with a hand. 'If the body is not named and Englishry proven, the Hundred will pay the fine, Father Prior. There is the law, and I will have it upheld.' He did not add that in uncertain times such as these, a small slice of that fine would not meet the Royal Treasury.

'I understand, my lord. At least the amercement will fall upon all, and not just Cotheridge. It is a small, but profitable, manor for our House. We will pray that the lord Bradecote and Serjeant Catchpoll are fortunate in their enquiries.'

'Your prayers will be needed,' muttered de Beauchamp, as the prior departed, passing Hugh Bradecote in the passage outside the hall. Secular authority acknowledged spiritual.

'I am sorry, my lord,' sighed the prior, which left Bradecote wondering. However, as he entered the hall, Catchpoll approached from the other direction and fell into step beside him.

'Looks like the lord Sheriff does not fancy riding in the heat, my lord.' He sounded cheerful, although had one heard his string of expletives upon hearing of the reason for the prior's visit, his true feelings would have been known.

'What has happened, Catchpoll?'

'A body, that is what, my lord, on the Bromyard road, or near to it as makes no difference, and not fresh either, as I hear.'

'No wonder the lord Sheriff has no desire for the ride, then.' Bradecote wrinkled his nose. 'Sometimes you wish murder was confined to cold months, assuming, that is, the corpse is not some soul who simply felt ill and expired. At which point we just hope his complaint was not one we might catch.'

'True enough, my lord, though often enough murder does seem to spread like a plague. Once you see one, it is more likely you will see another, like magpies.'

The two men looked to de Beauchamp, who had a small, grim smile playing about the corners of his mouth.

'There is a body by the Hundred border, just beyond Cotheridge. Go and see what you can make of it, and if the trail is as cold as the corpse, report back to me.' He managed to make it sound as if the body had been left to occasion him some minor inconvenience.

'Yes, my lord. Do we know—' Bradecote began.

'We know nothing, and like as not we will still know nothing when you have poked about, but we have to make the attempt. Or rather,' he shrugged, 'you will. It is but four miles distant. Take up the village reeve with you as you go, and he will show you the place.' De Beauchamp brushed away a fly, but Catchpoll felt the gesture was also waving them away. Serjeant and undersheriff bowed and set about obeying their instruction. Catchpoll decided he did not want Godwin the Reeve up behind him, and so they brought Walkelin, the serjeanting apprentice, and made sure his horse was sturdy.

Keen to show that the body was barely within their Hundred, the villagers had not removed it to the church, but had covered it with old sacking, and a villager stood 'guard' at a suitable distance upwind. The man made an obeisance that verged upon cringing, as if he expected to be beaten for his pains, and did not look the undersheriff in the face, but gazed at the level of his lordly boots. He said nothing.

'Was this the man who found the corpse?' Bradecote looked to the reeve.

'No, my lord. That was Edwin, but he is working the priory's land today. This is Ulf. He neither speaks nor hears.'

'And this was just as it was found? You have not, perhaps, moved it closer to the boundary?' Bradecote raised an interrogative eyebrow, and looked towards where the ground

11

fell away sharply to the tributary stream of the Teme that marked the Hundred boundary. It cut its way through the high ground in a narrow, vee-shaped ravine. In this summer weather it was barely more than mud with a sluggish trickle of water slipping over it, and where the trackway from Bromyard crossed it the sides were shallower. If the body was over a horse, or on some wagon, there would be no hardship in moving it from one side to the other.

'Not an inch, my lord,' declared the reeve, as though such a thought had never entered his virtuous and law-abiding head. 'All we did was cover him, decent.'

'Thank you. You and . . . Ulf may leave us now.'

The reeve had no wish to linger. He had been close to the body once, and once was enough. He took Ulf by the arm, and, bowing deeply, withdrew to where a lad stood with a handcart. Before he had gone a dozen paces, Catchpoll was drawing back the sacks to reveal the body of a man, lying upon his back, naked as Adam before the Fall. He was clean-shaven, with light-brown hair, and a nose broad in nostril and inclined to the aquiline.

'So all we have is a stripped corpse that could be anyone,' bemoaned Walkelin.

Bradecote looked at Catchpoll. He knew the serjeant could get more than that from their dead man.

'Don't speak foolish.' The serjeant shook his head. 'Sometimes I wonder why I spends so much time a-teaching of you, Walkelin.' He screwed up his eyes and stared at the body. 'I can do this on my own, and I am sure the lord Bradecote here sees what I does, mostly, but let us get you to add your mite. We have a man, but what sort of man? How did he die?'

'He was robbed of everything, so he wasn't a beggar, and he wasn't tonsured so he was not a holy brother.'

'Right, and wrong too. I agree he was no monk, but if you wanted a man to remain unknown, you would take everything from him anyway, wouldn't you? Say "yes, Serjeant".'

'Yes, Serjeant,' mumbled Walkelin.

'So perhaps he was wealthy and robbed, or perhaps he was just got rid of, quiet like, and has had the Hundreds playing "pass the body" these last days.'

'The corpse shows that.' Bradecote phrased it as a fact, but it was half a question.

'Aye, my lord. He has been dead a while, judging by the smell, and the wild beasts have nosed about him.' Catchpoll turned the corpse onto its side. The back was dust-dirty, and the flesh scratched in places. 'He has lain upon his back, else there would be bites here, and whichever Hundred he met his death in, it was not so close by. Tell us why, Walkelin.'

There was a moment of silence, and Bradecote could almost imagine he heard the serjeant's apprentice thinking.

'Because of the colour in the face, hands and feet, Serjeant. They're darker, so he hung over a horse just after he met his death, perhaps even his own.'

'The heavens be praised, he learns!' Catchpoll's smile would have hell-fiends worried. 'Three Hundreds meet within corpse-moving distance here, but even with a low summer level, I would doubt he was brought across the Teme, and if he was, dragging a man up here would be a labour for two men, and suspicious if seen. He might have been killed elsewhere in this parish, or in Broadwas parish next door, though he might have come further than that, even. You would have to ask why, if that were so. So, "not too far" is my thought.' Catchpoll paused. 'But let us go back to who he was. I would say he was what, about thirty, average height, not a peasant, because he was well fed to look at him, and most peasants are thin in the summer before the harvest. It is a time of scarcity and empty bellies. Our man here did not go without.'

'I see now, Serjeant.' Walkelin nodded. He looked more closely, ignoring the smell as much as he could. 'I would say he was used to handling a weapon, or using heavy tools, because his arms are well muscled.'

'Good lad.'

'I would say the former, Walkelin,' added Bradecote. 'There's a scar on the leg that came from something sharp, and since he was no peasant, that was not a careless sickle cut. That is what you would get if struck by a man on foot if you were mounted.'

'I might as well go back to Worcester and sit in an alehouse till the wife has dinner on the table,' grinned Catchpoll. 'You'll be thinking yourselves up to every trick soon enough.' He stood up, easing his back, and folded his arms. 'Go on, then, what else?'

'He was murdered for sure, because, even though you will tell me there are those who would steal from a corpse that died natural and say nothing, Serjeant, he could not have stabbed himself in the back.' Walkelin brushed the dirt away from a distinct tear in the flesh below the ribs on the back. 'No dragging across the ground made that.'

'And there is further proof he was moved. The wound has dry blood about it, but no earth stuck in that blood.' Bradecote could not quite keep the eagerness from his voice. Catchpoll's grin lengthened.

'So what do we do now, Serjeant?' Walkelin looked at him, rather than the undersheriff.

'We takes him to the local priest and gets him buried. What we have seen we remember, and if we are fortunate, someone will report a man of his description who has not arrived where he should, be that home or duty. If we is out of luck, he was off to Compostela on pilgrimage and will not be expected home for months.'

'Which leaves us with two, or possibly three, Hundreds still complaining that the fine, if due, lies not upon them.' The undersheriff looked glum.

'Well, I reckon as the lord Sheriff would be happy enough to make the two only pay up, but as like he will divide it between them.'

'The trouble I see, Catchpoll, is that nobody would be willing to tell us anything in case they bring down the fine upon their own Hundred alone, and are berated by their neighbours for it. It must have seemed a good idea when it was brought into law, but this proof of Englishry is a hindrance to us.'

'We deals with what we have, my lord, good or bad. It would be easier, aye, if all and sundry were keen to tell us anything out of the ordinary, but that's as likely as frost in August.' He pulled at his earlobe, thoughtfully. 'He would have had a horse, as well as clothes, and a sword, too. I doubt they are buried like the squirrels' nuts for winter.'

'And the wound implies he was not on the horse when he died. He might have been dragged off and stabbed in the back, but to me that wound says he was unmounted and taken unawares or distracted.' Bradecote wanted everything they could to lay before de Beauchamp.

'Put a wench before a man, and have her ask his aid and flutter her lashes, and a killer could come up behind easy enough, and our man none the wiser.' Catchpoll shook his head at the folly of his fellows.

'So, it could well be that more than one person is involved in this death.' Bradecote sighed.

'If this man was lordly, he would travel with a servant, at the least. There is no servant now.' Walkelin aired his thought aloud.

'And if the killing was several days past, the chances of finding him in our jurisdiction are . . . non-existent.' Bradecote rubbed his chin. 'What we can give the lord Sheriff is about as much use as bellows with a hole in them.'

'We give what we have. He knows as we do, some crimes remain just crimes where only the Almighty knows the culprit, and the only judgement is His. We asks, mind you, upon the Bromyard road that passes so close, if a man with two horses, one animal better than you would expect for the manner of man, has been seen in the last few days, or one with a burdened beast that ought not to be a pack animal. That might give us the chance to say the direction from which the body came.' Catchpoll was pragmatic. 'The two villages neighbouring along the road, and no more, since I still say why would any take a body further?' He shook his head. 'In truth, the trail is as cold as our friend here.'

Hugh Bradecote's lips twitched. It was one of the peculiarities of Catchpoll that he so often referred to the body as 'our friend'. Sometimes he even talked to them direct, but the answers he got from them were delivered without words.

The little church at Cotheridge was a neat stone building of no great age, and Godwin the Reeve, walking ahead and upwind of the handcart, was eager to tell Hugh Bradecote about its erection. It was clearly a source of village pride. The villagers were out about their labours with the hay being brought in. Father Wulstan, their priest, was sat upon a bench beside the church, taking the warmth of the sun to old bones. He looked up when hailed, and Bradecote thought he had been dozing.

'Good morrow, Father.'

'Good morrow, my son.' The old man lifted a slightly shaky hand in benediction, though the undersheriff was not certain as to whether it was for him or the cloak-covered shape on the handcart. 'My flock are bringing in the cut hay, but you bring not grass stalks but a man cut down, as I hear.'

'Indeed, Father.'

'I did not go to him,' sighed the priest, softly, 'for I would have taken young William from the haymaking. He acts as my eyes, you see, for although I am blessed by the Light of God, He has chosen to dim the vision of my eyes. I see shapes against the light, but deliver the sacrament more by touch and sound.'

Bradecote could see now the cloudy whiteness of his eyes, that matched the babe-soft ring of white hair about his pate.

'The man we bring you, Father, has no name to him, but we adjudge him of some standing, though he has nothing upon him.'

'God has his name, and how he "stood" in this world has no meaning beyond. Serf or seigneur matters not to the All Highest. He shall be interred with due solemnity and respect, but if you find a name to give him for our prayers, all to the good. Bring him into the church.'

Father Wulstan led them into the cool of the building. The nave was not large, but then nor was the village. The chancel arch was crisply carved, its zigzagging lines brightened with red and ochre. The chancel itself was so small as to be almost homely, and the priest moved within it with complete confidence. Until trestles could be brought, the body was simply laid before the altar upon the old sacking. In the confined space the smell of putrefaction was heightened. The priest appeared not to notice it.

'I fear his soul departed some days past, Father,' grunted Catchpoll.

'No matter. His mortal remains are at least to be interred in consecrated ground, and if he died with his sins still upon him, then we will pray the more assiduously for that soul.'

The shrieval party withdrew to the nave, where the smell was less strong, and the priest intoned prayers for the dead. At their conclusion he came to them.

'Father, we do not know if this man was a traveller, waylaid upon the road, nor even from which direction he might hail. The reeve here has said he is unknown to the village, but as undersheriff I ask him and you both, are there any of Cotheridge who might be capable of this deed?'

'None, my lord Undersheriff. I have served this community for the better part of forty years and baptised the majority of my congregation. Man is sinful, and Satan may drag one into the Pit, but to kill a man and steal from his body is not the act of sudden rage or evil. If you had said might any steal an egg or two, or take a roebuck, then honesty would have me say it was possible, but not this crime, not with these folk.'

Godwin the Reeve nodded, his expression solemn.

'To say none could commit a crime would be foolishness, but I agree with Father Wulstan. No man in this village would kill a man like this, not a cold-blooded crime.'

'Thank you, both of you. It is not an unexpected answer, but useful, nonetheless. If we discover the man's identity, you will be told, as will Father Prior in Worcester, where I know prayers will also be offered. We would also know,' Bradecote continued, 'if any villager here saw a man upon a horse, and leading another saddled horse, these past few days. We will not go to the fields and interrupt the haymaking, but ask today and send report – whether yea or nay – to the castle.'

The sheriff's men looked towards altar and corpse, and genuflected, crossing themselves, and then, with a nod to reeve and priest, went out into the warm sunshine and clear air, where the birds had yet a few hours of song within them. They took lungfuls of sweet summer air, mounted their horses, and Bradecote took the road direct towards Worcester, whilst Catchpoll and Walkelin cantered back past the coppice and Hundred boundary, to ask their questions in Broadwas. They rejoined Hugh Bradecote awaiting the ferry across the Severn into Worcester, the tide being too high for fording, and with no positive news.

* * *

'That, I am sorry to say, is all we can tell you, my lord, and how you wish to apportion the murdrum . . .' Bradecote left that hanging. He stood, with Catchpoll one pace to his rear, in the castle hall.

'I see.' William de Beauchamp leant back, a half-smile upon his face. 'Which means you think you can take your lady back to Bradecote and see your hay cut.'

'Well, my lord, we can see no further in this. That is it, unless such a man is reported missing, and even then who killed him is likely to remain hidden.'

'I hate to disappoint your lady, but she will be going home alone, Bradecote.'

'She will?' Bradecote looked startled, and Catchpoll sucked his teeth. Trust de Beauchamp to keep his own counsel until the end.

'I think so. You see, I have received a message from Robert of Gloucester, shortly after you left. The noble earl wishes to know if I have given hospitality this last week to a messenger from the Prince of Powys. He was expecting one to arrive in Gloucester, and he has failed to do so.'

Catchpoll made an unhappy growling noise and spat into the rushes upon the floor. De Beauchamp's own inclination was for the Empress not King Stephen, and he was now thus allied with the lady's bastard brother and chief supporter, Earl Robert of Gloucester, whilst still taking his due for collecting King Stephen's taxes and administering his laws. The earl's name was not popular in Worcester. Only five years ago he had come and fired the town because it had been given to Earl Waleran de Meulan, who was then fighting for the

King. There had been no deaths, for there was some warning of the catastrophe, and the people of Worcester had taken what mattered most to them in chattels and crowded into the sanctuary of the cathedral as the flames took home and business. The only good thing was that there had been not a breath of wind, and before evening a steady rain fell that limited the damage so that some premises remained and others were not in total ruination. Despite this, many had been forced to take shelter with kin or more fortunate neighbour, and rebuilding had taken some months.

'You think the dead man was this messenger, my lord?' Bradecote rubbed his chin. 'Well, it depends upon what sort of messenger Madog ap Maredudd sent, but if it was a man of status . . . It would fit, although I would have thought he would have taken the Hereford route rather than coming this side of the Malverns. If we but knew his description . . .'

'Which is why I am sending you to find out.' De Beauchamp noted the increasing unhappiness of his serjeant. 'And I care not how little you like the Welsh, Catchpoll.'

'It complicates matters, my lord,' declared Catchpoll, grimly. 'We have a dead man, killed for perhaps what he had of value in coin, or what he was, or had done, but this adds the possibility that he was killed for the message itself, and that is politics, my lord.' He said the word as if it were black witchcraft.

'True, Catchpoll. But if Earl Robert wants to know what happened to that messenger, I would like to tell him, even if I say he is dead. That knowledge might give him help or hindrance, I know not which, and have meaning to him.'

21

'And if the man is proved Welsh, does the murdrum fine stand? He would not be proved English, but he would not be Norman "foreign".' Bradecote was thinking of unwilling witnesses.

'A fine is useful coin in hand, Bradecote.'

'Indeed, my lord, but witnesses might be more forthcoming without the threat of losing coin from their own hand.'

'Ah, I see what you mean. Well, I would happily forego it if the crime were thus solved. Yes, encourage tongues with that, on your way back from Mathrafal. You ought to be able to reach the monks at Leominster by tonight if you leave within the hour, and the night thereafter you can take your meat at Bishop's Castle, or Ludlow if you make slower progress. I will give you a letter for the constables there.'

'Er, and what about when we get to Mathrafal, my lord? We do not speak Welsh.'

'What man in his right mind would, barring a Welshman? The prince is bound to have someone who speaks a language you can understand, and at worst Latin. Just be polite, and remember it may be a pisspot of a realm, but he is royalty.'

'Then should you not g—' Bradecote saw the sheriff's lips compress and thought better of the suggestion. 'Very well, my lord, within the hour. I would have an escort for my lady, though.'

'One will be provided, I promise you. Now, give her your news, and make your preparations.'

'I am sorry, Christina.' Hugh Bradecote took his wife's hands in his own.

'I am married to the Undersheriff of the Shire. Such things must be, but have a care, my love, in Wales.'

'Do not tell me you have a dread of it like Catchpoll?' He smiled at her.

'Not a dread, no, but where people can be open with each other and yet closed to you, much that goes on may be hidden, and if this man was killed by one who followed from that court . . .'

'I shall have a care, fear not. Now, de Beauchamp has promised me an escort for you back to Bradecote. Take it, and tell Thurstan the Steward that if the weather holds, I want the hay brought in next week.'

'Yes, my lord.' She dimpled, and dipped in a curtsey, from which he pulled her up and into his arms.

It could not be said that Mistress Catchpoll was as sanguine, when Catchpoll was gathering spare raiment, and a large oiled cloth.

'Wales?' She sounded amazed.

'Do not you start upon that also. I know, I swore I would never go there, but this is at the lord Sheriff's command, so I has no choice in it.'

'Why must all of you go? Why not send just the lord Bradecote?'

'Why? To watch his back, of course. You cannot trust anything Welsh, the weather, the tongue, nor the princes neither.'

Mistress Catchpoll pursed her lips. Her husband's vocal and violent objection to Wales had been known to her since before they were wed, but the cause of it had remained secret all these years, and she had no expectation of it being disclosed now. Her advice sounded remarkably like that of the lady Bradecote.

'Well, have a care. You will need all your wits and more if they say one thing to him, and another to each other.'

'Aye, but I "translate" faces better than most. Whatever the twisting of the tongue, I will know if they speak God's good truth or Welsh lies.'

'Then Godspeed, and mind you do not sleep with wet feet.'

With which prosaic advice, Mistress Catchpoll kissed him upon the cheek, and sent him upon his way.

Chapter Two

Walkelin wore a smile of anticipation for the first five miles, until Catchpoll threatened to wipe it from his visage with the back of his hand. He had never been as far north as Ludlow, which he had heard possessed a fine position and a castle of impressive strength. He thought he had been into Wales, having crossed the Wye as a man-at-arms when William de Beauchamp had visited some kinsman, and there were certainly people there who spoke Welsh, but in truth he was not quite certain whether having a Norman overlord made it England. It felt better to say he had been somewhere 'different' though, and his mother had been impressed. Eluned, the servant girl in the castle kitchens, had merely giggled when he told her of his adventure, but that might have been because he was trying to kiss her at the same time.

His companions were not smiling. Hugh Bradecote was trying to work out how to ask questions without upsetting royalty, and Catchpoll was ruminating upon having to cross the border into Wales.

They crossed the Hundred boundary without so much as a glance into the coppice upon their right-hand side. The corpse would be shrouded by now, even if none were available to dig the good earth before eventide, and before the sun was well risen on the morrow the body would be buried. Summer was not a time to leave the dead above ground. Having learnt all that they could from 'our friend', his physical remains were of no further use, and were cast from mind. It was one of the things that Catchpoll advised, and both his superior and apprentice had learnt swiftly, 'for dwelling upon them as we cannot bring back mars thinking how to catch them what did for them'.

'You realise also we will be too late to eat when we reach Leominster Priory,' grumbled Catchpoll.

'Then we pay good coin for bread and ale when we pass through Bromyard.' Bradecote was not going to let Catchpoll wallow in his morose mood for the entire journey, lest it dull his 'serjeanting' senses. 'All we need is a bed for the night and a break of fast in the morning.'

'Should we be asking about our dead man along this road, my lord?' enquired Walkelin.

'We have little enough to go upon, and if we ask all upon the road, we will not get the bed. Better we ask once we have found out if our victim is this Welsh envoy, when we might have a name, a horse described, and details of his companion, if he had one.'

'And if he is not?'

'In truth, we can report to the lord Sheriff, and thence to

Earl Robert of Gloucester that it was not a messenger to him, whereupon important people lose interest, and with a crime so old and a nameless corpse, we leave justice to God alone.' Experience was making a cynic even of Hugh Bradecote, of which Catchpoll approved.

'But—'

'If you start a-thinking that every death can be paid for, you will drive yourself mad as a hare in spring, young Walkelin. The lord Undersheriff is right. We do what we can, the best we can, but this crime was mayhap four or five days old when we saw the corpse, and every day after that makes it harder.'

'But we found who killed the horse dealer of Evesham.' Walkelin frowned.

'Aye, we did, and against the odds, in my view, but we got a name and he was not far from home. Since most men know who does for 'em, that was a great help. If this man remains nameless, we have no place to ferret, no kin to gain from his death, or lose by it.'

'But if he is the Welshman?' Walkelin now hoped this was the case.

'He might well have stopped at Leominster Priory himself, of course,' suggested Catchpoll. 'Welshmen, of the grander sort, are not so common they would not be noted, and if he stayed the night, they would have spoken with him and known his origin. That would give us a day on which he was alive, and a direction.'

'Where else would he stay if coming from Mathrafal?' Bradecote settled his horse, as it shied from a partridge flying up by the trackway. 'He would either come through Shrewsbury and down to Ludlow, or across as we go, past Bishop's Castle, and either route brings you to Leominster, if he was found between there and Worcester.'

It was, as Catchpoll had anticipated, after Compline, when the three sheriff's men rode into Leominster. On a summer eve, when travellers made good use of the day, however, Brother Porter was excused the first night offices, and remained until the sun dipped in the heavens before taking to his cot. For late arrivals, he acted as guest-master, and bade them a cheery welcome, and even, when their rank and role was declared, disappeared to bring them beakers of small beer to slake the dust from their throats. He was round of face and body, and clearly found the world, sinful as it was, a place full of joys.

'Tell me, good Brother, have you had a Welshman, a man of substance, and probably with at least one retainer, take advantage of your hospitality this last week?'

'Of a certainty, no, my lord. I see all who come and go, and if I missed the one, then I catch the other. We have had a Flemish wool merchant, some pilgrims upon their way to the shrine of St Oswald at Gloucester, and a widow bringing her son to give to God's service here. No Welshman, of whatever rank, has entered the enclave.'

There was no reason why the Benedictine should tell them false, but it muddied matters. Of all the resting points along the potential route, this was the one that was common, this was the one where the man must surely have stopped.

'No sense to it, no sense at all,' sighed Catchpoll, as he rubbed down his horse in the stable. He would not hear of the lord Bradecote seeing to his own mount, and had designated Walkelin to see the animal fed, watered and stalled, but the undersheriff had remained in the horse-smelling warmth, leaning against a stall post, arms folded.

'There is nowhere likelier, even if he turned to the Worcester road upon a whim, instead of going down through Hereford, and it is a steady day's ride to Ludlow, or Bromfield, if you want to conserve your horse, and he would, for it had to get him to Gloucester and back. To go further, well, you would be hard-pressed to reach anywhere else without riding at pace.'

'Unless he knew a place of old,' offered Walkelin.

'But he was Welsh,' snorted Catchpoll, and sneezed.

'Even Welshmen may have kindred in England. Look at the castle in Worcester. There is Nesta, the cook's wife, and Walkelin's wench.' Bradecote tried to find a reason.

'If that is so, we may yet find ourselves upon our return journey stopping every few miles to ask if anyone has Welsh kin. Holy Virgin save us from that.' With which Catchpoll crossed himself, and then spat into the dusty straw.

Brother Porter made sure that Father Prior knew of his important guests, however transient, and their departure next morning was delayed a little whilst the cleric made a gentle fuss of them, and made much of the new buildings in what was a very young house, an offshoot of Reading.

'What he hoped for was more than a gift for a night's lodging,' remarked Catchpoll, sapiently, as they trotted away.

'Well, if he thought I was wealthy he was sadly mistaken,' replied Bradecote, with a wry smile. 'We had a good harvest last year, and there are no rumbling bellies in Bradecote, or my other holdings, but the surplus was not such that I have bounty to dispense to new laid stone.'

'Reading cannot be poor, after what the old King did for it, and this daughter house does not look as if it is suffering. Treasuries always wants more treasure, be they royal coffers or the Church, and think everyone else should provide it.' Catchpoll sniffed.

Walkelin, whose relationship with silver pennies was tenuous, since any time he was paid his mother took the coin from him to keep it 'safe' and keep him from 'alehouses and whores', had lost interest, and was thinking about their victim.

'We need to think backwards, or rather forwards.'

'What?' Catchpoll cast him a look which questioned his wits.

'If it was a Welsh envoy, how far could he have got on his first day, assuming he set off in a morning?'

'Which has itself to be only a good guess,' Bradecote reminded him, 'and there is a huge difference between what a man might choose to do, what a man could do, and what he might be asked to do, in a day. Even the weather would affect it, and we had those summer storms scarce over a week back. My steward was worried about the hay.'

'We have too many unknowns, lad. Give us a few things as fact and we can make good guesses, but at present, you will make your head spin to no good purpose,' Catchpoll advised.

The day grew hot, and their pace, perforce, slackened. Where there was dappled shade there was some relief, but even there the air was still and heavy, smelling of warm leaf litter, and in the open the sun was merciless. They climbed the hill into Ludlow about noon, and went first to the castle, where, within the cool of thick stone walls, Bradecote made enquiry, in case the Welsh messenger had been foolish enough to come into contact with the King's supporters there, or had been reported to them. As expected, he learnt nothing, but was offered meat and wine, and it gave them the chance to rest for the noontide hour before pressing on to Bromfield. William de Beauchamp had given them a note of introduction for the castellan of Bishop's Castle, but both undersheriff and serjeant were already doubting that they could make that far in the conditions.

They reached the priory at Bromfield as the brothers finished None and the guest-master met them, courteous but seeming preoccupied. Bradecote asked after any Welshman who might have passed through about a week gone.

'We often have those with the Welsh lilt here, but there was a man, of some rank and means, here a week ago.'

'Can you describe this man, and was he alone?'

'He was well dressed, about thirty years, light-brown hair, quite a definite nose to him, and he had a servant, small weasel of a man.'

'Can you fix upon the day he came, Brother?'

'Oh yes, my lord, for he arrived late on the Feast of St Alban, and stayed the day after also, for his horse needed shoeing, and was spent. He said he had seen the forge at the roadside, but the blacksmith told him he would not shoe a horse so blown for fear it would fall down upon him and he be blamed if it was dead. And the man said that he would not reach his destination for the night after the work was completed so would rest the

31

day here. Brother Porter can confirm all this. I will call him.'

Catchpoll frowned, but said nothing, as a novice was sent to the gate. Brother Porter was the antithesis of his counterpart at Leominster, being a beanpole of a man, with a stoop, and a long, rather disconsolate-looking face. His eyes had a dullness, and his voice was a heavy monotone of miserable disapproval.

'Yes, the proud Welshman rode in late of an evening a week past, his horse weary, and with a shoe near casting, so he said. His servant's mount was in a worse condition, and it was no wonder that they remained a second night. I thought the beast might collapse before it reached the stable.'

'Then it would help us to speak with the smith,' remarked Bradecote.

'You will get nothing from him today, my lord.' The guest-master looked grim, and Bradecote was aware of a feeling of foreboding.

'He brought in the body of his wife to the church but two hours since and is gone to help dig her grave.'

'She is to be buried so soon?' Bradecote could feel Catchpoll as tense as he was himself.

'Father Prior dare not wait, for the corpse is . . . she went missing, you see.'

'When?' Catchpoll was terse.

'The day after St Alban's. She was going to visit her ailing mother but a mile away, and never returned, nor reached it either, as was found. Gyrth has been searching for her all the hours of daylight, and more, since. He found her, half-covered in branches.'

Undersheriff and serjeant exchanged glances.

'You have sent to Shrewsbury?'

'Indeed, but I heard from a traveller but yesterday there was some trouble in the north of the shire, near Ellesmere, so . . .'

'May we see the body? It is not in our jurisdiction, but at least something may be gained that can be writ down for any who come after to seek truth for her.' Bradecote added his own question.

'I will ask Father Prior, my lord, and you will need strong stomachs or weak noses.'

The brother went in search of the Prior Osbert, and returned a few minutes later, accompanied by a small, bird-like cleric and a grey-faced man in his forties; a strong, muscular man but one at the end of his physical and mental strength. His shoulders sagged, his arms hung loosely at his sides and his head looked too heavy to lift. Bradecote wondered how he had the energy to help dig a grave.

'This is Gyrth the Blacksmith, my lord, and Father Prior, who has given his permission as long as Gyrth agrees.'

The prior inclined his head, but the man barely acknowledged them. His eyes were blank.

'We would see the body, that it might help discover what happened, and who was involved.' Bradecote spoke gently to the man, who simply nodded.

The prior and the grieving widower led the way to the church, which had become part of the priory, but of which the western end was still for the use of the parish. They passed into the south transept, for there was a chapel where a body might be kept discreetly. Neither man passed beyond the blankets that had been erected as a swift screen to hide what lay within, although no blanket could contain the smell. The air was heavy with incense and all the sweet herbs they could muster, but death, old death, overpowered everything else. Bradecote had become used to the smell of death in the year since he had assumed the position of undersheriff, but even he felt his gorge threaten to rise. Walkelin choked and turned away. Only Catchpoll remained apparently unaffected. He approached the covered corpse and drew back the sheet. The smell hit them afresh. Bradecote crossed himself, and swallowed hard, trying not to breathe through his nose, but finding the smell caught in his throat anyway.

The body was in a poor state, and blackening. What surprised Bradecote was the age of the woman. He thought, though he could not be certain, she was perhaps no more than late twenties, and he had somehow imagined her older. The priests spoke of 'the corruption of the body' but it was unpleasant to stand within feet of it. Catchpoll moved closer than Bradecote could dare, and spoke softly.

'Poor wench. What happened to you, then?'

He touched the neck. The discolouration would have long ago concealed any marks made before death, but he grunted.

'She was strangled, choked hard, I would say. The voice box is crushed, and had she been found earlier I would swear there would be black bruises before this black.'

'I do not understand the gown,' murmured Bradecote. 'The bodice and shift are ripped, but the skirts have been cut clean top to bottom with a knife.'

The body had not been stripped, for none wished to deal more than needful with it, and the skirts were gathered over the lower part of the body like a shroud, but one side folded over the other.

'We must ask the smith how she lay when she was found, but my guess is the bodice was ripped while she lived, and struggled, but the skirts . . .' He looked grimly at Bradecote, whose slightly green tinge paled. There was silence as they both considered the meaning.

'Sweet Jesu, a man would do . . . that?'

'There are some as would. If he were fired enough by her, by her fear even, and she just beyond breathing . . .' His hand went to the folds of the gown, and Bradecote looked away. He had seen bodies naked, but this was too much.

'Too far gone to tell,' grunted Catchpoll, and Bradecote was conscious of relief.

'Do we need more?'

'No, my lord, she can tell us nothing else, may God have mercy upon her.' The clothing was made decent again, and Catchpoll stepped back from the body. They turned and went out through the archway, where Walkelin waited, shamefaced, and the prior stood in whispered conversation with the bereft husband.

'Master Smith,' Bradecote showed the man courtesy, 'we must ask where you found the body, and how it lay.'

'I wonder I did not find her three days past, for I searched the coppice that runs beside the trackway north to Onibury.' His voice sounded distant. 'There was branches over her, see, and . . . It was the air as told me.' He swallowed hard. 'She was on her back. You don't need to tell me what happened . . . I can guess easy enough. If I finds him, I'll slit his codd and roast—'

'We think your wife tried to defend herself, and any . . . dishonour, was after she could know aught of it, if comfort that can be.'

'She was a good woman. Men said as I was fortunate to have so comely a wife, but look what it led to. I wish she had been ugly, before God I do.' The blacksmith buried his head in his large hands and wept.

Bradecote asked the prior to send a monk who could scribe for them, that a message might be left for those with jurisdiction who came later. Prior Osbert nodded, sending Gyrth back to his grave digging, and walking slowly into the sunshine that seemed too cheerful for what they had just seen. He beckoned a brother, who went hurriedly away.

'This is very bad for our community, for the parish community also. Such evil as men do.' He sighed.

Bradecote looked at Catchpoll, who nodded.

'Father Prior, we are on our way to the Prince of Powys, concerning a messenger who did not arrive in Gloucester, and a body found by the road between Leominster and Worcester. The Welshman who was here on the Feast of St Alban is likely to be that body.' The prior crossed himself. 'However, we know that the man also had dealings with the smith about his horse, so there is a connection, and the woman,' he paused, 'I am sorry, we never heard her name . . .'

'Leofeva.'

'Leofeva went missing the day after the feast day, when the Welshman had his horse shoed. We cannot discount the possibility, if not probability, that the man who committed the crimes against her is now also dead.'

'We should pray for him also, but, do you know, today that is very hard,' sighed the monk.

'I will leave what Serjeant Catchpoll found from the body, and our thoughts, though they cannot be proved, for any who come to see about justice for the smith's wife. Beyond that, Father Prior, we would ask only your hospitality for the night, and will be upon our journey to Mathrafal early in the morning. If the man rode here in one day, and I doubt he set off at dawn, we can do so without crippling our mounts, and there is always Bishop's Castle if we need to break the journey for one more night.'

'I will have Brother Cellarer have bread and cheese provided for you, however early you depart, my lord.'

'Thank you. Here is the scribe, I take it?' Bradecote watched a youthful brother bustling towards them with inkpot, quill and vellum.

'Brother Laurence, yes. He has the best hand in our small community. Brother, come to my lodging and set down all that the lord Undersheriff dictates, and if you wish to see me afterwards, I am willing to speak with you.' Prior Osbert looked at Bradecote, and that look said that he thought the monk might find his duty harrowing.

So it proved to be, and several times the young Benedictine paused, his hand shaking. Bradecote spoke quietly, and firmly. He had to be accurate as best he was able, however upset it might make the innocent monk. When he had finished, he thanked him, and sent him, as a command, to his prior.

Outside, Walkelin, now a much better colour, was still apologising to his serjeant.

'I should be hardier of stomach, Serjeant. How can I . . . ?'

Catchpoll looked over Walkelin's shoulder, and gave Bradecote a small, grim smile.

'You had best tell him, my lord, as stomachs do not obey heads, not all the time.'

'No, they do not, Serjeant. Walkelin, it was all I could do not to be sick at the stench, and if Serjeant Catchpoll was the stronger, put it down to his nose being older and dulled by the odours of many years.'

'Thank you, my lord.' Catchpoll's lips twitched. 'I was going to say it was experience, but there.'

They departed a little after dawn, about the fifth hour, when the day was cool, and made good time, stopping only to let their horses drink at a stream, where they ate the bread and cheese from the priory, and then at Bishop's Castle, mid morning, where they checked whether any had seen a Welshman of lordly mien with a servant 'like a weasel', and were not at all surprised to hear a negative answer. They were offered ale, and a rest for their horses, and took only the former, wanting to travel as far as possible before noon.

They halted about midday where there was a clearing with dappled light and good grass, unsaddled the horses, and let them graze for over an hour, with Walkelin set to hold the reins, on the grounds that they did not want something sending their animals off and leaving them in the middle of nowhere. As Catchpoll explained also, holding reins was not a lordly task, and sergeants were too long in the tooth to do so. Instead, he lay with his head against his saddle and snored gently. Hugh Bradecote did not sleep, but wondered if the hay was being cut at Bradecote, and how his Christina and baby Gilbert were faring in the heat. The reverie was pleasant, but had to be limited. He kicked the saddle under Catchpoll's head, which woke him with a start and expletives, for above the canopy of trees a dark grey cloud presaged a heavy shower. They mounted, and set off, shortly afterwards hunching against a vicious patter of droplets.

'Must be in Wales now,' grumbled Catchpoll. 'Wet, miserable, and that is just the men.'

Bradecote shook his head. Catchpoll was just about the most sensible and pragmatic man he knew, but his loathing of the Welsh was both irrational and unshakeable.

'So how do we tell the Prince of Powys his man was quite possibly a rapist and murderer, without him cutting our bollocks off for . . . treason?' Walkelin sounded nervous.

'I thought you liked the Welsh,' murmured Catchpoll.

'I like Eluned, who is Welsh, which is not the same thing.' Walkelin now sounded aggrieved.

'Well, let me see, how about we do not tell him that at all? How about we act as if we know nothing and see what they reveal to us?' Catchpoll sneered.

'But—'

'Serjeant Catchpoll is right. We see what they tell us, because they may have pieces of this tale we do not, and may also have pieces that we do, but they choose to conceal, which also tells us things.' Bradecote urged his horse to a trot.

'Now that,' remarked Catchpoll, with a sudden death's head grin, 'is the way a sheriff's man ought to think. Mark you that, young Cabbage for Brains.'

* * *

Mathrafal, seat of the Prince of Powys, lay on the left bank of the Banwy, but by the time the sheriff's men reached it they were beyond caring about its location or defensibility. They were wet, very wet, for although the rain had ceased a good three miles beforehand, they were skin-soaked and cold, and the sun refused to come from behind a Welsh cloud and warm them. They arrived, Bradecote realised, looking like drowned rats, and hardly impressive. They were met at the outer gate by a guard that looked as if it knew its business, and were suitably wary, especially when the visitors spoke in languages they did not understand. Bradecote tried English, Norman-French and Latin, with little hope. He resorted to pointing at himself, giving his name and saying very clearly 'Sheriff of Worcestershire'. He would rather be mistaken for William de Beauchamp than kept out as a nobody.

After a few minutes, and several huddled conversations, the guard indicated they should dismount, and advance. At that point another man appeared, to whom the guards spoke as one, and he, without saying a word, beckoned them into the outer bailey, where lads came to take their horses. Lacking a means of escape gave them a feeling of vulnerability, but there was no alternative. Bradecote looked at Catchpoll and shrugged.

Chapter Three

Having been passed up the chain of command until somebody felt senior enough to make a decision about them, the trio were led through an inner bailey to a large hall, which was clearly where Madog ap Maredudd held court. How they were announced, Hugh Bradecote could not say, but the murmur of voices ceased, and all eyes fell upon them, some blatantly hostile. He stepped forward, with Catchpoll and Walkelin a little to his rear, and presented himself to the man upon a heavily carved seat that stood on a dais. Bradecote made a low obeisance. Treat him as if he were King Stephen and he cannot be offended, he told himself.

'Noble Prince, I am Hugh Bradecote, Undersheriff of Worcestershire, and I come at the behest of William de Beauchamp to discover if a man found dead in our shire is your man, or not.' He spoke clearly, and not too slowly, lest it sound patronising. If nothing was understood, then surely they would seek out an interpreter, as de Beauchamp had suggested.

Madog ap Maredudd simply stared at him blankly, and the lady at his side glowered as if he had said something offensive. There was a heavy silence, but Bradecote felt it was some game being played as to who would 'break' first. A man coughed, a woman giggled somewhere in the background, and Bradecote caught movement out of the corner of his eye.

Walkelin, ignoring a growling noise from Catchpoll, stepped beside the undersheriff, bowed so low his face nearly met his knees, and then announced in a nervously overloud voice, 'Trowin mower.'

Madog ap Maredudd frowned in perplexity at the mangled Welsh, but as comprehension dawned that changed to displeasure.

'What in the name of the Rood did you say?' whispered Bradecote, scarcely moving his lips.

'Big nose,' murmured Walkelin, reddening.

Catchpoll gave an anguished sigh. Walkelin realised that his words had been taken as an insult, and thought fast. He mimed a big nose, and then tried another word he had asked Eluned to give him, and which he had been trying under his breath these last few days.

'Shovrithiyess?' He fell upon the floor and lay on his back with eyes wide open, and acted a knife being stabbed into his chest.

The prince looked to a heavy-set man at his right hand, who shrugged. Then a voice from among the courtiers was heard.

'*Llofruddiaeth!*'

There was a collective intake of breath, followed by an

exhalation of understanding. Madog ap Maredudd looked Bradecote in the eye and spoke.

'I have your tongue, a little. I understand more. I was at Lincoln.' His words were accented and with a peculiar lilt, but intelligible.

Bradecote cursed himself. It made sense enough. If Madog had fought beside the Earl of Chester and William of Roumare he would have learnt at least a smattering of Norman-French.

'We end this . . .' Madog gestured at Walkelin, now flushed of cheek and dusting down his cotte, and said something which Bradecote took to be a name. A man with wavy hair and a close-cropped beard came forward, bowed low to his prince, and then very slightly to Bradecote.

'I am Rhys ap Iorwerth. My mother was from Chirbury. I will say your words true to my prince.'

'Thank you, Rhys ap Iorwerth. Tell him that a messenger he sent to Earl Robert of Gloucester did not arrive as expected, and that the body of a man, and a man used to bearing arms, and well fed, was found near the road from Bromyard to Worcester. We wonder if it is the same man.'

Madog had pricked up his ears at the name of his 'ally' Robert of Gloucester. Catchpoll watched him carefully as Rhys translated. His face registered surprise and thoughtfulness, and Catchpoll would have sworn the news was indeed news to him. A question was asked in return, which came swiftly to the sheriff's men.

'He had a big nose, you say. What else would you say of him?'

'Of his height,' Bradecote pointed out a man, 'and beardless. His hair was like unto his.' His finger moved to another. 'He

43

had a scar upon his right leg, calf to shin.' He waited for the words to be given in Welsh. From somewhere in the hall came a woman's muted cry, and many crossed themselves. That needed no translation.

'My prince says that the man you found indeed sounds like Hywel ap Rhodri, whom he sent to Earl Robert. He wishes to know how and why his man was murdered, for murder was the word your man used.'

'His body was found naked, some days dead, and stabbed in the back. We would ask if he had others with him, a companion, a man-at-arms or servant?' Bradecote decided saying that they had no idea as to motive was not helpful.

'He left with Rhydian, his servant. I saw that myself.'

'There has been no sign of this Rhydian.' Bradecote did not state the obvious conclusion to be drawn.

The lady seated beside Madog spoke to him, ignoring the sheriff's men.

'May I ask what the noble Lady said?' Bradecote judged her to be Madog's wife. She was not young, but still possessed a certain cold beauty.

'She said that Rhydian was a faithful servant, faithful even unto death.'

'Yet we have no second body. Hywel ap Rhodri's body was moved, but it makes no sense to move one corpse but not the other.' Bradecote spoke half to himself. 'If Rhydian should return, perhaps wounded, would the lord Prince send to Worcester with that news?'

Rhys asked, and Madog nodded, and spoke at length.

'My prince says that Hywel ap Rhodri was a true and loyal

man, a man of courage, and he would have justice for him. He says that if some Englishman killed him because he was Welsh, it is an insult to Powys and to him as his overlord.'

'Tell the noble Prince that we will do everything we can to find out who killed his man, and why. Having a name to him is a start. You may tell him he was buried decently and that the monks of Worcester, who hold the manor in which he was found, offer prayers for his soul.' Bradecote paused, and then continued. 'I swear that we will make every effort to find his killer, from whichever side of the border they may come.' Rhys scowled, but Bradecote drove home his point. 'If there is anything here that has a bearing, then for the sake of justice, the prince's as much as my king's, we must know of it. Chasing about Worcestershire for a killer is of no use if Hywel ap Rhodri had enemies, or rather, one enemy, here. More murders are committed by someone the victim knew than otherwise, and that applies in all realms.'

Rhys did not look mollified, but repeated the words for Madog's benefit. The Prince of Powys nodded again, and his wife cast Bradecote a look of loathing, which Catchpoll thought interesting.

'Upon which day did Hywel ap Rhodri leave?'

'I can tell you that, my lord Undersheriff. He left on the Feast of St Alban,' Rhys answered swiftly.

'And I would ask the lord Prince, not of what he wished to send to Earl Robert, but how the Earl Robert knew to expect a messenger, and thus knew him to be late?'

This Rhys translated, and Madog ap Mareddud's face became stormy. He was silent for a minute, and then, very slowly, spoke.

'My prince says you pry, but he says this also, that he

arranged some time since that he would send a messenger upon the Feast of St Alban, with a decision to the Earl Robert upon a matter which is no concern of yours.'

Which puts me in my place, thought Bradecote.

'I am not concerned with the politics of the mighty, only justice for the murdered.' He made sure his voice was calm, reasonable. It did not aid them, alienating royalty, not when they stood in their hall.

Madog looked hard at the undersheriff as he heard the interpreter, and gave a slow nod, perhaps of acceptance. He then informed them that they would be accorded all due hospitality, at which he also looked about his court, making it clear they were under his protection, and followed it with a vague speech about kingship and responsibility, which Bradecote also took to be for local consumption. The audience was then at an end, and Bradecote, Catchpoll and Walkelin withdrew. They were shown to a small, and rather gloomy, chamber off the inner court. A man-at-arms waited outside.

'Do you get the idea we are meant to think we are "honoured prisoners"?' murmured Bradecote.

'It is so we will not contaminate their pure Welshness,' scoffed Catchpoll. He turned to Walkelin and cuffed him about the ear. 'And that is for speaking without leave and very nearly getting us killed through simple stupidity.'

'Ow!' Walkelin rubbed the injured ear and looked to Bradecote. 'I am sorry, my lord. I meant no disrespect, but it was so . . . it felt like the air was being sucked away. I thought I could help, but then I realised I was actually talking to a prince and I forgot most of the words I had.'

'Help and hindrance start with the same letter,' grumbled Catchpoll. 'If he had not decided you were as entertaining as a fool with a sheep's bladder on a stick, they would be throwing our remains to the wolves that undoubtedly inhabit the forests hereabout.'

'Enough.' Bradecote raised a hand. 'We survived, and now we have to sort out how far what has been handed to us aids our hunt.'

'If this Hywel ap Rhodri was the flower of nobility the Prince of Powys describes, then he must have been killed for what he had about him, or what someone thought he might have,' asserted Walkelin, glad to get away from his own failings.

'Or that was praising him too high, to cover "politics".' Catchpoll sucked his teeth. 'Mind you, I would swear the news of the death came as a surprise to his overlord.'

'And Madog would not arrange to send a messenger to Earl Robert and then have him killed on the way. If you are a prince who has suddenly cause to distrust a vassal, but have no proof, simply send him on some minor military duty and arrange he is found by an arrow.' Bradecote shook his head.

'Then what about a rival, who wants to be more in favour with the prince and saw him as in the way?' Walkelin was dogged. 'You could not see every face among the court, Serjeant Catchpoll.'

'No, I could not, and from the sounds of it, there was a woman who took the news badly.'

'I did not think to ask if he was wed,' murmured Bradecote to himself.

'If he was, then it was his prince's choice not to tell us, and his duty to see her treated properly.' Catchpoll was thinking of something else.

47

'Ah, but might it then be that it was she who had him killed, paying the servant to do the deed?' Walkelin brightened.

'The one problem I have with all these ideas is why wait until he was in Worcestershire, not just over the Shropshire border?' Catchpoll's eyes narrowed. 'It makes no sense, no sense at all.'

'Then the killing was not ordered from Powys?' Bradecote accepted Catchpoll's reasoning.

'It would seem less likely, unless very devious, my lord.'

'If that is so, he was not killed for his message, since none would know he carried it, outside of Mathrafal, and not because of who he was, since he would be just a passing stranger. That means we are indeed back to Walkelin's idea of him being murdered for horse, sword and scrip.'

'And do not ask me why that sits ill also, my lord, because I cannot say why, but it does.'

'Which leaves us with no reason at all, and if it were a madman, such a fellow would leave the body where it fell.'

'Ah, but his neighbours would have moved the body because of the fine, and if they feared he was dangerous, well, there is always an accident with a scythe whilst cutting the hay . . .' Catchpoll was in gloomy mood. Bradecote wondered if he would brighten when they crossed back into England.

'Thus, we have a name to please priest and monks, but new people, important people, wanting answers we cannot provide.' Bradecote raised his eyes to heaven and prayed.

Having kicked their heels in the bare chamber for some minutes, they heard an interchange in muttered Welsh, and the man-at-arms peered round the door and beckoned them to follow him once more. They were led to a larger room where they found their bedrolls rolled out, Bradecote's upon the narrow cot against the wall of the chamber.

'Ah, the reason for our waiting. What odds they went through all we have?' Catchpoll asked, miserably.

'Of course they did. They trust us as little as we trust them, I doubt not.' Bradecote was sanguine about it. 'But we have nothing to hide, and it is possible that someone here does. Having learnt to be as suspicious a bastard as you are, Catchpoll, I suggest we check our possessions for ourselves, lest anything has been "added" to incriminate us if we sniff too close to a truth.'

This appeared to cheer Catchpoll, in a perverse way. He set to inspecting his meagre baggage with zest, although whether he was pleased because his superior had developed such a level of cynical suspicion, or because it all proved how devious, dastardly and downright untrustworthy were their hosts, Bradecote could not say.

Just as these precautions were completed there came the sound of footsteps on the stone flags outside, and a knock upon the oaken door, although the door opened before Bradecote could invite anyone in. A burly man-at-arms pointed at the undersheriff and said something that may or may not have been a request. Bradecote looked blankly at him. The speech was repeated, with the addition of a beckoning finger, and a raised hand that indicated the other two were not to join him.

'You will not go alone, my lord?' Walkelin's voice belied his nervousness.

'I am under Madog ap Maredudd's protection,' declared Bradecote calmly, but using the name that the burly man would understand as a shield, and shrugged. He nodded to the burly man and followed him from the chamber.

'What do we do now, Serjeant?' asked Walkelin.

'We wait.'

Hugh Bradecote followed the broad back of his guide to a spiral stair, which the man almost blocked with his bulk, and up to a chamber, where the man halted, and then realised that not to enter would mean Bradecote squeezing past him in a manner that would please neither of them. With every indication of not wanting to open the door, he nevertheless lifted the latch and opened it wide enough for him to step within, have the 'Englishman' pass him, and withdraw swiftly, so that he might perhaps be forgotten.

The chamber was furnished for a lady. There were hangings upon two walls, a heavy chest, a curtained-off box bed, and a carved chair set by a brazier, which heated the cold chamber, whose stone held no warmth from the summer outside. In the chair sat the lady from Madog's side, her expression imperious. Bradecote could understand her pride, for it came with royal blood, but not the revulsion that mingled with it. A little apart, and with eyes downcast, stood Rhys the Interpreter. The lady spoke, her eyes upon her visitor, and when the translation was made, Bradecote felt that however correct the words, they lacked the antagonism of the originals.

'My lady asks, what is your true reason for coming to Powys?' Rhys looked uncomfortable.

'The reason is the one I gave before all. We seek the name of a murdered man, and from that knowledge, if possible, to catch his killer.' Bradecote copied the lady, and looked at her, not Rhys ap Iorwerth.

'If you think him a man of Wales, why did you bother?' The lady's sarcasm needed no translation.

'Because our King's justice applies to all within his kingdom,' replied Bradecote, diplomatically, 'and because also Earl Robert of Gloucester wishes to know what happened to the messenger he was expecting. Earl Robert is . . .' He paused for a moment, as Rhys ap Iorwerth caught up in translation, and, as he finished, the lady interjected.

'He is a king's son, a son acknowledged.'

Bradecote remembered then. Bastardy was different in Wales. If a man was content to call his by-blow 'son', and have him accepted, he might inherit, or share inheritance.

'Indeed. So we are here in good faith, noble Lady, and with no underhand motive.' He kept his voice calm. 'Is there any aid you might give us?' It was impertinent to ask, but in private it might be easier to hear facts than in a hall full of power and aspiration, doubt and double meaning. She stared at him. 'Forgive me, lady, but when the noble Prince spoke of Hywel ap Rhodri with such praise, you did not look as though you agreed.'

She looked irritated when the words were given to her in Welsh, but answered.

'My lord judges a man as a man. The virtues of courage and loyalty to his lord I would grant to Hywel ap Rhodri, but he has, or had, a fault.'

'Which is?'

She spoke, calmly, but her words evidently shocked the interpreter.

'He . . . my lady?' Rhys ap Iowerth gasped and stared at her. She nodded, her lips compressed, and he continued his translation as though the words were wrung from him. 'He cannot keep his hands off women. He uses honeyed words to seduce, but if honeyed words do not succeed . . . he does not understand "No".'

'You have . . .' Bradecote faltered. He could scarce ask a royal dame if she had been molested.

The lady Susanna's voice dropped to as near a growl as a woman's voice could go, and that passion echoed into the translation, 'If you were thinking to ask if he had dared to even look upon me, I can assure you he valued his skin too much for that impertinence, and if he had . . . Then it would have been me, personally, who would have flayed every inch of it from his back. No, he laid hand upon one of my ladies. The Holy Virgin be praised he was disturbed before he could do more than upset and frighten her.' She looked directly at Rhys the Interpreter, and spoke rapidly, a command, not something to translate. It was no more than a few phrases, and Bradecote did not need to understand the words to get her meaning. The man paled and gabbled some assurance. No doubt he had been warned that spreading any word of what was said would see his tongue cut out. Then she returned her gaze to his own face. 'If Hywel ap Rhodri has met a violent death, look you to someone whose woman he has dishonoured.'

'In this court?'

'Not to my knowledge, but one does not hear all things. If it were so, why wait until he was so far into England?' She said the word as if England were situated at the gates of hell, on the wrong side, and Rhys ap Iorwerth also gave it weight. 'Mayhap it is just common English thievery and killing.' Her lip curled.

'Thievery and killing are common to all lands, and all peoples.' Bradecote felt unnaturally piqued at her animosity to his land. 'When we were at Bromfield, they spoke of a Welshman who was undoubtedly this Hywel ap Rhodri, and a woman went missing the day he was there. She was found the day we arrived, dead the day she went missing from the state of the body, strangled and . . . dishonoured, probably after death.'

Rhys did not at first translate. He stared at Bradecote, and spoke softly. 'I cannot tell her that.'

'Tell her.' Bradecote was firm, and, hesitantly, Rhys ap Iorwerth did so.

'You say this to shock me?' She looked at Bradecote.

'I say only what I believe is true.'

'To blame a Welshman.'

'Welsh or English, men are the same beneath. There are bad Welshmen, lady, and good Englishmen.'

'Do you know so little, Undersheriff? You speak to Susanna ferch Gruffydd.' Rhys spoke without prompting.

Bradecote looked blankly at him, and the lady demanded that Rhys keep nothing concealed. When he repeated both his words and Bradecote's she rose from the fur-draped seat upon which she had been sitting very erect, and said but one word, hissed at Bradecote.

'*Cydweli.*'

He frowned, and then slowly coloured. Kidwelly. It had not been what he would have done, but Gwenllian ferch Gruffydd, wife of the Prince of Deheubarth, had led a small army, and after a bloody battle hard men do hard things. The 'English' lords had beheaded her on the field of her defeat, beheaded a woman. It sat badly with him, but . . . From the names he assumed they must have been sisters.

'I am sorry.' He wished the words unsaid, even as Rhys spoke them in Welsh. This woman did not want his sympathy, would no doubt find it insulting and pointless, and he could not deny the latter. A muscle quivered in her cheek, and her eyes burned. He tried to return to the situation of the present. 'I did not ask before the lord Prince, but was Hywel ap Rhodri, however he strayed, a married man?'

'Yes.' The answer came from Rhys, without him translating to the lady Susanna, who spoke sharply to him again, clearly wanting every word passed to her. Bradecote looked at the man. One fist was clenched, and his expression was one of repressed emotion, though which emotions it was hard to tell.

'Was she the lady who cried out at our news?'

This time the words were translated before Rhys replied in the affirmative.

'May I speak with her?'

'No!' This time the answer was a cry from the heart. The lady Susanna looked as surprised as Bradecote. She spoke to Rhys, firmly, but without heat, and he answered her. Bradecote wished he could read faces as well as Catchpoll. His guess was that she was either the interpreter's kinswoman, or he thought softly of her. The lady spoke again, and this time Rhys ap Iorwerth translated.

'She is distraught, and she knows nothing beyond the fact that she has lost a husband.'

'May I have at least her name?'

There was a silence, then another exchange in Welsh.

'Her name is Angharad, Angharad ferch Caradoc.' Rhys bent his head, as if in defeat. The lady Susanna spoke again, and he translated with his head still bent, and his voice dead.

'Go back to England, where your king is scarce a king and you have an empress not quite a queen, and find out who killed Hywel ap Rhodri. You may scrabble in the dirt and find nothing, Englishman, but if you do, send here the truth.' Susanna ferch Gruffydd got up from her chair and turned away from him. He was dismissed.

Bradecote reported the extraordinary interview to his companions.

'Shame it is we cannot understand their tongue, else we could ferret good and proper over this.' Catchpoll sucked his teeth. 'A good, sound motive for a killing is the dishonouring of a woman, and we can include them as enjoyed the process with them as didn't, if you are looking at vengeful men, be they fathers, brothers, or husbands.'

'It still makes no sense for it to be a killing that springs from here, though.' Bradecote shook his head. 'They understand blood feud well enough. It would have happened here, or just into Shropshire.'

'Unless the family wanted the shame kept quiet. What if the maid, as was, looked like to contract a good marriage?' Catchpoll was thinking.

'And did the servant, Rhydian, have a sister, or a wife?' suggested Walkelin.

'Or it could be that Hywel ap Rhodri thought his mission to Gloucester provided more opportunities, more nameless maids, and someone did for him because of it?' Bradecote was almost talking to himself.

'Leastways, we have another motive other than base theft, or court intrigue.' Catchpoll tried to sound optimistic.

'If the last one, we must also look to England too. We discounted anyone killing the messenger for the message, but if someone fiercely for King Stephen, and with knowledge that Powys and Gloucester both side with the Empress, heard of a boast to impress a wench . . .' Hugh Bradecote rubbed his chin, and sighed.

It could not be said that the trio felt that the evening meal would be convivial. Hugh Bradecote would be most likely accorded the status of honoured guest, despite the prevalent animosity, and he would be at least treated with outward courtesy. Catchpoll was not so sure he and Walkelin would be as fortunate, and warned his apprentice to be wary of any food he did not recognise.

'You never know. Something peculiar might have them all laughing at us, whether we seem to like it or loathe it. We are under the prince's protection, so poisoning us is not an option, but making a laughing stock of us is well within the boundaries. And remember not to try your youthful lustiness in gawping at maids. That wench you have in the castle kitchens,' and Catchpoll's leer was pronounced, 'is enough Welsh female to make eyes at.'

Walkelin looked suitably cautious, though it went against

the grain in a young man who appreciated his food, and vowed his total devotion to Eluned of the kitchen.

They thus departed to eat according to their station, and Bradecote felt that if none would ply him with unpleasant 'delicacies', he knew that he was watched even more than he was watching, and would need a clear head and politic tongue all evening. His host wanted to know of the situation between King and Empress, and the undersheriff had no problem in sounding confused. Who knew, he thought, how things would unfold, although his own view was that the Empress herself had lost her chance back in '41, when she had held King Stephen her prisoner, but had alienated the citizens of London and failed to have the crown placed upon her head. She had made enemies, and more was said against a woman's rule, but she was the mother of a son, and one day, if Eustace, son of the King, proved weak . . . No, sounding unsure was no deception.

He ate, though at times he thought the glare of Susanna ferch Gruffydd willed him to choke upon his meat. He wondered if Angharad ferch Caradoc was present, or whether, in her fresh grief, she eschewed food. He could scarcely stare at all the ladies present and try to deduce if one sat with a broken heart. If truth was spontaneous, then she had not expected bad news about her spouse. The cry had sounded natural enough, but . . . Bradecote was recalled to the present by Rhys asking a question from a man who asked if it was true all English lords had hoards of silver buried beneath their manors. Bradecote blinked in surprise and laughed.

'If that were so, then there would be nobody taking sides with King or Empress either. It would simply be neighbour against neighbour and the winnings to the biggest "wolf". My only "gold" is that of the grain of the harvest, and my silver pennies will cover the cost of a length of good wool for a new winter gown for my lady.'

'You are married?' The question came from a woman.

'Married, and with a son, still a babe in arms. Wife and heir are my precious jewels.'

'He speaks like a bard,' laughed a man down the table, and amidst the laughter, Rhys translated that sally back at least.

Bradecote watched his subordinates 'roll in' to the chamber, Walkelin singing a song his mother would undoubtedly have clipped him smartly about the ears for even knowing. The door shut behind them, and the song continued only as long as the footsteps could be heard in the passageway outside. At which point Catchpoll, digging Walkelin sharply in the ribs, bade him cease forthwith, though less politely.

The words of censure on Hugh Bradecote's lips died, and he smiled ruefully.

'So, whilst I was watching everything I said, and scrabbling for even useful hints, you were soaking up more information than ale, I presume?'

'That was our intention, my lord.' Catchpoll was at least in a more cheerful mood. 'We had to imboo . . . drink, a little more than we wanted, just to make it look good. We are not ale-soaked.'

'Not,' confirmed Walkelin, with the hint of a hiccough.

'Sit down, and let us hear what you have discovered, if anything. Pox on it that it was all in a foreign language.'

'I heard the word "peck-her-diris", after Hywel ap Rhodri's name,' declared Walkelin, with a touch of pride, and little slurring of the words.

'Sounds something the priest would give you penance for,' grinned Catchpoll.

'Well, he would.' Walkelin looked almost smug. 'It means sinful, or wicked.'

'Just why did your kitchen-wench feel the need to teach you that one, Walkelin?' The grin widened, and Walkelin blushed.

'We know he "sinned", so does that really help us?' Bradecote frowned.

'I could not understand the rest of what was said, but there were sounds of agreement, and head nodding. I think his reputation was known widely.' Walkelin desperately wanted his information to be a grain of use.

'Which means fathers and husbands would keep an eye upon their womenfolk, given the chance.' Catchpoll was serious once more.

'Sometimes the chance dissolves like mist, and men like Hywel ap Rhodri, who take advantage, ofttimes do it when there is an unexpected hint of opportunity. It gives them added excitement.' Bradecote's distaste was obvious. 'They may even like the woman to be fearful.'

'True enough, my lord.' Catchpoll rubbed his eyes. 'I caught no words, but when they weren't talking about us, and none too admiringly either, our man was present like a ghost at the feasting. I could smell it, sense it. It rankles that he died in England, and mayhap by an English hand, but among the lower sort, I would say few will pray for his soul.'

'And I am not so sure that is not true among the upper levels of this court either. For all that Madog made much of his good points, and may have shut eye and ear to his weakness, he did not spend time at the meal bemoaning his loss of a good man, through Rhys the Interpreter, who still looked as happy as a kicked dog. You know, I think we are unlikely to get more from Mathrafal. Best we get back and report what we have, and set to work at home.'

'God and his saints be praised,' murmured Catchpoll devoutly, and crossed himself, then belched.

Chapter Four

They awoke cold, but not hung-over, and Catchpoll needed no encouragement to pack his chattels ready for departure. Walkelin disappeared to the kitchens, where his ability to mangle the word for bread, combined with mime and a cheeky grin, brought them a loaf and a good portion of cheese. Bradecote wanted to show they were keen to depart, and if Madog ap Maredudd thought that meant without food, they would look so much the keener. They went to the great hall, when he thought prince and court might break fast, and indicated they sought admittance. The guard simply stood aside and the undersheriff strode in with his subordinates behind him, more confident than the day before. Bradecote made deep obeisance.

'We would take our leave of you and be about finding the murderer before the trail becomes colder still, lord Prince, but would ask for any knowledge which might aid us as we depart.

Do you know whether he took the route through Shrewsbury, or through Bishop's Castle, and did he carry upon him a letter of introduction that marked him as a royal envoy? What horse did he ride, and what manner of man is his servant, Rhydian, to look upon?'

Catchpoll gave a slight movement of the hand, which stilled Walkelin, who was wondering why the undersheriff asked a question to which he already knew the answer.

The questions were translated. Some discussion followed between Madog and three men who looked to be trusted counsellors. Then Rhys ap Iorwerth gave the replies.

'My prince says that Hywel ap Rhodri was to stay at the abbey of the Benedictines in Shrewsbury, and then at the priory in Bromfield, to avoid King Stephen's castellans, and travelled as a man about private business. He would be circumspect. Lords change sides, so it was better than none know that he bore messages for Earl Robert of Gloucester.'

Bradecote acknowledged this as wise.

'And his horse? His man?'

'The horse was just a brown horse, but it had a star upon its forehead, and a white stocking to one hind leg. Rhydian rode a grey pony. Rhydian is of small stature, looking more youth than man, and has dark hair.'

'Thank you. That will help us.'

There was a short, uncomfortable silence where nobody seemed to know what to say, then the Prince of Powys spoke directly to Bradecote, slowly but clearly.

'I send Rhys ap Iorwerth with you.'

Bradecote opened his mouth, but said nothing, and glanced

at the interpreter, who looked as if he had been sent to fend off the slavers of Dublin single-handed. Madog ap Maredudd spoke to his man, so that the rest of his speech was plain to the court, and made so to the Englishmen. Rhys did not care to look Bradecote in the eye.

'My prince sends me with you into England, so that I may report back when you have discovered who killed Hywel ap Rhodri, to save the lord Sheriff of Worcestershire sending word,' he paused for a moment, then continued, 'and to see that English justice is fair.'

There came a snort of derision from Susanna ferch Gruffydd, but Bradecote looked to her husband, and held him eye to eye.

'Noble Prince, the laws of England give even greater weight to the lives of those not of its breeding' – he did not say that those laws were to protect the overlords, and bring in coin to the Royal Treasury – 'and a death such as that of Hywel ap Rhodri cannot be emended. It is an offence against our lord King, and as his officer, it is my duty to see that all is done to discover the culprit and bring them to punishment. I do my duty.' He spoke heavily, slowly. It was important that everyone understood that he had not merely come to spout diplomatic nothings.

Rhys ap Iorwerth translated, and it sounded to Bradecote that he gave similar weight to the words, however incomprehensible. Madog nodded.

'Then God grant you success, King's man,' he paused, 'for no prince commends failure.'

Bradecote wondered if the hint of threat was real, or for the benefit of the rest of his audience. He bowed, low and with a degree of flourish. Let Madog decide if that was real or for show, he thought. He could sense Catchpoll bristling behind him and hoped he would follow his lead.

'I would leave within the hour, Rhys ap Iorwerth.' He wanted to assert that if the interpreter came with him, he was under his command, and if Madog had underlying motives for sending him along, then perhaps a swift departure would limit the amount of instructions that might be given, unless the man had been closeted with his prince long before the audience, which looked most unlikely from his reaction. Bradecote backed away for several paces, bowed again and turned on his heel to stride decisively from the hall.

Catchpoll was muttering before they reached their 'cell'.

'English justice!' he fumed. 'A Welshman to doubt English justice!' Catchpoll kicked his tidied bedroll. 'Not that the bastard is sending a spy to find out all he can for himself.'

'"Lord Bastard Prince" to you, Catchpoll,' admonished Bradecote, gently. 'It complicates matters, but we deal with the crime as we always do, discuss it as we always do. Whatever he learns, he cannot report back until all is over, and I would have him see we have nought to hide in this.'

'And what if Prince Madog is connected to the death? Think how easy it would be to ensure nobody is found, or worse, an innocent made to look guilty.' Catchpoll's expression was grim.

'You said yourself, Madog ap Maredudd looked surprised at the news of the death.'

'Aye, I did. But that is not to say he might not have done some thinking, and asking of questions, and already know the answers we are sent to seek. We dabbles with politics, here, my lord. Justice, English or Welsh, may come second to the plans of princes. Does the Prince of Powys want the murderer found? Does he want it to seem as if his man was killed because he was Welsh, and provide a flame to fan that would lead Welsh bowmen and spearmen into England to thieve and burn upon the "reason" of mistreatment of a well-born countryman?'

'You are the one who says "we deal with what we have", Catchpoll. Neither you nor I can influence what goes on above our level.' Hugh Bradecote gathered his accoutrements and smiled wryly at Serjeant Catchpoll. 'Just be pleased we are leaving Wales, yes?'

'I am, but wish we were not bringing part of it with us, that is all,' grumbled Catchpoll, unappeased.

They left Mathrafal, knowing more than the eyes of the gate guard followed them, and initially in silence. It gave gravity, thought Bradecote, and an awful lot of what had taken place within the walls had been for show. He wondered if that was how life was in the entourage of any prince and gave thanks that he was spared such a life. They trotted along the trackway and Rhys kept his own silence until he realised that they were not taking the road to Shrewsbury.

'But that is where Hywel ap Rhodri stopped. Do you have such confidence that you need not follow his path . . . my lord?'

'We already know his path, Master Interpreter, and he did not ride to Shrewsbury and thence to Bromfield, but direct to Bromfield in the one day, nearly killing his horse in the process.'

'There is no sense to that.'

'There was if he thought there was an opportunity to take advantage of a woman, where he would be swift gone and swift forgotten.' Hugh Bradecote spoke sternly. 'You heard the words of Susanna ferch Gruffydd. Hywel had a failing, when it came to women. You heard what we had found also. At first the murder and rape looked as if they were the crime of a moment, an opportunity taken, but now we know he saved a day of his journey for no other sane purpose, it looks very much as if he felt confident he would find some woman to use in Bromfield. He planned his foul crime.'

'This is just linking two things you "hope" connect, my lord Undersheriff.'

'Do not be so sure. Hywel saw a forge at Bromfield where he might have his horse shod. He went there on the day he stayed, and it was the smith's wife who went missing. He had been there, almost certainly seen her, and selected her as a likely victim.'

'Victim you say, but he wooed with words, he was a seducer. He had no time.'

'He was "one who did not understand 'No'," remember?' There was an almost imperceptible pause. 'A man who gets used to taking what is not fully offered, or offered at all, can learn to like it, prefer it, like to see the panic, the fear, and may come to see seduction as a time-wasting preamble.' Bradecote spoke with bitter anger, thinking of his Christina's treatment at the hands of her first husband, who was another such man.

'You paint the picture of a monster, and I never saw a monster in Hywel ap Rhodri.'

'But you are not a woman.' Walkelin thought the point worth stressing.

'I still cannot believe—'

'Believe,' growled Catchpoll.

'We will not force on to Bromfield,' announced Bradecote, after another hour, 'since we departed well into the morning. Better for us to stay at Bishop's Castle tonight, Ludlow tomorrow, and then have two longer rides, to Leominster and then back to Worcester. We can stop at Cotheridge and give a name to the priest in passing.'

'Then what do we do, my lord?' Walkelin questioned.

'Well, we ask west of Cotheridge about the two men, and now one man and the horses. Someone must have seen something, and if Rhydian was the loyal servant as described, there is another corpse yet to be discovered.'

'Perhaps he was buried?' Walkelin suggested.

'Why bury one and merely hide the other? No, if this Rhydian was "faithful unto death", he must be above ground, howsoever hidden,' Catchpoll gave a grim smile, 'and summer will aid us, because what we will find now will not be easy to recognise, but easy to smell.'

Rhys ap Iorwerth crossed himself. He was shocked at the way these Englishmen could discuss murder and corpses with so little concern.

'We try all the nearby manors, and this time it will not be a casual questioning, so Broadwas, Knightwick, Doddenham . . .' Bradecote wanted to sound as if he had a plan, however thin.

'Doddenham?' Rhys repeated, and all three sheriff's men stared at him.

'You have heard of it?' Bradecote asked.

'I have heard the name, somewhere.' Rhys ap Iorwerth frowned, and repeated the name to himself. The others waited, in hope. 'It was to do with Hywel ap Rhodri,' he shouted, as if he had found a great treasure.

'And . . . ?' Catchpoll encouraged.

'Some relative. My mother being from Chirbury, he mentioned it once. I think perhaps his mother's sister, or mother's brother, or a cousin. He had English connections and that was the place.'

'Then I think we have an answer to a question, at the least.' Bradecote sounded relieved. 'We wondered where Hywel ap Rhodri stayed if he went from Bromfield and yet did not stop at Leominster. He could not have reached Worcester, and there was no other likely point, but if he had kin, where better to break the journey, even if it meant a long day from Bromfield.'

'So do we stop there instead of Leominster?' wondered Walkelin.

'And alert any who needs to find themselves proofs that whoever killed the man it was not them? I think we had as well report to the lord Sheriff, and then return. What say you, my lord?' Catchpoll looked at Bradecote.

'I agree. There is nothing so fresh we must find it immediately, unless that be the body of Rhydian, but a day will not be such a difference now. We ride with our news to the lord Sheriff, and he can at least send to Earl Robert of Gloucester to confirm the messenger is not coming.'

'And I can sleep in my own bed,' said Catchpoll, with a smile.

* * *

They reached Bishop's Castle in the afternoon and were greeted with recognition. Rhys ap Iorwerth dismounted a little stiffly, and Bradecote guessed that he did not often travel far beyond Mathrafal. Catchpoll made much of sending the lord Undersheriff to the constable of the castle, and having Walkelin see to his horse once again, but also indicated Rhys should also remain and care for his own animal. The question of the man's status was open. He was not, Bradecote would swear, from among Catchpoll and Walkelin's 'sort', but as the interpreter he had been treated more as a servant than advisor, and his demeanour was not assertive. In Catchpoll's eyes, a man who did not act like a lord, and was Welsh to boot, was not going to get deference. Bradecote was a little surprised that the man seemed to accept this.

The constable was keen to hear of the atmosphere at Mathrafal. Powys was like having a large and irascible dog as a neighbour, and when it snapped, Bishop's Castle was in easy range of its teeth.

'We have had it quiet for some time, and the longer it remains so, the more I wonder. The safest thing for us is when the Welsh forget us and fight among themselves. Then we relax.' Raoul the Constable sighed. 'Thus it has always been along the Marches, before ever we arrived.'

Hugh Bradecote made vague agreement, but was secretly a little surprised at the man retaining what was clearly a sense of being 'alien' to the land. Then he smiled secretly to himself. The truth of the matter was that, after a year as undersheriff, and Catchpoll's influence, in his mind 'them' and 'us' had the 'us' as the sheriff's men, and the 'them' as everyone else. How delighted this would make the serjeant.

It could not be said that Catchpoll was feeling particularly delighted at that moment, although the beaker of beer in his hand was very welcome. Catchpoll was thinking, and was frustrated at how much was pure conjecture. Knowing as much as possible about the victim was always a great asset in finding out who killed them and why, so the journey to, and into, Wales had not been a waste of time. They had a name, and very useful detail about the man's character, which provided a very solid motive if anyone had discovered him molesting a woman. That might be seen as a perfectly legitimate killing, but might have been hidden to cover the dishonour to the woman and the shame to the family.

Walkelin found him with a frown of concentration.

'Serjeant? You have thought of a problem?'

'Problem? No. I tries not to do that, because the more you looks at problems, the more problems you finds. So I do not deal in problems, I deals in solutions.'

'So have you thought of any solutions?' Walkelin enquired.

'More I am sorting out what solutions are . . . available, though I think our visit to Doddenham will be what takes us ahead. What we will find out there, I do not know, but that must be the key, because that is where he was killed.'

'Not nearer where we found him, Serjeant?'

'It would be too strange a coincidence. No, something he did there, said there, or perhaps even just being there at that time, was the thing that got him killed.'

'But if what Rhys ap Iorwerth says is true, they are kin.'

'So? More folk are killed by people they know than strangers.'

Catchpoll shrugged and set down his empty beaker. 'You have learnt that, well enough.'

'But not kin who knew him. They may not even have known he was kin until he arrived and declared himself, gave his lineage. They are kin without such deep feelings that might include hatred.'

'We know none of this for sure. Bear all in mind, but keep that mind alert to possibilities.'

The next day to Ludlow was not going to test them, although Rhys ap Iowerth grimaced as he settled himself upon his horse, which made Catchpoll grin behind his back. Bradecote worked upon the sound premise that men were men, whatever their language and culture, and made an effort to engage the Welshman in conversation, giving a little and learning a lot, trying to see if there were differences that might alter the way they looked at the situation before them, and more especially whether Madog ap Maredudd would do so.

'Your laws, laws upon rape and murder, they do not treat them as less than the worst sort of crimes?'

'We follow the Cyfraith Hywel. They are undoubtedly of the worst sort, but it means in general a heavy *galanas*, what you would have as wergild, according to the victim's rank. The same applies to rape, but if the man cannot pay then he loses the contents of his codd.'

Bradecote nodded, for that seemed similar to English laws, where castration was an accepted penalty.

'If a man is poisoned, the poisoner suffers death.' Rhys paused. 'I suppose that is because one could not poison someone

71

upon an instant urge from anger, or in self-defence, but must plan it beforehand.'

'A death that is concealed, the body hidden away, cannot be paid for under our law, which is why the death of Hywel ap Rhodri is accounted unemendable. It must be from the same reasoning, for hiding the body of the victim implies neither accident nor defence, but intent and foul purpose. I cannot say whether the lord Sheriff will judge that your wergild fine will be paid to Hywel's kindred. The man was killed in England. If it should turn out that Rhydian killed him, mayhap your prince will arrange matters in Powys. I do not know, and I cannot guess.'

'But Rhydian was loyal, my lord.'

'And how many times in history has a man been killed by his closest friend, servant, advisor? We cannot discount him until or unless we find him as dead as his master.'

Rhys crossed himself, and then thought of another unpleasant question.

'If this woman, the wife of the smith, was indeed killed by Hywel, is he also shown guilty of defiling her . . . If she was dead already?'

'He killed her in the process of defilement, so whether she was unconscious or had just ceased living, I call him guilty of both, though you can argue your fines. I tell you true enough, Master Interpreter, if he had committed such crimes in my shire, and was not yet dead . . . he would wish he were, even before arraigned before the Justices.' Bradecote spoke between gritted teeth.

Rhys looked at Bradecote's profile, and felt his own guts knot, for the undersheriff's face was implacable, merciless. He paled, and Catchpoll, listening and observing, smiled inwardly. It was good that the Welshman should know that the lord Bradecote could be that hard, and it was good that the lord Bradecote had hardened. Only a year ago, he had been a well-meaning novice, full of moral certainty, and 'we do not treat prisoners roughly'. He was still somewhat inclined to that idea, but in certain cases . . . the smile became overt.

Catchpoll retained the ghost of that smile as they rode into Bromfield. They came to the forge, where the sound of hammer upon anvil was reassuringly normal, but when they saw the face of Gyrth the Smith, that lie was exposed. He might beat the red-hot iron, but in his heart every blow was upon the man who had taken his wife.

'My lord.' Gyrth nodded his head in brief deference, and thrust the cooling iron back into his fire.

'Master Smith. We are on our way back from Powys and have a name to the Welshman whose horse you shod, and who was found killed in our jurisdiction. His name was Hywel ap Rhodri.'

'Was it indeed? I doubt he died shriven, and assuredly I hope not, for I curse his name and would see him burn in such hellfire as makes my forge the warmth of sun upon grass.'

'Are you so sure it was him?' Rhys ap Iorwerth asked, hesitantly. The smith stiffened at the Welsh accent.

'He was here the night before I shoed his horse, poor beast. He saw my Leofeva, spoke to her, though she answered not, and he saw her, when she told me she was about to depart to see her mother, as he waited for the shoeing next day. What more do you need, Welshman?' The appellation was spat at Rhys.

'Could you show us where you found the body of your wife,' Catchpoll suggested, 'just in case anything upon the ground adds to that proof?'

Gyrth nodded, lips compressed, and called out. A lad of about ten emerged from the cottage and came to him. The child looked, like his father, rather lost.

'Keep the fire from hunger, Alwi. I will be back very soon.'

The boy said nothing and looked at the strangers nervously. The smith jerked his head and led the way back along the trackway and, after about five minutes, took little more than an animal's path, that showed repeated use by fox or badger, through the undergrowth to a gap where a fallen tree had created a space too small to call a clearing. He pointed to one side where twiggy branches had been cast at all angles.

'I found her over there. The branches covered her. Must I remain?'

'No need, Master Smith. Thank you.' Bradecote gave him dismissal, for which he seemed very grateful. Rhys just stood in the patch of sunlight that added glints of red-gold to his trimmed beard. The sheriff's men stood also for a moment, and then Catchpoll squatted onto his haunches with a groan of aching bones and touched the ground where the body had lain. His eyes searched.

'Look hard, Walkelin, in all this space. If the smith's wife resisted, and I think she did, for there are broken bramble stems on that track no wild thing ever made, then mayhap a trace remains of him who harmed her.' He did not sound hopeful, and was thus most surprised when, after about five minutes,

Walkelin let out a cry of success. He turned. Walkelin stood up, something between finger and thumb.

'What is it, Walkelin?' asked Bradecote.

'A silver coin, my lord.'

'Such a thing could—' began Rhys, and then stopped.

'This coin was not minted in England,' announced Walkelin, turning it over and over. 'It is not of the King, nor older kings.'

'Let me see it.' Bradecote held out his hand, and Walkelin placed it gently in his palm.

'It is very old. Many hundreds of years old. I saw a coin like this once, and it was from when the Romans were here.'

'So it is still no proof,' Rhys suggested, but his tone was not convincing.

'Have you ever seen such a coin, Rhys ap Iowerth?' Bradecote stared at the interpreter, who sighed, and nodded.

'We are the true people of Britain, the people here when the power of Rome came, and when it left. We were pushed by the fair men from across the sea and retreated into the West. Those that could took their silver with them. Sometimes it is found among old walls, old settlements. I cannot say it did not come out of Wales, but, my lord, you said yourself you saw one such in England.'

'I did, but this one has a small hole in it. I think it was worn about a neck. We can ask the smith but . . .' Bradecote saw Rhys redden. 'Was it Hywel ap Rhodri's?'

'I do not know, I swear that upon oath, my lord, but something silver and small as a coin was about his neck, for he touched it sometimes. I never saw it close, and would say none other did either.'

'But it is sufficient to quash any doubts, Rhys ap Iorwerth.' Bradecote did not pose it as a question.

'It is sufficient, my lord.' Rhys crossed himself again. 'Shamed am I that a Welshman did this, and I will pray for the woman.'

'And her motherless son, and wifeless husband.'

'For them too, my lord.'

Bradecote thought the point had been made enough. He nodded to Catchpoll, and they retraced their steps to the road, and thence to the forge, where the smith's son was now whispering blandishments to the velvet nose of the undersheriff's horse. The smith looked up, and his hammer was held ready to fall. His eyes questioned.

'We found a proof.' Bradecote would say no more with the boy before him, and the smith closed his eyes for a moment, and the hammer fell, like a clapper on a tolling bell, thought Bradecote.

The Welshman was very quiet as they rode into Ludlow, and clearly overawed by the castle's size and magnificence. Rhys ap Iorwerth was watched, quite overtly, by one of the castellan's men, lest he pry where he ought not, and pass such information as he might find to his prince. The castellan smiled when Bradecote told him how impressed the interpreter was by the castle. They rose early next morning, the Worcestershire men keen to return to home ground, and passed through Leominster before noontide. They rode into Cotheridge as the late afternoon saw the shadows begin to lengthen and the sun's heat dissipate into a more pleasant warmth. The horses were tired, too tired when they halted to shake away the flies that gathered about their heads. Bradecote took Rhys ap Iorwerth to the little dwelling next to the church, where they found Father Wulstan among his fowls, talking as to children. He heard the firm footsteps, and turned, asking who approached, for they were not steps he knew.

'Hugh Bradecote, Undersheriff, good Father, and Rhys ap Iowerth out of Powys. We can name the man you buried that came to you dead by murder as Hywel ap Rhodri, and the man with me would see where he lies, that he might report back to the man's kin in Mathrafal.'

'God be praised that is so. Our prayers are as valued even without a name for the poor man, but this is good news indeed.' He stretched out an arm and trod towards his own door, where he could follow the line of the wall, and then stepped with a disturbing confidence past his church door as though his eyes were cleared of their fog, and thence about the north-west corner and to where Bradecote and Rhys ap Iorwerth could see the recently turned earth.

'You see, my lords?'

'We see, Father Wulstan. Thank you.' Bradecote wondered if he ought to mention that the man might be in more need of prayers than the elderly priest could ever imagine, but decided against it. Why tell the good man that a rapist and killer lay in his consecrated ground?

Rhys ap Iorwerth pressed silver into the priest's palm.

'For Masses for his soul, Father.'

'Fear not, my son. They shall be said.'

It was a very quiet Rhys who mounted with the sheriff's men

shortly afterwards. They set off eastwards towards Worcester, and he appeared lost in his own thoughts.

'I wondered, look you, if it was right to give money for prayers for one who had done so much evil,' he murmured eventually.

'Surely, such a man has more need of intercessions?' Bradecote glanced sideways at him.

'But perhaps he deserves to pay. We all of us sin,' and Rhys coloured, thinking perhaps of his own sins, confessed or not, 'but few so coldly – so repeatedly, as it seems – and beneath a surface of being as every man.'

'If you were asked to give coin, you gave coin.' Bradecote shrugged.

Rhys did not reply. A mile on, he halted his horse, with a request that they wait, and some show of embarrassment. He dismounted and forced his way from view into a patch of elder and cobnut.

'He seems a reasonable sort of man,' murmured Walkelin, as they waited, and, seeing the expression on Catchpoll's face, added, 'for a foreigner, of course.'

'And what counts as "foreign", Walkelin?' enquired Bradecote, with studied casualness.

'Why, a man from across the borders.'

'Of Worcestershire, or England?' The tone remained the same, and Walkelin, focussed upon the question, did not catch Catchpoll's warning look.

'Ah, now, my lord, I knows better than to say my shire, for that just makes a man not local. No, "foreign" is them from over the borders.'

'His mother was from Shropshire.'

'Then he is but half-foreign,' beamed Walkelin.

Catchpoll groaned.

'So it is down to parts, Walkelin, eh? Makes it difficult for me, of course.' Bradecote ignored Catchpoll, but for a different reason.

'My lord?' Walkelin was all open innocence.

'Well, you see, my father's sire was born in Normandy, and my mother's was a Breton. What does that make me?'

'Lord of Bradecote,' replied Catchpoll, swiftly, as Walkelin's eyes widened in horror, and he flushed to the roots of his hair.

Hugh Bradecote laughed loud, and his horse skittered at the unexpected noise.

'Next time you want to dig a hole, Walkelin, use a spade,' growled Catchpoll, as the undersheriff calmed his mount, 'and be thankful the lord Bradecote possesses a good humour.'

'But I only answ—'

'Shut up, and look stupid, which should not take much effort.'

Rhys returned, with further apologies, and the quartet trotted to the Worcester ford, with castle and priory beckoning them from the far side.

Chapter Five

William de Beauchamp looked at the four weary men before him and listened. When Bradecote finished speaking he sat in silence for a minute.

'I shall send to Earl Robert and tell him the news, though by now he must know something untoward befell the messenger.'

'My lord Sheriff, my prince would have me go to the Earl Robert, for I carry the message lost with the death of Hywel ap Rhodri.' Rhys spoke up, and the three men who had travelled with him turned to look at him in surprise. 'Upon my return I would go to wherever the lord Bradecote is asking his questions, and can then report back afterwards as my prince commanded me.'

'Kept that dark,' muttered Catchpoll, and Rhys looked almost apologetically at him.

'No deception was intended, but my prince could not discount that someone knew Hywel ap Rhodri was his

80

messenger, and sought to prevent him for that reason. Travelling as I have has been protection in numbers and by disguise, if you will. I was ordered to do so by my prince.'

William de Beauchamp remained expressionless.

'You will have escort there, but if you have cause to await some answer, that returns with you alone. Madog ap Maredudd's business is with the Earl Robert, not this shire.'

'As you see fit, my lord Sheriff.' Rhys bowed low.

'I would speak with my men, privately.' De Beauchamp gave the command, and the Welshman withdrew. 'Well?' The sheriff looked at Bradecote and Catchpoll.

'My lord?' Bradecote frowned.

'Could there be anything in the idea that the messenger was killed for the message?'

'I doubt it, my lord.' Catchpoll pulled a cogitating face. 'Knowing he had a message means someone from Wales knew why he was sent, and we comes back to why wait until into Worcestershire to kill him? None upon the journey would know of his role, and the bastard's habits mean that we might suspect any man within three miles of the death who has wife, or daughter, sister, or even mother.'

'I agree with Catchpoll, my lord. It stretches belief too far to imagine a political murder.' Bradecote shook his head. 'We can but try in Doddenham and see what we can unearth.'

'Which may be Rhydian the servant,' added Walkelin. Catchpoll glared at him, but the serjeant's apprentice had lost his initial terror of the lord Sheriff when perforce he had to work alone with him, and, although very respectful, no longer shook silently in the background hoping not to be noticed.

'Which certainly might be the messenger's horse. A good horse would be kept, and if our arrival is not suspected, it will not be hidden.' Bradecote stifled a yawn. 'My lord, we have ridden the day long, and would be back to Doddenham early on the morrow. With your permission . . .'

'Get to your beds, yes. If Earl Robert gets his message, from whatever man, and knows the previous one is dead, we have done all he would want of us. As for Madog ap Maredudd, well, Powys is thankfully not our neighbour, not our problem.'

'Amen to that,' growled Catchpoll.

Bradecote, Catchpoll and Walkelin set off next morning, yet again on the road to Leominster, which was becoming depressingly familiar. For Walkelin and Catchpoll at least, the night had been spent in their own beds and with home cooking, though Catchpoll did not reveal what Mistress Catchpoll said to relighting her cook fire long after she had damped it down. Bradecote had eaten well, from what the castle kitchens could provide, but wished he could have gone further by a few miles and slept in the comfort of his manorial bed and with his loving wife.

As they reached Broadwas they went to the fields and asked after any horses of the description given of Hywel ap Rhodri's white-stockinged brown, and the smaller grey. The villagers were hot, and toiling hard, and the trio got shaking heads and blank looks in answer.

'You realise, my lord, that if Hywel ap Rhodri was killed in Doddenham, then him turning up in Cotheridge is almost funny.' Catchpoll looked sideways at the undersheriff.

'Why?'

'Because Cotheridge is an outlier, so to speak, an isolated parish of the same Doddingtree Hundred as Doddenham.'

'You jest.'

'Not on such things as Hundred boundaries, my lord.'

'Would everyone in Doddenham know this?'

'That I cannot say, though they would know Broadwas is across their boundary and in Oswaldslow Hundred, so why take it so far?'

'Mayhap the person who took it did not know, but thought that going even further into the next Hundred, as they saw it, would make it seem not like some corpse-over-the-border game,' offered Walkelin.

'It is to be hoped that is true, or else we have to go back and speak severely with all those honest-looking liars in the Broadwas fields.' Bradecote swore, softly and in English, which made Catchpoll smile.

The manor of Doddenham was held by one Thorold FitzRoger, and William de Beauchamp described him as 'a man of small stature, clever, but not as clever as he thinks himself'. Bradecote had a vague image of a man in his mind, which was confirmed when they rode into the bailey of a neat manor with a well-kept wooden palisade, and found the lord about to go hawking, for a man stood close by with a falcon upon his gauntleted hand. FitzRoger was of average height, but of slender, almost delicate, build, his hair fair and fine as an infant's, and his eyes had a hooded look.

'Thorold FitzRoger?' Bradecote questioned, but with authority.

'Yes.' The man looked at the undersheriff, with a similar vague idea of having seen him before.

'I am Hugh Bradecote, de Beauchamp's undersheriff. We come seeking information on one Hywel ap Rhodri.'

'Hah!' snorted FitzRoger. 'Do not tell me, for I will guess. He has been straying with maids across half the shire, yes? And there are men aplenty after his blood.'

'One at least achieved his goal, for Hywel ap Rhodri is dead, stabbed in the back.' FitzRoger looked mildly surprised, but not at all upset. 'We heard he was a kinsman of yours.' Bradecote kept his tone casual.

'Kinsman, yes, but not one I would choose to take into my hall a second time.'

'He was here, then, a little under two weeks past?'

'About then.' FitzRoger made no attempt to deny it, but sounded vague. He dismounted and sent his horse back to the stables. 'You will want all, no doubt. Best you come within.' It was an invitation, but made without enthusiasm. The sheriff's men dismounted, and followed him into a hall that was wooden framed, but with a stone solar and upper chamber at one end, with battlements above it. The tower end would provide security in times of peril, but there had either been lack of manpower or inclination to replace the rest of the hall in stone. The window shutters were opened wide to let in the summer air, and pools of sunlight flooded across the rush-strewn floor. A sparrow chirruped in the eaves. FitzRoger waved a hand at a bench against one wall, and Bradecote sat, though Catchpoll and Walkelin remained standing, leaning a little against the wall itself. FitzRoger took his own seat.

'He arrived the better part of two weeks ago, late one evening, as you said, and declared himself my cousin.'

'You had no reason to doubt him?' Bradecote asked.

'None. You see, he could give accurate account of his ancestry, knew much of my mother, and even the month of my own birth. Besides, my mother confirmed all he said. He was kin, and hospitality his due.'

'But you did not like him.' It was a statement.

'At the first I had neither liking nor dislike.' FitzRoger shrugged. 'All I knew was what stood before me. It did not take him long, however, to raise hackles. Free he was, with the serving maids, as if they were there to amuse him. That Welsh tongue of his spouted sweet words, but it might as well have been a serpent's forked tongue, and he was patting and fondling them, as I discovered, whether encouraged or not. He made mischief in the two full days he was here, and glad I was that he was gone on the morning of the third day.'

'Did he give a reason for being in Worcestershire?' Bradecote wondered if the man had gone willingly or been ejected.

'I did not ask, and no reason was offered,' replied FitzRoger, easily.

At this point the oak door of the solar opened, and a shapely young woman with large dark eyes, and raven plait showing from beneath the folds of her coif, emerged. She stared at Hugh Bradecote for a long moment and then transferred her gaze to FitzRoger. It was not a gaze of love and adoration. Bradecote rose.

'My lady FitzRoger?' From garb and demeanour she could be no other.

She nodded, but said nothing.

'This is the Undersheriff of the Shire, Avelina, come to report that my disreputable cousin has met with an untimely, though perhaps not unexpected, end.' There was, thought Catchpoll, a peculiar relish to the way the man gave the information, and the lady paled.

'He is dead?'

'He is, and by intent,' confirmed Bradecote. 'Your lord says that he spent two days here, about two weeks past, and was gone upon the third day. It is our guess he was dead within hours of departure . . . if not earlier.' There was the suggestion, the hint that the manor of Doddenham itself lay under suspicion.

'What do you mean, Bradecote?' FitzRoger rose, his arms braced upon those of his chair. 'You said he was dead, but not where, nor when.'

'What I say. His stripped corpse was found, rotting, some days later, hidden just over the border of Cotheridge parish. He did not ride that far.'

The lady pressed her fingers to her lips.

'Then he was attacked by robbers, and murdered for horse and raiment. In days such as these, men travel at risk.' FitzRoger was dismissive.

'Indeed, but he did not travel alone, did he, but with a servant, one Rhydian.'

'He had a man, but I did not know his name. He was but a servant, and if he is not found then it is perfectly clear what occurred. The man killed his master and made away with all he had. Yet you have the audacity to come here . . .' FitzRoger's voice rose, 'and accuse . . .'

'I have accused nobody. I come with questions and seek answers. We,' he indicated his companions, 'would speak freely with those in this manor, within the bailey and in the village without, to find all we can about what was seen and heard during the visit of Hywel ap Rhodri.' He paused for a moment, and added, softly, 'That is telling you what we will do, not asking your permission for it.' For no obvious reason, he did not take to FitzRoger.

'Then I cannot prevent you. How long will you remain?'

'As long as needful.'

'I see little need for you to remain, now the news is given. Had you any real thought that the crime originated here, you would have come sooner,' declared FitzRoger, huffily, and Bradecote thought the man was trying to calm himself.

'Our hall is at your disposal, my lord,' offered the lady FitzRoger, before her husband could exacerbate matters further. 'Such a foul death must see the culprit brought to the King's justice.' Her voice was silken-soft, and she contrived to look both approachable and alluring, and yet out of reach at one and the same time. Catchpoll thought it said a lot about both the woman and her marriage. Of course, the majority of unions at the manorial level were not based upon mutual passion and affection, but this one had little barbs about it. He wondered if Bradecote would declare his own wedded state, or let her play her tricks and see if it led them deeper into the reality of life in Doddenham.

FitzRoger himself made a vague assent that lacked any conviction.

'Thank you, my lady. We shall be as discreet as the circumstances permit, and would not cause unnecessary upheaval. Should we remain for some time, space upon your hall floor, and simple fare will suffice us.' Bradecote's voice lost all shrieval authority and was 'grateful guest'. Catchpoll kept a straight face.

'Have you anything more you need to ask of me, or will you now keep my steward and all others from their duties?' enquired FitzRoger, petulantly.

'There is nothing that is obvious at present, but we would speak with your lady here, and you mentioned your mother.'

'My mother is busy.' There was annoyance, and something more, in FitzRoger's voice.

'Too busy to speak to the sheriff's men?' Bradecote raised an eyebrow. 'What possi—'

'She attends my lord's brother, my lord, who lies sick of some undulant fever. She and I have been nursing him several weeks. He came here from his lord, Gilbert de Clare, about a month ago, and is again confined to his bed, in much pain.'

'I am sorry. However, if you and she share his care, I would have speech with her, after yourself. Might she be fetched?'

'I will see, my lord, but . . .' the lady Avelina FitzRoger gave a wry smile, 'my lord's lady mother is not one who can be commanded.'

'Then stress that I do not command, but request, my lady.' Bradecote smiled at her, and then looked to her lord. 'You may go hawking as you planned, FitzRoger.' He dismissed the man in his own hall, knowing it would rankle, and that he could either obey the command, and look inferior, or remain and look like a sullen child. FitzRoger left, reminding Bradecote that his brother was of the household of a lord in favour with the King.

* * *

Bradecote sent Catchpoll and Walkelin to begin talking to the manor servants and was left with the lady Avelina. She came to the bench upon which he had been seated, and placed herself further along it, the folds of her skirt carefully arranged. She was closer than needful, but far enough away to be decent. She turned herself slightly towards him so that she presented her face in half-profile, and it was a comely one at that. She folded her hands in her lap, meekly.

'I scarce think I can assist you, my lord, but ask your questions.' The silkiness of voice was pronounced.

A year ago, thought Bradecote, I would have found this act unsettling. He found women who were more 'want to be chased' than 'chaste' difficult, for they had an obvious physical appeal but were entirely false, in his view. They exuded a neediness, yet were rapacious, bold, dangerous. His Christina was bold, but in a different way, more independent, and not needy. Loving her, having her love, he could stand back the further from such as the lady Avelina, play her game without embarrassment, and use her wiles against her. He lowered his gaze for a moment, as if both attracted and unsure. This pleased her, for, when he looked at her again there was the hint of a smile playing about her mouth.

'My lady, I would ask if there is anything you recall from your husband's kinsman's visit that might help us. Did he argue with his servant, or anyone else? Was he at ease?' The questions seemed general, unthreatening.

'He was our guest.' She stressed the 'our'. 'His servant I saw but upon the edges of my view, if you understand me. He was attentive, almost,' she paused, and a delicate frown appeared between her brows, 'as if guarding him, protective, which was foolish, since the master was strong of limb and body, and the servant puny, more like . . .' She did not make the comparison with her lord, but Bradecote heard it, unsaid. 'I think he, Hywel . . . ap Rhodri, found that irritating. I presume the man had served him from when both were in their youth, though his master was older. I saw Hywel ap Rhodri wave him away upon occasion, but what he said I cannot tell, for it was in Welsh. There was no sign that the servant was angered by a little lordly shouting.'

'Sometimes one need not understand words to get the meaning of a conversation. Ladies, especially, are good at listening.' Bradecote supported the flattery with a smile that brought a soft colouring to the lady Avelina's cheek.

'The servant sounded like a nursemaid.' The lady giggled. 'You know, they fuss and warn, and sigh, and shake their heads.'

'So you would be surprised if he had murdered his master?' Bradecote said, softly, bringing her straight back to the ending of events. She crossed herself.

'I cannot see it, I cannot.' She spoke truthfully, he would swear.

'I have to ask, my lady . . . your lord said that Hywel ap Rhodri upset the maidservants, by being over familiar with them. Did they complain to you?'

'Complain?' There was a hint of surprise in her voice. 'They are serving maids.' She tried to sound imperious, but did not quite manage it, and under his firm gaze, faltered, blushed. 'Some men are more . . . manly, their appetites greater.' She shrugged. 'It is their nature, and both a blessing and a curse. He apologised to me, said it was something he had made confession for too many times to number, but that it meant nothing, was just him obeying nature. "It is the sin of being a man", he said. I forgave him.' The blush deepened, and she lowered her gaze to her lap.

Bradecote noted that she had said the apology was to her, not before her, and that 'she' forgave him. He could almost imagine the man with his lilting blandishments, persuading the lady that it had all been light-hearted nonsense, sport that harmed none except himself, when he made those confessions and did penance. Bradecote doubted he made confession for what he had done to Leofeva, the smith's wife. Had Avelina FitzRoger faced him with the accusations in pique, because he had been plying her with seductive words also, if nothing more? He would have been that daring, but would she? He tried to take one step further back in his mind to evaluate her. Had she made eyes at him to tease, or because she was a wife more in name than act, and her 'neediness' was not just for admiration? There had been some deep resentment between husband and wife, for certain, but whether it was him seeing her as generous in her looks to others, or her resenting him for lack of 'verve' he could not say. His own first impression of Thorold FitzRoger was not one of those slight, sinewy men who defy their physique and would be found at the forefront of any fight, wreaking havoc upon their opponents. The man had been about to go hawking, and hawking struck Bradecote as his ideal sport, watching something else do the killing, and not exerting himself. Of course, appearances could deceive. The lady Avelina was watching him, waiting. He focussed on events.

'And when he left, did your lord intimate that he would not be welcome if he returned by this way?'

'I do not know what my lord might have said upon the second evening, after he had bid me retire, but Hywel was gone early in the morning, before the manor was even awake. My husband said that no doubt he ought not have remained the second day here, and was keen to make up time on the good Old Road from Worcester to Gloucester, for it runs true and can be travelled at some pace.'

'I see. Thank you, my lady.'

'If there is no more, my lord, shall I go to my lord's mother, and ask . . .'

'Please.'

She stood up, smoothed her skirts in a way that he now thought looked habitual, and went to the solar door. As her hand touched it, she turned, and her voice lost the purr.

'Whatever sins he committed, Hywel ap Rhodri did not deserve to die by violence.'

Hugh Bradecote said nothing. The law was the law, and taking it into one's own hand led down the road to no law at all, but Hywel ap Rhodri should have met death for his crimes in another way, and perhaps a stab in the back was too swift an end.

He resumed his seat and awaited the older lady of the manor. He waited some time, and was wondering how much of the delay was caused by the sickness of the patient, and how much by a lady showing she had a will of her own and was subservient to none. Eventually, the solar door opened, and a woman emerged. Having seen the son, Bradecote had expected someone bird-like and frail, but the lady before him was inclined to the plump in face and form, and, had her expression been more accommodating, looked the motherly sort.

'You are the undersheriff.' The statement was bald.

'I am, lady.'

'I am Matilda FitzGilbert.' She sat herself in the chair made vacant by her son, her hands upon the arms. She looked very at home in it. Bradecote wondered how much power she might yet wield in the manor. 'You wished to speak with me concerning Hywel ap Rhodri, my nephew, who is dead.'

'I do, and his death was murder.' Bradecote could speak as plainly. 'Your son tells me he arrived here about two weeks past. You had no previous contact with him?'

'None.'

'Yet he was your sister's son.'

'My sister and I took different paths. We did not meet after she wed and went into Wales.'

'Was that because she married a Welshman? I know that on the border, in the past, marriage has been made the way it is permitted in Wales, by the abduction of a maid, and the paying of her price thereafter.'

'No, not that. My father, Osbern, held Byton, which lies but a few miles from the Welsh border, as it stands now. Welsh or English, there was little made of the difference there. My father sought Rhodri ap Arwel as a son-in-law, for he was in rising favour in Powys, and a friend over the border is good protection.'

'So he gave him your older sister.'

'Younger.' Matilda FitzGilbert's face showed no emotion, but Bradecote thought there was the faintest trace of annoyance in her answer.

'Your younger sister, then.' She was not being very forthcoming thus far, and he was struck by what he later described to Catchpoll as 'a gut feeling'. 'Did this Rhodri come wooing, or was your sister sent to him?'

'She was not a horse for trade, lord Undersheriff, not quite. He came, he wooed, he won, he took. From what I gather he did that a lot even after he married, so I doubt Emma had much happiness as a wife.' There was no regret visible about this. 'It transpired from his manner here that the son was in the mould of the father.'

'He was undoubtedly that son, your sister's son, lady? You had no doubts?'

'None at all. He could name his lineage, upon the English side, back to the Conquest and before. He named the year and month of my elder son's birth.' This seemed to offend her, as though it had been a private thing.

'If there was no contact, how did he know it?' Bradecote seized upon the fact.

'Because my father visited Rhodri and my sister several times in the first two years of their marriage, as he came here also.'

'And not thereafter?'

'No, for he died. I did not know of the son, Hywel, because he is some three years younger than my Thorold. There was a girl-child born first, but perhaps she died, or is wed long since in Wales, which is as good as dead to me.'

'What did you make of your nephew?' Bradecote persisted.

'What should I have made of him? He was like his father in looks, as I recall the man, and as sweet-tongued. Could not keep that tongue, or his hands, to himself, as we found within the day.' The lady looked him straight in the eye, and Bradecote wondered if she meant to shock.

'So if he had come upon his return from Gloucester . . . ?'

'He would not have tried to get within the gates,' snorted the lady, and Bradecote gave an inner cheer of delight. It was something. 'If you have no more to ask, my son Durand is mightily sick of a fever, and must be attended at all times.' She rose from the seat.

'I would not keep you from your charge, my lady, though the patient is not left alone, with the lady Avelina to tend him.'

The look he got suggested that the lady Matilda did not think so much to her daughter-in-law's care.

'She lacks experience by a sickbed.'

'Then thank you for coming to me, but if there should be questions that arise, be sure I shall request speech with you again.' He went to the solar door, and began to open it for her. She moved, for a woman in her fifties, and with a slightly rolling gait, remarkably swiftly, and passed him before the door was even fully open, with a grudging acknowledgement.

Hugh Bradecote rubbed his chin, stood pondering for a moment, and went to find Catchpoll.

Chapter Six

Serjeant Catchpoll had everything under control. Their presence in the manor had caused flutterings as soon as the reason was made known, and Catchpoll liked 'flutterings', for they made for things being said that might otherwise have lain concealed. His first instruction to Walkelin was to play his role as 'innocent man-at-arms dragged along by his superiors' and work his 'red-haired magic' upon the maidservants.

'For if Hywel ap Rhodri acted true to character, they will have things to say about the man, and forthright ones at that.'

'Or be too silent, Serjeant, if he took advantage to their shame.'

'True enough, but then you have to judge whether the "maid" would have told anyone else, and women are bad at secrets, or whether the wench might wield a knife herself, in revenge, though if she did so, then someone else had to have helped move the body.'

'And we still have no news of Rhydian.' Walkelin chewed his lip. 'And there is the matter of two horses and their harness. I do not like those missing things.' He spoke almost to himself.

'Well, then, best you find out about them. I am sure the lord Bradecote would hate to think of you a-worrying over them,' replied Catchpoll, sarcastically. 'I am first for the steward.'

Brictmer the Steward was a man in late middle age, a little stooped of shoulder, and thoughtful of demeanour. He shook his head over the 'bad thing' that had happened.

'A quiet manor is this, with everyone about their own tasks, at least these last dozen years since the lordling Durand took himself off to the great lord he serves now. In his youth he was,' Brictmer gave a wry smile, 'difficult to have about the place.'

'Tempersome, was he? Young lords without responsibilities . . .' Catchpoll sounded as if he knew all about such.

'Not tempersome, particularly, but idleness breeds foolishness, I say. He was inclined to do things upon the spur of the moment, upon a whim, regardless of what would follow. His sire could not control him, and he enjoyed annoying his brother, who does not do things without careful thought, and is thus a good lord to serve. Only person Durand FitzRoger ever attended was his dam, and the lady Matilda could bring him to heel like a dog when she chose. Once he went upon his way, we settled good and peaceful, even when the lord Roger died and the lord Thorold took his place.'

'And now you have a new lady too. Pretty piece, though it is not for the likes of me to say it.' Catchpoll winked at the steward.

'Aye, she is, poor lady.'

'Poor? How so?'

'What woman would want to be lady of a manor where there is a lady still in authority? The lady Matilda is not one to cross, nor has she wanted to step back.' His voice dropped to a whisper. 'And she has been wed these three years with no sign of a child. I know as it is the woman who is blamed but . . . I think both parents wished the lord Thorold had been more like his younger brother. He is a good master, a good lord, but not . . . strong in body, alas.' He shook his head. 'My woman, God have mercy upon her, gave me three sons and two daughters, though two of the boys was taken from us by a spotted fever when small. Children are a blessing.'

'That they are,' agreed Catchpoll, nodding in agreement. 'I doubt the lord Thorold has liked mother and wife both taken up with duties at the bedside of his brother, or did they become close by being parted? Often happens that way.'

'Oh, I think both prefer the being apart, but fearful poorly was the lord Durand when he came home a month since. Came in a litter, he did, not being fit even to slump upon his horse. The servants were afeared he came with some evil disease that would spread among all, but it has not done so. The ladies cared for him most careful, and but a couple of weeks ago he looked much the better for it, pale but up and about the manor, but then, when he was even thinking of returning to his lord, the fever struck him down again, sweating and crying out in pain he was. Terrible to hear, were his groans. The lady Avelina, I think she believes he will die, but the lady Matilda says no. She says as she has seen such fevers that come and go and give such pains, and the man recovered, in time. Myself, I think if the lady Matilda has told him he shall not die, then he will not die because he would not disobey her.' Brictmer gave a sad smile.

'You do not think the death of Hywel, nephew to the lady Matilda, is linked to this manor?' Catchpoll moved the conversation to the direct.

'It will have been the servant as killed him. The man did not seem the sort, but then, who better than one who appears loyal.'

'What was he like, the servant?'

'Underfed, in the cook's opinion. She took pity upon him, sure enough, and tried to ply him with extra bowls of pottage. His thin frame made him look a stripling, though I heard his master claim he was full five and twenty years, and it brought out the motherly in her. He was very alert, I thought . . . reminded me of a stoat, truth to tell.'

'So we hunt a very tall stoat, do we?' laughed Catchpoll, watching the man closely.

'Stoats are not easy to catch, so you had best hope not.' Brictmer grinned, but Catchpoll thought his eyes wary.

'We will speak to all in Doddenham, in case anyone saw the Welshmen depart, or heard them in argument. Sometimes things mean nothing until events afterwards show them in a new light, and there is nothing wrong in not having worried over them before. It is the small things as lead to the greater ones, in our work.' Catchpoll let that sink in, and could sense rather than see a hint of concern in the steward. 'But there, I must not delay you in your duty. If you would tell me how many work within the palisade, and at what, I shall be about the lord Sheriff's business.'

* * *

Walkelin had found the stables empty of all but horseflesh, and therefore moved on to the kitchen. He liked kitchens, for they smelt good, and a pleasant young man could often get titbits, not just of information. The cook was the age of his mother, and he knew how to handle her, calling her 'mistress', very deferentially, and giving her 'gossip' about how 'this body of some Welshman' had been found, and that because of it he had been dragged all the way to Wales, where the cooking was awful, so that the lord Undersheriff could put a name to the victim, and the Prince of Powys had said the man was good and loyal. This, as intended, got the cook quite agitated.

'Good? Him? Well, I care not what some prince says. I saw, with my own eyes, the way the man was when here, and he was far from good. His poor servant, now there was a decent lad, though blind to his master's faults, so blind he was trying to persuade himself that his master could not resist a wench making eyes at him, but I knows better. The girls here are good, honest girls, and one is my niece. Twelve, she is, and yet to look upon any man in that way at all. He made her cry . . .' her voice trailed off and she shook her head, 'so I kept her in the kitchen the rest of the time he was here, and told her if a man such as he dared enter, I would hit him with the skillet.' The cook fairly bristled with indignation. 'Look at her, poor lambkin.' She pointed her ladle as a girl – and Walkelin would not have described her as a woman – entered the kitchen, head down, shoulders hunched.

'A man would not—' He spoke what was uppermost in his mind, and stopped short, reddening. It did him little harm in the eyes of the cook, who approved of his disbelief, though it made the girl tremble.

'No decent man, that is for sure,' she corrected, but gently.

'He did not harm you . . . hurt you . . . just frighten you, yes?' Walkelin, for all he was asking a serjeant's apprentice's questions, wanted reassurance as any honest young man might seek.

'Is not frightening more than enough?' The cook gave the answer, and gripped her ladle as though imagining the assailant.

'Yes, yes it is but . . . I hope you can come to know all men are not . . . like that.' He spoke to the girl, but she did not lift her head, nor make any sign that she heard him. Walkelin's open and generally happy face wore a grim expression. 'I think only his prince will mourn such a man's death.'

'Evil comes upon the innocent,' declared the cook, 'but them that does it must pay in the hereafter.' She crossed herself.

'And should pay here, an' all.' A young woman, willowy of stature, and with a strand of fair hair escaped from her coif, brought in a basket of pease. She looked at Walkelin, judging him, and decided he was not one to object to that sentiment. 'He tried it with me, putting his hand where none but a husband might and I slapped his face, good and hard, lord or no lord. He swore at me, as I guess, but in his own natural tongue, and I care not what he said. To think us free for his using!'

'He is dead, Aldith,' said the cook, and Walkelin heard warning rather than admonition in her voice.

'Good.' Aldith dumped the basket of pease upon the kitchen floor with an angry flounce, and took a wooden bowl from a shelf. 'The lord Sheriff might be here, but who is he looking for justice for? Not for the likes of me, for sure.'

'It is the lord Undersheriff who has come, and the sheriff's serjeant,' murmured Walkelin, feeling almost guilty.

'And would they care that I was molested by that Welsh lecher? No, because I am nobody, and he was somebody, even if only in Wales.' She took a handful of pods from the basket and began to shell the pease with a vicious enthusiasm that Walkelin found slightly unnerving.

'You were glad he went, then?' He stated the obvious, but with a reason.

'Glad? I never saw the going of him, or I would have left burrs under his saddle and hoped his horse would throw him in a ditch, even a dry summer ditch. Slunk off, he did, in my opinion, tail between his legs, and I wish that was all he had there, for the sake of every maid in the shire.'

'But his servant, you said, mistress, was not a bad man, yet spoke not against him?' Walkelin looked back at the cook.

'Some good men are blinkered to the sinful,' replied the cook, virtuously, 'or rather they try to be. I heard them together, voices raised, that first evening, outside the hall, but it was all in Welsh foreign, so . . . The servant, his name was Riddeann I think, had little English, but said his lord was "a good man" – more in hope than belief, I would say. He said he was the one always being led on, well did this little mummery really, and it was funny to see. He fluttered his eyelashes and made like a woman being forward, and sighed, and shook his head.'

'Then he was a fool, good-hearted or not.' Aldith shelled another pod and the peas rattled in the dish. They smelt sweet and fresh and at odds with everything to do with Hywel ap Rhodri, which was linked only with corruption and death.

'Well, I must go and see what my superiors want to do with me,' sighed Walkelin, sounding suitably put upon. 'I will leave you to your labours, ladies all.' He made them a little bow, which made the cook smile, but Aldith just sniffed.

The sheriff's men walked out into the cluster of cottages that made the village of Doddenham, but did not set about knocking at doors, since few, unless decrepit, would be found at home with the hay at least cut, and probably being turned. Instead they went to the little church, which was cool and empty.

'So what have we got, Catchpoll?' Bradecote leant his arms on the stone of the font and looked at his serjeant.

'Bits, my lord, small bits, but interesting ones. The men-at-arms are idle in my view, of mind and body, from lack of use and training also. They could give me nothing. From Brictmer the Steward I have it that the lady Matilda still rules the roost.'

'No surprise there. I met the woman,' grinned Bradecote.

'Not only that, though. The lady Avelina has been wed three years, and no babe in her cradle, and the steward clearly thinks his lord not up to the task, shall we say. The lady is thwarted then, in several ways. She has a manor in which she cannot be the lady, and a husband who is not enough of a husband to her.'

'A less than contented wife is nothing new, and I guessed the same, but of what use is it to us?' Bradecote's brow furrowed.

'We shall see as to that, my lord, for I am not yet of any view upon it. However, there is more. The sick man we did not see, attended by the two ladies, is Durand, the lord Thorold's younger brother, and far more "able", at least from repute, if the hints were true. He and his brother are not close. They were at odds often enough when Durand was young and in the manor, but he left to join the lord Gilbert de Clare, and no

103

doubt wished to get advancement that way, being landless. The only person he ever attended was his mother. He was a man who acted first and thought later, the opposite of his brother. The feeling is that he was always favoured by his parents, who thought Thorold more the litter runt than sturdy firstborn. Durand returned a month back, ailing good and proper with a fever. Brictmer thinks the lady Avelina fears he will die, which makes me wonder how fond she is of her brother by marriage, but that the lady Matilda is convinced he will live and he will not disappoint her.'

'If the lady Avelina is more caring than illness alone demands, I doubt the other lady in the case would turn a blind eye,' murmured Bradecote.

'If she has seen. Mayhap she has not. They must take it in turn to nurse the man. Now, the interesting thing is that our sick man was not so sick about two weeks past, and was up and about to the point of thinking of returning to his lord, but was then struck back down.'

'For real?' Bradecote queried.

'I have seen such a fever, my lord. A neighbour of ours, he was very sick of a fever that came upon him, and seemed to leave, but returned three times more within a few months. He sweated bad, and had pains, even in his . . .' Walkelin winced.

'That would keep a man to his bed, for sure,' Catchpoll grimaced, 'but if he was healthy enough to have met with Hywel ap Rhodri, did he perhaps have an argument with him, over a wench?'

'It would have to be very serious to end in a killing.' Bradecote sounded doubtful. 'Yet it is possible. From the lady Matilda I got a story in words and a story that was not told.' Bradecote took a deep breath. 'Whether this has bearing or not, I too do not know, but . . . The lady Matilda had a younger sister, Emma. A younger sister, mark you, and I think that rankled, for she was wed first. Her sire held Byton, west of Leominster, in land that is so close to Powys that Wales is not "foreign". She said he liked the idea of a son-in-law who was powerful over that border, as protection in awkward times, and it makes sense. She said Rhodri ap Arwel "came, wooed, won, and took" and she said he too was a roving man with women. There was something in the way she spoke makes me think he wooed her too, either for sport or to test, and then had the younger sister to wife. She said that after the marriage she and her sister did not meet, but that for a couple of years her father went to each and brought news. She had no knowledge of Hywel ap Rhodri, only a firstborn girl, but that her sister knew of Thorold's birth. She said Hywel was able to recite his ancestry and she had no doubt he was her nephew, but that he would not have stepped into Doddenham if he had been upon his return journey. She was quite open that he was not safe with women.'

'And the lady Avelina looked quite upset when she heard of his death,' muttered Catchpoll. 'She may be tender-hearted, of course, or there was an attraction to having a "real" man about the place, however briefly, and if she thought Durand ailing . . .'

'But he was better then, Serjeant,' Walkelin reminded him.

'True enough, so I will leave that one merely a thought, but her lord liked telling her, that I swear.'

'He did,' agreed Bradecote. 'Which leaves us with the FitzRoger's family as follows.' He ticked off his long fingers.

'Thorold disliked his new cousin, dislikes his brother, is afraid of his mother, and jealous about his wife, even if he does not bed her. Brother Durand is favoured by his mother, and his brother's wife, perhaps, and, when well, is impulsive. I doubt he liked having Hywel about the place doing what he used to do, but more thoroughly. Youthful maid chasing is not the same as hunting the way Hywel clearly did. The lady Avelina is frustrated as lady and wife, favours the brother, but when he is sick he cannot give her "comfort". She was distressed to hear Hywel ap Rhodri was dead, but not heartbroken. Losing her heart would be unlikely in two days, but it might indicate he took advantage as it was offered.' Bradecote reassessed what he had heard from the lady's pretty lips.

'I asked her if the maids made complaint about Hywel ap Rhodri and his wandering hands, if no more. They might well have come to lady rather than lord. She stalled, then talked of the stronger appetite as a blessing as well as a curse, and I felt that she had responded to that, which makes sense if she was starved of it in the lordly bed. Had she enjoyed his blandishments, his attentions? Had she been tempted to more, or indeed given in to that temptation?' Bradecote pondered. Many lordly couples did not love each other, but muddled along, as he knew from experience, but he had sensed a desire in her husband to hurt her, and she liked him as little. 'There is no love lost between lord and lady here. Adultery is a great risk as well as sin, but did she weigh it against frustrated boredom, and think that Thorold would be glad to show he was not impotent, if there were results from that sinning? What better way to make an unfulfilling husband pay, and if the child were male, then it would supplant the brother with whom he did not get on, as heir. Yes, she might have taken her chance.'

'Even if she has feelings for the brother, Durand?' Walkelin had his doubts.

'If it is as the steward believes, and she thinks him likely to die, she might have thought it her one chance for real excitement, or even a revenge.' Bradecote shrugged.

'And Hywel ap Rhodri sounds the sort to enjoy cuckolding a relative who probably showed his dislike and played superior,' added Catchpoll.

'I doubt mightily if the lady Avelina wanted him dead, but she might be a reason to kill. The lady Matilda might have ordered his death, for she has the stomach for it, I am sure, and something in the past pricks her like a thorn in a horse's frog. What is more, Thorold declared he had no idea why Hywel was in the shire, but when I gently asked his mother if Hywel might have returned "on his way back from Gloucester", she turned not one hair. She knew, and so did Thorold, because his lady told me he had said Hywel ap Rhodri must have left before the household was risen because he had lingered too long upon his task and could make up time on the good road from Worcester to Gloucester.'

'They knew his mission?' Catchpoll asked.

'She looks no fool, and nor is Thorold, and sense says even if the Welshman tried to keep that quiet, if she knew it was to Gloucester, and knows Madog ap Maredudd was at Lincoln, then she guessed aright. The thing is, Thorold knew also, yet he lied. Why?'

'The man has shown no interest in either side, so what reason would that be for murder?' grumbled Catchpoll.

'We have but possibility, many possibilities. If there is more beneath the surface, and somehow I think there is, either brother might have had motive.'

Catchpoll sighed, and scratched his ear.

'Well, whoever did it, it was here,' announced Walkelin, who had been concealing his news with difficulty. It got just the reception he hoped to see. Both his superiors stared at him.

'Why?' asked Catchpoll.

'Because the stables have five horses within. Two are riding horses for men, so the lord Durand's horse was brought back when he came home sick, in case he died no doubt, one is a lady's mount, and two look for work, if they wants horses not oxen for carts and such. All were stalled. There was another stall, but it was empty, of a horse. However, there was straw upon the ground and horse dung among it, fresh.'

'Interesting. Go on.' Bradecote nodded at Walkelin.

'I counted the bridles, my lord. There were six, though I saw no sixth saddle, I admit. I would say there was another horse in that stable this morning, and it was removed while we were in the lord's hall.'

'A fair assumption, young Walkelin. Well spotted.' Walkelin blushed at Catchpoll's praise. 'The trouble is, that shows others in the manor know something, if not all. I would swear the steward was too keen to say that the servant killed the master, as his lord had done before him.'

'And with the villagers in the fields, who would see a horse led, or more likely ridden, out of the manor itself?' Bradecote frowned. 'Though I would have thought better bridled and bareback, rather than saddled and in a halter.'

'Mayhap the saddle was on, and the rider told to hurry up and not worry about the bridle.'

'So we need to find out who rode the horse, and where. Finding the animal would make denying involvement with the death very difficult.' Bradecote was thinking.

'But if everyone is involved, at least after the event, who is guilty?' Walkelin felt a little deflated that his good news provided more of a problem than an aid.

'There was one wound in his back, Walkelin. One man – and it was more likely to be a man who had the weapon in hand – actually killed Hywel ap Rhodri, whosoever ordered it.' Bradecote wanted things as simple as possible. 'If half the shire were complicit, well, would you bring them before the Justices, if they helped hide the killing of a rapist and murderer?'

'But we have no proof they knew he was either, nothing proven beyond they thought he was lecherous with serving maids.' Catchpoll sucked his teeth.

'My lord, I spoke with the cook, and she had no good word to say of the man. She said he had made her niece cry, and her a girl of but a dozen years, and modest too. Whether that was casual groping of the girl, or worse, was not said, and when I tried to speak a little to the girl it was with the aunt present, and the girl was very shy and said nothing.'

'We ought to try and speak with her alone, then, but gently.' Bradecote sighed. 'There would have been others, by what was said in the hall.'

'I think, my lord, she is too scared to speak to anyone. She looked at me as if I were a wolf.' Walkelin was very unlike a wolf, and the sort of young man most women confided in with little compunction. If the girl was scared of him, it had meaning. 'I heard from another servant girl though, older, but not old. Aldith was aggrieved, and told me she had slapped Rhodri's face, "lord or not, for placing his hand where none but a husband might", and I would say it was she who reported him to the lady Avelina.'

'In view of his previous behaviour she was lucky to live,' murmured Bradecote.

'Aye, but it was likely within the manor buildings, so perhaps he dare not, my lord,' offered Catchpoll.

'There is one thing more, my lord.' Walkelin paused. 'I think the cook knew Hywel ap Rhodri was dead before I told her, and not because she learnt of it swiftly, after we arrived. She was interested in the detail of us finding him, and that I am sure was new to her, but when Aldith was ranting on about him, she said, "He is dead" to her, not like someone revealing news, but reminding her to be wary of sounding too delighted.'

'Lucky for the cook he was stabbed, then, not beaten over the head with something flat and heavy, else she would be a suspect.' Catchpoll gave a death's head grin, but was thinking. 'Trouble is, my lord, as I says, we have no proof Hywel ap Rhodri was killed because of his way with women, but if that is the belief here, they will lie until Doomsday to protect whoever they think gave real justice to maids like this Aldith.'

'And we cannot be sure it was the true motive. No.' Bradecote shook his head. 'We need to find things, namely a brown horse, a grey pony, and Rhydian the loyal servant, who argued with his master . . . yet was "faithful unto death".'

'Whose death is worth considering, my lord,' offered Catchpoll.

'But they know of Hywel's death here, have had the horse here, Catchpoll.'

'Aye, my lord, but if Rhydian did for his master, and they knew, even connived at the hiding of the corpse, they might have bid him depart with thanks for the deed, not wanting him taken up for the killing.'

'I had not thought of that, true enough. I had it either the killer was of the manor and it was done here, or Rhydian did it, and somewhere upon the road to Worcester. This ought to be simple, and yet it is not.'

'Simple things is sometimes more complicated than you would guess, and difficult prove easy.' Upon which philosophical pronouncement Catchpoll folded his arms, and turned, as the church door opened with a clunking of the hinges.

Chapter Seven

A thin, ascetic-looking man entered, his expression questioning, but not unfriendly. Tonsure and garb proclaimed his calling.

'Good morrow, Father.' Bradecote smiled at the priest.

'A good morrow to you, also. May I be of help to you?' His voice was soft, but not weak.

'In all seriousness, a prayer for us to find things would be an aid.'

'You have lost something, my son?'

'Specifically, one horse, one pony, a man who may well have departed this life, and the truth, which is not so much lost as hidden from view.' The smile twisted.

'That is quite a list.' The priest blinked. 'I am Father Dunstan, priest of this parish, and since truth is always a good thing, I will assuredly aid you to find it.'

'Alas, Father, sometimes the finding of it means discovering evil, and pain to even the innocent.' Bradecote became more serious. 'A man was murdered, almost certainly within this manor, about two weeks past. His body is found, and buried, and prayers said over him, although he probably needs more prayers than a parish might provide. We seek why he was killed, and who killed him.'

'Yet you said you need to find a man who may be dead, so another man also?'

'Father, the missing man was servant to the first, but if he did not kill his master, then the chances are he is dead.' Catchpoll had been watching the priest closely.

'I am about to recite the Office, but if you would join me, I am sure your prayers will be heard, and I can offer you some cider, bread and good butter, if you would care to eat thereafter.'

With the promise of food, and perhaps background information upon the manor, within and without, they stayed.

Father Dunstan ate little but was unstinting in his hospitality. In the soft gloom of his simple dwelling, Hugh Bradecote asked questions, but circumspectly.

'We know you cannot reveal anything learnt from confession, but we have several problems, as we said. One is that a horse has gone missing from the manor stable, and it is likely to be the horse of the man that was murdered. If It is, and we find it, then that is proof that what happened is known here. At the least, we need to know what sort of manor Doddenham is – contented, or at odds with itself, whether one might hold grudge against another and implicate them out of malice, that sort of thing.'

'I have not seen a new horse, but then I do not go to the stables, and it would have to be very unusual to have attracted my attention if it has been ridden. I look at people, not the animals of God's creation. As to this manor, well, it is a very close community, and the warp and weft of kinship bind it.'

'The cook said her niece was one of the serving maids,' corroborated Walkelin, hoping that Father Dunstan would expand upon the relationships, and earning an approving look from Catchpoll.

'Ah yes, Milburga, the daughter of her brother, Tovi the Wheelwright. And his wife was sister to Brictmer the Steward, whose son Corbin will follow him, and in the end marry Aldith, once he has . . .' The priest paused.

'Father? You said truth is a good thing.' Bradecote reminded him gently.

'It is.' Father Dunstan sighed. 'And he is guilty of no more than youthful adoration. He is nineteen, and full of youth's excitability, and the lady Avelina means nothing by it, it is just her manner.'

'Fallen under her spell, has he?' suggested Catchpoll, in a fatherly voice. 'Calf-love, no doubt.'

'Indeed. I am sure he does not lust after her, at least, not much,' the priest blushed, 'but he has her set very high. Aldith and he, well, they have always been close, but perhaps so close neither can see what is before them, and now he is in thrall to his lady, Aldith has to sit second in his affections, which has, for the while, put her off all of the male sex.'

'Bit of a fancy name, Corbin, for a son of Brictmer.' Walkelin was thinking upon a single point that niggled.

'Ah yes, but his wife, may she rest in peace, gave him two sons before Corbin, alas also departed this life. Brictmer loved her dearly, and gave in to her wish to name the third son Corbin. She said as how it might help him advance in life, not thinking he would follow his father as steward, if his name was not "the old sort".'

'No cause to give a decent Englishman a foreign name, though,' grumbled Catchpoll, without thinking, and then screwed up his features as Hugh Bradecote laughed.

'And you berated Walkelin for insulting me, Catchpoll. As you say, good job I have a sense of humour.'

Father Dunstan looked from one to the other and smiled. There was an ease between the three men, though divided by both rank, and ancestry, and a strong bond existed also. In times of division that pleased him.

'Father, the lady Matilda I have met, and from report also hear that she is one who finds stepping back from commanding a hard task. How do her son and his wife cope?' Bradecote made the question sound more rhetorical, and shook his head a little to aid that impression.

'Ah, well in honesty, I do not think that she ever tried to "stand back". Even when her lord was alive, she was the rod of iron and he the willow that bent.' The priest sighed. 'It is difficult for her, of course.'

'Difficult? How so?' Catchpoll queried.

'I came after she was wed to the lord Roger, but I always felt that . . . she concealed some disappointment. I fear she despised her husband, however much she remained dutiful at his side. He was not a strong man, in will, and she . . .'

'She is the tough sort, aye. But surely she would be happier with a man who let her rule the roost?' Catchpoll persisted.

'I always assumed she was the style of woman who would have preferred a strong husband and been pleased to show subservience, submitting her own will to that strength like an offering, but in its absence could not bear to watch weakness and took over.'

'That is an interesting thought, Father.' Bradecote had not considered that option before, but it had a sense to it. 'So in a way she resents doing what she does well, and despises those unable to match her.'

'Alas for her, the lord Thorold is the elder son. He was an eighth-month child, always sickly as a lad, and one who, though I hate to say it, cannot fit the role. He plans, he acts, but always the lady Matilda watches and makes him feel his inferiority. She doted upon the younger son, the lordling Durand, who is stronger of body and attitude, though not strong in faith, I fear. She is most anxious of late, since he has returned to us in such poor health.'

'She and the lady Avelina tend him, we hear.' Walkelin added his mite.

'They do, and have had young Corbin to assist them when strength was needed to lift the poor man. He has been sick of an undulant fever, and in much pain of the body, which has distressed both ladies.' Father Dunstan shook his head. 'Such afflictions are sent to try us.'

'It must be bad when a man thinks he is recovering, and slips back into an ague,' suggested Catchpoll. 'Hard upon the spirit.'

'His spirit,' responded the priest, with the first sign of acerbity they had heard from him, 'is rebellious. He rebels against his God, and his body, and has to learn that both cannot be treated with contempt.' He coloured. 'When he was at his worst, I went to offer extreme unction, and he swore at me, and at the Almighty, though I hope that was the fever yelling. However, he has refused to make confession since, and it worries me. The lady Matilda has told me to be patient, and that he will recover as long as I pester him not.'

'And the lady Avelina?' Bradecote pushed her name back into the conversation.

'She is not so sure he will become again his old self, and it makes her sad of heart. She has no malice to her, but she is the sort of woman who opens like a flower in sunshine with admiration and closes at rebuke.'

'And her brother by marriage admires her?' Catchpoll suggested.

'Durand has always admired her.' Father Dunstan sounded regretful.

'You do not suggest more, Father? I have to ask.' Bradecote could not avoid the question.

'I do not, but, if you were to ask if it were unthinkable, I would have to admit it is not. I do not condone sin, but I know we are all fallen from grace, and in such a state . . . I pray that the worst has always been but both flattering the other, for she is a comely woman, and Durand more of a "man" than her lord. He has neither land nor wealth to achieve a good marriage, and she is in a marriage that is nothing but duty. Both are needy. So if they play with wooing words, that is wrong, but might be much worse, whether in the thought or the deed.'

'It cannot have pleased young Corbin, though, having to tend the man who is experienced with women, and whom the lady he sets upon a height weeps for.' Catchpoll pulled a face. 'That is cruel for a lad.'

'Ah, but the lady Avelina has showered him with soft praise, saying how much they "cannot do without him", that it offsets the pain, and of course it means he gets to see his lady more than he would normally do. He is both happy and unhappy at one time, as happens in youth.' Father Dunstan smiled then. 'I was not born tonsured. I remember the confusion of feelings when manhood is new, untested, and both keen and nervous.'

'Are you happy and unhappy at one and the same time, young Walkelin?' asked Catchpoll, grinning at his serjeanting apprentice.

'Indeed I am, Serjeant,' replied Walkelin, instantly. 'I am happy that I please my lord Bradecote, and unhappy that you still have fault to find in me, so often.' The tone was vaguely reproachful, but his eyes twinkled.

'It should be accounted a blessing by you, Father, that you do not have to train a youth to follow after. They are a great trial, a great trial.' Catchpoll's voice held a ripple of amusement.

The atmosphere was suddenly too light and jovial for the undersheriff.

'I think,' announced Bradecote, 'that we have trespassed upon your hospitality too long, Father Dunstan. We ought to be out, irritating the haymakers with our foolish questions.' He rose, and his companions took their lead from him. They thanked the priest, and went outside, where the blazing sun made them screw up their eyes at its glare.

'Useful,' remarked Catchpoll, laconically.

'Indeed,' agreed Bradecote. 'But we have two brothers with motive enough to cast the shadow of doubt upon the other, and yet that doubt might still be true, and one of them will not make confession. Obstinacy or guilt?'

'And a lad who might choose to play the "gallant knight" if he thought his lady was being insulted by the attentions of Hywel ap Rhodri,' Catchpoll added. 'Foolish it might be, but I have known such deadly foolishness before, and a knife is as oft a weapon of rage as of planned assault.'

'And if it was the steward's son, no doubt but all the manor would draw in upon itself in support. They would not see killing an outsider, one who had mistreated the servant girls, as worth a rope's length.' Walkelin warmed to his theme. 'Then they would have moved the body over the Hundred boundary and hoped never to have had anything mentioned again.'

'At which point we start looking for the servant, Rhydian,' Bradecote said, heavily. 'Your theory only works if he is dead, and what worries me is that if they took Hywel ap Rhodri over the boundary, they would not have left the other body behind, since it would be just as damning.' Bradecote rubbed his chin, meditatively. 'If the man spoke little English, how would they suggest he took his pony, whatever coin and things of value that his master possessed, but not his horse, and go . . . where? He could scarcely go back to Mathrafal and claim he had simply "lost" Hywel ap Rhodri. And what is more, even if he understood, why would he accept?'

'I cannot see he would, which brings us back to where is the body?' Catchpoll agreed.

'What about the Teme? A body pushed into the water in the evening might travel some way downstream before being noticed.' Walkelin spoke more in hope than belief.

'Bodies in water turn up eventually, and I would think well before now. Besides, the river is low at this season, even with that Welsh rain we just had.' Catchpoll dismissed the idea.

'Could they have buried the servant over the boundary and dumped the master because of fearing discovery?' Walkelin tried again.

'But they were not worried about digging a hole, in woodland with many roots, beforehand? That too does not ring true.' Catchpoll was even less impressed.

'Our trouble is that the evidence we have conflicts, all of it. I doubt the villagers will be of any help, but we ought to ask. Come on.' Hugh Bradecote led them towards the hayfield.

The pale-yellow gold of the field was dotted by the line of peasants, turning the drying hay. The recent rain had caught them with it cut and some had rotted, but the rest was salvageable, if less sweet. Now they wanted fair weather to dry it thoroughly before they brought it into ricks. They looked up for a moment as the three men approached, but did not stop their travail. Catchpoll stepped to the fore, wanting to make the most of Hugh Bradecote's station.

'Listen to me. This here is the lord Bradecote, Undersheriff of this shire. He seeks any information about the Welshmen who were at this manor but a few weeks past. If any of you spoke with them, saw them even, then come and tell the lord Bradecote what you saw, what was said.'

The faces remained largely blank.

'What cause would the likes of us have to speak with them?' grumbled a weathered-looking man.

'Someone must have at least seen them.' Catchpoll gave the villagers the benefit of his gimlet-eyed stare. A young woman moved, but an arm was stretched out before her, and she halted. 'If you have words to say, maid, say them, private or public, at your choice.' The serjeant did not threaten but his tone was commanding in a fatherly way. The girl braced herself and stepped forward.

'I saw him, the Welshman, the evening he rode into the manor, with the little man on the grey pony behind him. It was eventide, and we were coming in from the pease field. He looked at me as he passed, and he was well dressed and his horse good, so I lowered my eyes and bent the knee, and he laughed.' This had clearly annoyed the girl. 'Then . . . then he asked, with that voice that goes up and down, if my knee was all I would bend for him.' She shuddered, and stared at the ground, blushing. 'He came out of the manor gate an hour before sunset, and was looking about. I hid, because I feared he would be seeking me, and . . . He scared me, for his face was angry, but like a hunting animal.'

'A cautious maid stays a maid the longer, so you did not do wrong,' Catchpoll commended her, loudly enough so that some would hear and her name be less likely to be bandied in gossip.

'Did you see him again?' asked Bradecote.

'No . . . my lord.' The assertion was too vehement, and her eyes darted sideways along the line of workers.

So that was a lie, thought all three of the sheriff's men.

121

'Very well. Thank you . . . ?' He raised an interrogative eyebrow.

'Winfraeth, my lord.'

'Have any other of you seen the Welshman or his servant? Answer me.' Bradecote used the command, and looked at the peasantry before him.

'We work the fields, my lord,' came a placating voice, 'and have not time to waste in gazing.'

'But a stranger is always of interest, a source of good gossip to pass among friends.' Catchpoll could almost hear their reluctance in the silence. 'We come not to threaten or accuse, only to seek pieces of the broken pot of events. If you are unsure, or do not want your neighbour to know, then we will be about the manor a day or so yet, and have ears to hear.' It was the best he thought they could achieve, standing there in the hayfield. He glanced for the briefest moment at Hugh Bradecote, who gave the smallest of nods, and then turned away. Walkelin stepped in beside them.

'They are hiding something,' he said, with certainty.

'You don't need to tell us that,' mumbled Catchpoll. 'As soon as we reaches cover, and out of their sight, you comes back as close as you can and watch that girl, see if any accost her. We needs to know what and who is putting pressure upon her not to speak more, and whether it is the man we saw put out his arm or nay.'

'Yes, Serjeant.'

'Be swift, because as I reckon, they will want to speak with her now, not later. We will be back in the manor, won't we, my lord?' He looked at Bradecote, who was frowning.

'Yes. Yes, it is as good a place as any at present.'

Walkelin went about obeying the order and undersheriff and serjeant ambled slowly back towards the palisaded manor.

'Trouble is, Catchpoll, silence is a good weapon. If they all keep quiet, what can we prove?'

'As yet, little, my lord, but keeping silent is not as easy as you would suppose. We watches, we listens, we niggles them.'

'And we find that damned horse.'

'That, my lord, would be very useful indeed.'

'And I am wondering when I might speak with the ailing Durand FitzRoger, over whom such care is taken. I have a fancy that it should be now.'

'There is them that is sick, and them that is playing sick, you mean?'

'Possibly, Catchpoll, though a fever such as his might have him delirious one day and spry of mind a few days hence, and back again. His mother was mighty keen I did not set foot within the solar, which makes me suspicious.'

'Glad to hear it, my lord.' Catchpoll gave his death's head grin. 'Suspicious is what we needs to be, each and every day.'

'I shall keep that as my watchword, you old thief-ferret.' Bradecote shook his head and grew serious once more. 'There is much here, and yet nothing.'

'There should be more when we have spoken to the fancy-named Corbin, I think, my lord. There are links, and he is involved in many.'

'We ought to have asked in the field for him to come forward, if there. My fault.'

'Well, if he is lulled a little, not thinking we are keen to hear him, he may be lax. He attends the man who is ill, and dotes upon his lady who would undoubtedly have had Hywel leering at her. He is likely to visit the stables often, and he was not about the courtyard and buildings once we came from the hall. No youth was about, only the cook and maids.'

'But as logically he could be out in the field, lending a strong young body to the labour, Catchpoll.'

'True, but I have my doubts. He might be attending the sick man even now, of course. If you gain admittance to the solar, I would imagine he would be sent out to avoid him hearing the words of his betters.'

'And he will walk into the welcoming embrace of Serjeant Catchpoll?'

'I would not go that far, my lord, though it is an "embrace" many a man in Worcester has learnt to fear, I am glad to say.'

'So I am to flush him out if he is there. Fair enough. If he is not . . . ?'

'Then I will ask for him about the manor buildings, and if he is not about, return to the fields, by which time I hope Walkelin will have taken another step forward for us.'

Walkelin was at that moment crouched in the long grass of the field boundary, which was not an unpleasant place to be on a hot, sunny day, or at least it would not be if he had not found a place in close proximity to an ants' nest. He was trying to observe without being seen, whilst attempting to prevent the insects crawling inside his cotte. He was successful in the first and failing miserably in the second. It seemed that the fieldworkers had simply not had the time to halt and discuss the import of the sheriff's men coming among them, and had formed line again, turning the hay to dry more evenly. Walkelin wondered if Winfraeth had been approached even as they had turned their backs on the villagers, and he was thus wasting his time, and being bitten by ants for no good reason.

He watched, and wriggled, and sweated, but only for a few uncomfortable minutes before the line seemed to ripple about the girl, and she was flanked by two men, one young and the other, the one who had tried to forestall her in front of the lord Undersheriff, of middle age. He wondered if the latter were her father. Both men continued working, but appeared to draw closer to Winfraeth time and again, and Walkelin would swear that they spoke with her, for she shook her head repeatedly to each in turn. What he could not tell was whether they were themselves asking questions, or were receiving her assurance that she would say nothing more. He committed the men to memory by face and form, and waited for a few minutes, wondering whether he ought to remain in case there was more 'said', but it soon became clear that the practical task was once more all that occupied them. He slithered backwards, secretly hoping that he squashed a few ants in the process, to a point at which he might walk, bent low as if with a crippled back, until hidden by a clump of elder and holly. He straightened, wincing slightly, swore as he brushed a final ant from his neck, whence it had reached in the ascent to his cheek, and strode purposefully towards the manorial buildings. He hoped his report would satisfy his superiors.

Chapter Eight

Undersheriff and serjeant were admitted into the bailey without question, though they were watched every step by curious eyes. They entered the hall to find it empty, and walked to the door at the end, where Catchpoll beat a smart tattoo upon the heavy planks. It was opened by a man, or rather one just 'fledged' to manhood, muscled from a man's labour, but yet with a certain gangly untidiness of limb and uncertainty of jawline. This must be Corbin, Brictmer the Steward's hope and joy. He vacillated between looking respectful and bullish, as if he could not decide whether he should admit them or not. In the end he did what was wisest, and left the problem to someone more important.

'The lord Sheriff's men are here, my lady.' He did not specify which lady he addressed.

The lady Avelina emerged from the gloom, thrusting Corbin out of the way before her, and pulling the door closed behind her. She stood, head held high and bosom heaving, which pleased Catchpoll no end, before the solar door. Her arms were outstretched as if protecting it and its occupant with her body. Corbin looked even more unsure what he should do. The lady's pose looked very impressive until the door was opened behind her by the lady Matilda, whereupon the younger woman almost fell backwards into the chamber.

'Do not be a fool, girl,' she admonished, as if her daughter-in-law were a scullery maid, and stared at Bradecote. 'If you must speak with my son, lord Undersheriff, then speak, but be mindful that he is weak, and still confused of mind. If you press upon him too hard, I will have you leave.' Bradecote wondered if she might actually try to achieve that herself, forcibly. 'He,' and she pointed at Catchpoll, 'does not enter.'

Bradecote took breath to remonstrate at being given orders, but Catchpoll responded swiftly.

'Be sure I shall not, my lady.' It was unusually meek and mild of Catchpoll, but Bradecote did not so much as blink an eye, knowing the serjeant had never been interested in remaining for the interview, and now had Corbin on hand to ply with questions.

Bradecote stepped into the solar, and the smell of lavender and rosemary overlaid with illness, but he did not smell death. Just for a moment his brain marvelled that it was that particular sense that alerted him, more than sight or sound, to its presence, as if it whispered in the manner of a cooking odour, teasing with what was to come. The room was overwarm, with a brazier burning beyond the bed, and a man with sallow skin that looked as bloodless as vellum, lying beneath the covers. Well, there was not a doubt the man had been very ill. However, the

127

eyes, which were open but a little, did not, thought Bradecote, have the distant, bemused look he would have expected with such a complexion. They glinted in a surprisingly alert way.

'Durand FitzRoger, I am Hugh Bradecote, Undersheriff. I understand you are ill – have been ill – but I am investigating the death of an envoy of the Prince of Powys, almost certainly within this manor, and while your fever might have been in abeyance. I must therefore ask questions of you. Do you understand?'

The man wet his lips, and nodded, slowly.

'Hywel ap Rhodri was your cousin, the son of your mother's sister. He came here about two weeks since. You saw him.' Bradecote had no proof of this but did not offer it as a question. If the man refuted it, so be it.

'But a little.' The voice was tired.

'You supped with him, perhaps?'

Again Durand FitzRoger nodded.

'Was his manner towards the women, of rank or otherwise, seemly?'

'I cannot recall.'

No, thought Bradecote, you say the words, but memory makes those eyes glitter the more. You recall well enough.

'Did he tell you why he came?'

'No.'

'Did he ask to have speech with your brother alone?' Again, Bradecote had no proof, but he was interested as to whether Durand would immediately create distance between the murdered man and his brother, or not. He watched, watched as intently as a cat with a mouse, and was as still. There was a pause, very slight, when he would swear Durand was weighing up possibilities. There came the nod, and Bradecote heard a soft but sudden intake of breath from behind his back. Was that surprise at a truth admitted or a lie created?

'But you did not speak with him privately?'

'No. Saw him at dinner. Welshman.' Durand sounded suitably vague and confused, and his hand gripped the blanket convulsively. There was a swishing of skirts.

'You have learnt all you need, and can see my son is in no condition to be of use to you.' The lady Matilda's voice was low, but firm. Bradecote did not turn to look at her, but raised a hand to quiet her.

'One question more, my lady. FitzRoger, did you kill, or did you have killed, Hywel ap Rhodri?'

'No. I did not.'

'Thank you. I wish you a full recovery, and safe return to service with de Clare.' Bradecote turned, and found the lady Matilda glaring at him. The lady Avelina ignored him entirely, but went to the bed, and took up a cloth from a bowl of water set on a stand beside it, and began to bathe Durand's face, murmuring as a mother to a child, and Bradecote thought the curling lip of the older woman was more at that than at him.

'I could have answered your questions,' hissed the lady Matilda. 'What point was there in agitating a sick man?'

'I think, my lady, he is strong enough not to be "agitated" by the few questions I put to him.'

'And what weight can you give to the answers of a fevered brain, my lord? He is confused of mind, and nothing he says is assured.'

'Then you must corroborate. Did he only meet Hywel ap Rhodri at dinner?'

'Yes.'

'And he did not speak with him alone?'

'No.'

'How can you know that? Or do you watch your son as a hen with but a single chick, and never let him from your sight?'

'You are insulting, my lord.'

'No, it is you who are insulting, insulting my intelligence. If your son was well enough to be sat at table, he would not be under your eye for every minute, for he is a man grown, with his own will. He would not relish you acting as nursemaid.'

She coloured.

'When did you hear that Hywel was on his way to Gloucester?' Bradecote threw the unexpected question at her.

'I . . . do not recall.'

'It would seem a rash thing to make known, as his prince's envoy.'

'He was among kin.'

'Kin he had never met before, and if he knew Durand FitzRoger is of the household of Gilbert de Clare, then he may well know that de Clare is, for the present, sided with King Stephen.'

'He did not make any announcement. I must have heard it from his servant.' She looked flustered.

'What was the servant's name, lady?' He was pressing her, pressing her hard.

'How should I know or care?' She drew herself up, imperiously.

'Because I am wondering why you were present when his servant made such a declaration.'

'He said it to Hywel ap Rhodri, at . . .'

'Dinner?'

'The second night. Durand was not present upon the second night, for he was feeling unwell again.'

'How convenient.' Hugh Bradecote was not a man who sneered often, but when he did, it was impressive. It also achieved his aim. 'I am wondering also how you understood the man when he had almost no words other than Welsh.'

'You cannot speak to me in this manner. I am Matilda FitzGilbert, lady of this manor and . . .'

'Lady mother of the lord, Thorold FitzRoger, which is not quite the same, since he is wed.' Bradecote wanted this woman angry, for she was only going to betray things she wanted hidden when in ire. His voice was smooth. 'I wonder what Hywel ap Rhodri wanted to talk in private about, with your elder son?'

'Durand's mind wanders. There was no meeting.'

'Do not tell me you watch Thorold as closely as Durand, for it would be impossible if one were tied to a sickbed and the other entertaining a guest, however unwillingly.'

If looks could be weapons, Bradecote knew he would have a dagger at his throat by now.

'He would have been explaining his misdemeanours with the servant girls, no doubt.' It sounded a feeble reason even to the lady.

'A private interview over a subject that was probably raised by the lady Avelina telling her husband of his wandering hands in the first place?'

'She would not complain if a man's hands wandered over any part of her,' snapped the lady Matilda.

'Actually, I was referring to the maid Aldith having complained to her mistress, but we will let that pass, for now.' He concealed his interest. 'You see, if the lady of the manor,' he stressed the position, and saw her squirm, 'reported it to her husband, and you also were well aware of it, it sounds most unlikely that Hywel ap Rhodri would want to talk in private to make an apology.'

'I doubt he ever apologised for anything he did,' she spat.

'That, at the least, my lady, is probably very true. What did he do that made you so angered against him?'

She flushed, a deep, dark redness suffusing her cheeks, overlaying the mere spots that marked her anger. Bradecote would swear she was embarrassed, and suddenly he thought of what she had said earlier, that Hywel was like his father. He made a guess, but it was not a wild one.

'Did Rhodri ap Arwel ever apologise to you?'

Her response took him completely by surprise. She hit him, full across the face, very hard. His cheek stung, and he could feel the scarlet weal of her imprint rise upon his skin. Only by the slight flaring of his nostrils might one have seen that he had to control himself at that.

'Was that what you would have liked to do to him? Perhaps you did, all those years ago.' His voice was still even. 'Let me guess. If Hywel, and I am afraid we know an awful lot about Hywel ap Rhodri and women, was like his sire, then Rhodri ap Arwel would be bold enough to woo two sisters and find it exciting, and then choose one to the disappointment of the other. You were disappointed, weren't you, and then married off to Roger FitzGilbert, a man as exciting as a bucket and, I guess again, hardly youthful and vigorous. It must have been a great disappointment. I wonder at you being so dutiful.'

'She had no choice.'

Bradecote turned. Avelina FitzRoger stood in the doorway, and her mouth was twisted in disdain.

'But—'

'Rhodri ap Arwel preferred Hywel's mother, Emma, and I am sure I can see why, but not until after he had "tasted the pleasures" of the older sister. Not quite good enough, were you?' The lady Avelina laughed, and it was not a nice laugh. 'And there are consequences to that.'

'What would you know, Barren Wife.' Bradecote actually stepped back, letting the two women's mutual loathing crackle like lightning between them.

'Was Roger FitzGilbert paid well to take you, who had already been "taken"? Did he know? Or was the mewling rat of a son a shock so early in the marriage?'

'Thorold was an eight-month child. He came early to the world, and seemed like not to live, yet he did, however weak it made him. He had that strength, more is the pity.' The older woman sounded bitter.

'Aye, and pity for me. Barren Wife you call me, but what wife would not be with a husband like him. I am married to a man who should not even be master here.'

'No. He is Roger's son, Roger's blood. I did not wed until three months after my sister, and Thorold was an eight-month babe, I tell you. Upon the Holy Book I would swear that, as I told Dur—' She stopped, and blinked at Bradecote as if he had appeared out of nowhere.

'So Hywel ap Rhodri told Durand he was the rightful lord of Doddenham, did he? True or false, that was a dangerous thing to disclose, and mighty malicious too. Did you and your sister part on bad terms, lady, all those years ago? Did he make the claim out of spite, or revenge?'

'Both, I dare say. He was his father's son, and his mother's also. Between them they spawned a cross between a goat and a serpent, all hungry pizzle and false tongue. Thorold is my son, and the son of Roger FitzGilbert, oft though I have regretted it. And,' she looked back to her daughter-in-law, 'if you think Thorold would be glad of an heir of your body, even if through his brother's loins, think again. Is that why you whine and weep over Durand? Do you fear he might die and leave you unsatisfied, girl?' A thought hit her. 'Sweet Virgin, you did not let that Welsh ram tup you, did you? I told Thorold he was a fool to marry you.'

Bradecote had been congratulating himself upon finding out so much, but this was now but one step from a cat fight, and no man with any sense got involved in those. He said nothing, and simply walked out. In the fresh air he heaved a huge sigh of relief, and headed for the gate, just as Thorold FitzRoger trotted in, though there was no sign of his hawker. For a moment Bradecote considered warning him, but then decided if the man could not control either wife or mother he was not much of a man, and besides, he did not like the man. He was more concerned that the tingling handprint on his cheek should not linger enough for Catchpoll to notice.

Meanwhile, Catchpoll had been playing 'fatherly man of the world' with Corbin, with regard to women. The lad's brain was in a whirl, which was ideal for Catchpoll's purposes. As soon as Bradecote had disappeared into the solar, and the door shut to exclude all others, Catchpoll took Corbin gently by the arm and led him outside to a bench at the side of the hall.

'Can't say as you can ever understand 'em, lad, but a wise man learns when the best thing to do is get out of the way. Women!' He shook his head in mystification.

'She pushed me out of the way,' said Corbin, dreamily, though regretfully. He was torn between wishing she had ordered him to bar the door, and thus prove his devotion to her, and the fact that in shoving him through the doorway she had actually touched him. Catchpoll was no fool.

'Aye, which proves women do not think straight. If that door was to be barred and barred proper, it was you, not she, who could do it. But did the lady think? No, she did not, at least not like a man. They reacts, you see, like a startled horse, all feelings, not thinkings. Must be hard, being in a chamber with two such as the ladies of this hall.'

'They hates each other. Always picking on her is old lady Matilda, treating her like a child, or a servant, and my lady Avelina is doing so much, tending the lord Durand even in the night.'

'Doubt that delights her lord much, though, if she leaves his bed to—'

'The doubt is whether he would notice. The poor lady is much neglected, and what man, what real man, could neglect a lady as beautiful as she is?' Corbin tried not to think how wonderful the lady Avelina would be curled up beside him, because he was too lowly and unworthy to even sleep like a hound at the foot of her bed, and it was sinful, her being a married lady. On the other hand, thinking about it made him tingle, and he could not imagine actually wanting to waste time in sleeping at all if she were lying there . . .

Catchpoll read him as easily as he could the trail of a shod horse in soft ground. He let him have his moments of sinful pleasure. What he had not said to Corbin was that in the first flush of manhood, where the body had reached a peak but the mind was yet to lose the impetuosity of the child, the male could be as 'all feelings' as the female. Corbin was in just such a state, and Catchpoll knew that to be dangerous. The lad could be manipulated to do things in heat, and without thought to consequences.

'Has the lord Durand been so sick he needs nursing through the night?' Catchpoll dragged Corbin's thoughts reluctantly from the lady Avelina.

'He has that, poor man. At times he has thrashed about, his mind lost, his body tormented as by a fiend from hell,' Corbin crossed himself, 'and I have had to hold him down upon the bed. At others he was so weak I had to lift his head that he might be given the draughts my lady Matilda makes of willow and feverfew. And him such a strong and vital man in health.' There was a touch of admiration.

'But yet sometimes he is recovered, and then falls back into sickness?'

'It is strange, but so. My lady was jubilant when first he improved and could leave his bed, though weak, but the lady Matilda was watchful, and refused to give thanks for deliverance.'

'Well, she has the years to have seen such things and know, where the younger lady would not.'

'She was right, the lady Matilda. For some days he seemed upon the road to health, even ate within the hall when—And then of a sudden he was as bad as before.'

Catchpoll noted the omission of any mention of Hywel ap Rhodri and thought it time to introduce the name.

'When the Welshmen were here, so I heard.' It was worth seeing how Corbin reacted. He made no denial, perhaps eased by thinking the knowledge already in the open. 'Never trusted the Welsh, myself,' he added.

'Never met many before they came. "Riddian", that was the servant's name; he seemed decent enough, not that you could get much from him, but . . .' Corbin's face clouded.

'But . . . ?' Catchpoll waited, patiently, as the fisherman who has the fish investigating the bait.

'He was a bastard, lordly or not, that Hywel ab Roddy, who thought anything in a skirt was his.' Corbin's hands clenched into fists.

'Well, the lady Matilda wears a skirt, but I doubt he would have gone that far. A man would need to be lost of mind to fancy a woman of her ilk.' Catchpoll wanted any hint of whether Hywel had sniffed about the skirts of the lady Avelina, and thought this might get an indirect answer.

'No, he liked them young,' Corbin growled, and for a moment there was no youth, but man, revolted as Walkelin had been revolted. 'I am glad he is dead, by whatever means.' It was almost a cry.

'Not just a pat on the behind and a stolen kiss type, then?' Catchpoll knew all too well Hywel's 'type'.

Corbin just shook his head, brows gathered, a muscle moving in his cheek. Had he seen? Had he intervened? If Corbin had seen his cousin speechless, had heard that Aldith, the girl he grew up beside, had struck out at Hywel ap Rhodri to defend her honour, might he have acted if he saw the wench Winfraeth being molested? Was that what she was holding back? Such simple folk as these might not be certain that killing a man caught in the act of rape would not be a crime, just as with the man caught stealing the chickens or the scrip of coin. Killing him after, now that was different, and Catchpoll had no idea which might have occurred.

Bradecote found Catchpoll and Walkelin leaning against the east wall of the church, out of the sun.

'You look like the lord Sheriff when he has heard how much tax we have collected,' declared Catchpoll, grinning.

'Well, that may be good or bad, depending on whether it is enough.'

'Never enough, my lord, you can be sure of that, but usually enough to keep him in a decent humour. I take it the solar proved useful.'

'I certainly learnt much, within it and without, though where it takes us is as yet unclear. Have you discoveries also?'

'Aye, my lord, but let us see how they sits with yours.' Catchpoll moved to the side, thus creating a space for the undersheriff to join them in the shade.

'Well, some things were already guessed. The two ladies of the manor hate each other to the point where, when I left, it was a toss-up as to whether they might be found by Thorold FitzRoger brawling on the hall floor.'

'Then my money would be on the older dame,' laughed Catchpoll.

'Agreed. The lady Avelina dotes upon Durand, but not the way his mother does, just as the priest said, and that lady even made the suggestion that the lady Avelina might have let Hywel have his way with her too, out of excess of desire.'

'Or the fact that her lord is not up to the task, as young Corbin told me,' interjected Catchpoll. 'I would guess that was common knowledge in the manor.'

'Well, what I got from Durand was interesting. He is not a well man, it takes no physician to see that, and looks weak at present, but his head is not as confused as he, or his mother, tries to make out. I doubt he could walk or ride far this day, but he could think straight and fast enough. He admitted only to meeting Hywel ap Rhodri at dinner the first night, and claimed he knew nothing of the man's manner with women, of any rank. That was a lie written over his vellum cheeks and in his narrowed eyes.'

'Which means if he and the lady Avelina are . . . entangled, and he thought the Welshman had been taking the "rights" he had in turn taken from his brother, he has a motive for murder,' murmured Walkelin.

'He does, though whether his ailing on the second night was real or feigned, we do not know. If he did not kill him, he might have had Corbin do it, upon the pretence the man had insulted the lady, though he denied either, firmly.'

'It would work, my lord, as a trail of events. If the lady has been playing false with the brother . . .' Catchpoll scratched at his beard.

'But there is a hole in this bucket, Catchpoll.' Bradecote frowned. 'Durand FitzRoger must be nigh on thirty, and has been in the employ of Gilbert de Clare some years. I doubt he has lived here since his brother's marriage. The lady Avelina is not many years over a score, at a guess, and from one of the lady Matilda's insults, Thorold took not a child bride, but rather a woman grown to beauty, and has therefore wed since Durand left the manor.'

'Three years ago, so said Brictmer the Steward, remember,' interjected Catchpoll.

'Why?' asked Walkelin.

'What do you mean, "why"?' Catchpoll frowned at his serjeanting apprentice.

'I mean if Thorold FitzRoger scarcely beds his wife, why would a beauty interest him?'

'A fair point, Walkelin,' agreed Bradecote, 'but he would want an heir, especially if he and his brother are not close. It might be he thought a comely wife might inspire him, or even that it would conceal his failings, because others, lusting after her, would not be able to imagine that he did not. Things are not always simple. It does not help with the fact that the lady might never have met Durand until he returned ailing upon a litter, and too sick to lust after.'

'An awful lot of lusting in this murder, my lord,' remarked Catchpoll.

'There is.'

'Would not Durand have returned to see his mother, at least a few times over the years?' Walkelin, a good and dutiful son, could not imagine cutting all connection with his mother.

'My lord, you forget the priest. He said that he could not discount a bodily sinning between the two, but hoped it was just flattery and suggestion. He can only know that from previous encounters and rumour,' Catchpoll reminded them.

'There is that. I forgot. Let us accept, then, that they have met before, when he was in health and of full manliness. He comes home very ill, and she nurses him, but fears he will die. Hywel turns up, all Welsh charm . . .' Catchpoll guffawed derisively at this, 'and giving off signals like a stag in the rutting season. If she is starved of a man, and Durand, however much she loves him for his body, may be of no further use to her, might she show willing?'

'She would have to be a pretty heartless piece.' Walkelin was rather shocked at the thought of a woman effectively using men for her needs, at a base level.

'I doubt having a heart would aid her in her life at present, Walkelin. She is probably selfish, grown so if not born so, realising she is trapped, and not even having a child to give heart-love.' Bradecote tried to feel some sympathy for her situation.

'Which means Durand might have had a motive to kill Hywel ap Rhodri.'

'And what of the husband, my lord? Even a dog who does not want to eat his bone will snap at the hound that tries to steal it from him,' Walkelin added.

'The more so if he caught them at it.' Catchpoll nodded.

'If he had caught them thus, he would have killed the man at that moment, so they could not have been together the first night.'

'But Hywel was gone by the third morning, my lord, so if he found them the second night . . .' Walkelin did not give up.

'But Catchpoll and I saw the lady's reaction when Thorold told her Hywel was dead. She did not know. If he had killed him, stabbed him in the back, surely it would be when Thorold found them in adultery, and even if he found but did not kill then, she would guess that, dragged off, Hywel's treatment would be severe.'

'And Thorold liked telling her he was dead. If he had killed him, I think he would have taunted her with it before now, my lord.'

'That he did, Catchpoll. However, think on it another way. Thorold FitzRoger is not a man of strong body or fighting mind. He likes to watch. He likes his hawking, but have you seen a single hound about this manor? I doubt he hunts. Such a man might think it more appealing to wait, not even let the wife know he knows she is cuckolding him at this point, and has Corbin drag him off in the night, kill the man in front of him and hide the corpse, upon the reason that he had found the Welshman abusing the lady. That ensures the manor remains silent to protect Corbin. He can bring out the deed to taunt his wife at will.'

'Nasty, that, but . . . possible. So, both brothers might have good reason to see Hywel dead.' Catchpoll sucked his teeth.

'That is not all, though.' Bradecote raised a hand. 'We have to include the lady Matilda.'

'We do?' Walkelin blinked in surprise.

'She has reason. We knew she married Roger FitzGilbert after her sister went into Wales as the wife of Rhodri ap Arwel, and I had guessed he had made eyes at her too. But there is the possibility there were more than stolen kisses. Thorold was an early babe, and weak. The lady Avelina accused her of having borne Rhodri's brat, and that Durand was the rightful lord of Doddenham.'

Catchpoll whistled through his gapping teeth, which Bradecote interpreted correctly.

'Yes, dangerous talk. The lady Matilda swears she was wed three months after her sister, and that Thorold was born a month too soon. If that is true, then he has to be Roger FitzGilbert's. If she heard the words from Hywel ap Rhodri herself, who was told that tale by his mother, and with him wanting to make trouble for the aunt his mother hated, then the lady Matilda might have thought it just an attempt to blackmail or upset her. She might not have known Durand knew at the first, and told him it was a lie only later, even after Hywel left.'

'Do you believe her, my lord?' Catchpoll was pulling a 'thinking face'.

'I think it likely that Thorold is the rightful lord. She sounded regretful that it was so, but firm in her assertion. Whether she succumbed to Rhodri ap Arwel I do not know. Not every coupling ends in a child. When he chose her sister, she may have told her what had occurred, or Rhodri might have boasted of it to his wife to hurt her in an argument, or when the wine took him. We shall never know, but neither sister had direct contact ever again, and Matilda FitzGilbert is a very bitter and angry woman when it comes to Rhodri ap Arwel. If she heard the son was like the father with women, and he tried blackmailing her, she would have him removed without a second thought, both in revenge upon her sister and Rhodri, and because he might threaten Doddenham.'

'Would she do it herself, my lord? I have not seen the lady.' Walkelin did not find it easy to imagine her doing so.

'She has the strength of will, and if she caught him unsuspecting, from behind, she might have done it herself.' Catchpoll paused. 'But . . .'

'My "but" is that she has something that son Thorold shares, she would want to see the look in Hywel ap Rhodri's eyes as the blade bit, watch him die. If she did it herself, I would have thought she would do so to his front, not in the back, though she might as easily have decided to order the death, for dishonours in the manor, to show her power here, which is strong.' Bradecote sighed. 'So the only one of the lordly class we dismiss is the lady Avelina herself, and we did not suspect her anyway.'

'But we have better reasons now, my lord, and reasons we can prod and probe.' Catchpoll was positive. 'And young Walkelin has news from the hayfield also.'

'Yes, my lord, I did as—' Walkelin stopped. Winfraeth was coming into the village, a bucket in either hand, heading to the well. She was alone. Walkelin looked from serjeant to undersheriff, who both nodded. They slipped round the side of the church to sit upon the grass and think upon all they had learnt, whilst Walkelin would try and use his honest, decent face, to persuade the village girl to give up her secrets.

Chapter Nine

'May I draw the water for you?' asked Walkelin, with a shy smile. He had the ability to look remarkably unthreatening and trustworthy. Winfraeth was not immune to that charm. She nodded, and let him fall into step beside her as she walked to the well.

'Hot work, hay making, though I am from Worcester and not used to that labour, I confess.' He made it sound a failing, but Winfraeth saw a certain glamour in not having a life based upon the fields and crops.

'I have never been to Worcester,' she said, softly, as though it were Jerusalem. 'Is the cathedral as big as they say?'

'Oh yes,' Walkelin could not disguise his pride. 'The roof is so high inside you could put two houses on top of each other, even tall ones with a solar, at the least. And there is glass in the windows, lots of glass.'

'Oooh,' sighed Winfraeth, even more impressed, as Walkelin dropped the bucket down the well. He paused a moment.

'That Welshman, the one who came here. He is dead now.' Walkelin wanted to see her reaction. She said the right words, but they sounded rehearsed.

'He never is! Well, I ought to pray for his soul, but he was not a nice man.'

'My lord Undersheriff and Serjeant Catchpoll, they say that too. He would not keep his hands to himself, they say, and was a menace to decent women.'

'He was. I—' She stopped, but Walkelin looked the picture of sympathetic understanding, and he was only a lowly man-at-arms and not the lord Undersheriff or his rather frightening serjeant. Her resolve melted away. Here was a sympathetic ear, and with no connection to the folk among whom she lived. 'I saw him, the second morning after he came, by the twin oaks, and with the lady Avelina.' Her voice dropped. 'I was not looking, but I saw. She was in his arms, and . . . I would have said by choice, but for . . .'

'But for what?' Walkelin sounded more intrigued than interrogative.

'He saw me. I know he saw me, and I ran away, and I told nobody, not even my father or Ketel.'

'Ketel?'

'He is . . . I had hoped . . . And we are very fond . . . but . . .'

'You speak in riddles, Winfraeth, if I may use your name.'

'I ran away and I told him, when he, the Welshman, found me, that I had told nobody, but he did not believe me.' She was not truly attending to him now. 'I was in the field, and he must

146

have watched for me, for when I went to the thicket to—' She blushed. 'I never saw him until he grabbed me from behind, and his hand was over my mouth. He said as how I was a nosey wench and he ought to slice my nose right off as a warning.' She was silent for a moment. 'I almost wish he had, instead.' She bent her head, and a shudder ran through her.

'Sweet Jesu, your father and your man must have wanted to kill him. How did you stop them?'

'They would have . . . so I did not tell them, said I had caught my gown in a bramble and fallen, to account for tears to the cloth and the bruise on my face and . . . When I heard he was dead I could not let Ketel wed me with the lie in my heart. I told him, though not about the lady, and he said as he believed me, and . . . There will be no child from it, thank the Holy Virgin for hearing my prayers,' she crossed herself. 'He told my father it was his choice, and he would stand by me . . . But now I wonder if it is right to make him do so. What must he think? I could do nothing, nothing, but—'

Walkelin laid a tentative hand upon her arm, and when he spoke, it was not as a sheriff's man.

'If he said it was his choice, it was so, and he knows that you are maid at heart. If you blight his life, and yours, by keeping from him, then the Welshman has another victory over you, even though his body rots. Winfraeth, what you have told me is important, and I am duty-bound to tell the undersheriff, but I swear to you, no other person in Doddenham will know what you have said to me, nor shall we speak of it with Ketel or your father. It is further proof of the man, and his misdeeds, not of guilt that you or yours should feel.' Walkelin was perhaps

147

no more than eight or nine years her senior, but he felt as old as Serjeant Catchpoll, and as serious. 'Now, I will carry these buckets to where you leave the track, and no further, so none sees that you spoke with me.'

She looked at him through her tears, and his honesty was so patent that she sniffed, wiped her nose upon her sleeve, and nodded.

'Thank you.'

When his superiors saw the look upon Walkelin's face they knew, knew as clearly as if he had told them in words. It was rare to see him look other than an essentially kindly soul, and at this moment he looked like a man who had killing on his mind.

'So he did. We had to think it likely.' Catchpoll hawked, and spat into the grass.

'If he were not dead already, I would see him swing, Serjeant, but only after I had had my time with him, and he would want the rope by then.' Unthinkingly, Walkelin echoed Bradecote's words to Rhys ap Iorwerth. He proceeded to tell them Winfraeth's tale. 'I swore we would not make it known in Doddenham, not see her shamed.'

'Why should she suffer more? You did right, Walkelin. We can only be thankful that he let her live, and that her man is sensible and understanding. But it gives us more to think upon.' Bradecote was grim.

'Not least where the bastard got the stamina,' grumbled Catchpoll. 'He seems to have needed women like most men need bread.'

'He cannot have gone about like this in Mathrafal, my lord, else there would not be a woman untouched.' Walkelin was still seething.

'I think he saw this time in England as his chance to do what he wanted as often as he wanted, without fear of consequences, since he had no intention of returning. I, like you both, think the knife was too swift a death, but that is what he got.'

'Pity it is that a knife in the back cannot be self-defence, for even if it went before the Justices for the killing, if the man – or woman – did for him to keep his own life, the penalty would be light. That is if any at all, especially if we gave it that Hywel ap Rhodri had raped and murdered his way through our shires.' Catchpoll shook his head.

'Which helps us not at all now,' remarked Bradecote, stretching. 'Winfraeth saw him with the lady Avelina, but told nobody. What we need to know is whether any other saw their indiscretion, and whether husband or ailing lover, in thought or deed, saw them. Might Durand have followed her, seen her with Hywel, and feigned illness to cover his plans for later that day?'

'The ladies nursing him would have known, at the least,' Catchpoll reminded him.

'But the lady Matilda only said he fell ill the second day, not when upon that day, and . . . could he have left the solar in the night, murdered Hywel ap Rhodri and his servant and . . . He could not have got the bodies away, though, not without people knowing.'

'But they did know, within the manor walls and in the village. Winfraeth said she told her swain Ketel when it was known the Welshman was dead, and we did not say to them he was dead. Besides, everyone in the manor would be happy

149

if he were dead and gone after the things he did. If Durand killed "the Welsh bastard" and his servant, he need not even have admitted it, my lord. Come the morning, the bodies are discovered. The lord Thorold decides it is best hidden and forgotten, since whoever had cause had a just one, and arranges for the disposal of the bodies. In which case Rhydian might lie as far as the shire boundary.' Walkelin warmed to the theory.

'So why keep one horse, and where is the pony, Walkelin?' asked Bradecote.

'Rhydian's body was taken under a cloth on a cart, with produce or wood, or some other disguising reason. The pony was used to take Hywel ap Rhodri's body over the border into Oswaldslow Hundred, or on as far as the woods by Cotheridge, and then taken perhaps and sold in Worcester before any of us knew of the death. One grey pony sold by a man is not worthy of questioning, in the way of everyday. The horse is more distinctive, and worth more also, and so if nobody is like to come sniffing about in Doddenham, the horse is best kept until the lord Durand takes it with him to Gilbert de Clare, as his spare horse or to sell to another knight.'

'Now that, young Walkelin, is at least a sound reasoning. Beasts change hands often enough in Worcester that the animal, if ever there, might be long gone, and other than it was grey, we have no description of it. We cannot trace it.' Catchpoll shrugged.

'And if we ask who left the village for several days, let alone with a pony that did not return, we will get blank looks again, pox on it.' Bradecote frowned. 'Did you get anything new from Corbin, son of the steward?'

'He is clearly smitten by the lady Avelina, and spoke as if it were common knowledge that the lord Thorold is lacking as a husband, as I said. He also said Hywel was a bastard who "liked them young" so he knows, at least after the event, of what happened to Aldith and also, as I guess, Milburga. Winfraeth we can discount on this, since she kept her tongue in her head until after the death, and only spoke to man and father.' Catchpoll pulled one earlobe. 'He was very aggrieved, so if he did not see, then he saw the results in Aldith's anger or the girl's muteness. If someone had told him the Welshman had laid hand on his adored lady Avelina, he would have been capable on that score too, but in the run of things he is an ordinary lad, and not the killing type without cause.'

'But perhaps he had cause, or was given it. One man we have not spoken to by name is Tovi, father to the silent Milburga. He would have cause enough by any reasoning. I should have asked for him in the field, since he might well be with his fellows in their time of need for every strong arm.' Bradecote chastised himself for forgetting another man by name.

'I think not, my lord, for I heard the sound of hammer upon iron when we went to the field to ask our questions. I would say his workshop lies on the west side of the village and set a little apart in case of fire.'

'Keeping your ears open, good lad,' nodded Catchpoll, approvingly, and Walkelin relaxed a little, and smiled.

The wheelwright's was in fact perfectly obvious from the fact that there was a new wheel lying on the bare earth beside it, and from the sound of sawing within. They entered, and saw the wheelwright and a lad who was almost certainly his son, from colour and build. Tovi the Wheelwright was a big man, with a mane of hair that was plastered, at the front, to his sweat-beaded forehead. Bradecote expected a booming voice to match, but he spoke with diffidence, in a slow, deep voice. He was also very wary, and as soon as Bradecote identified himself, sent the boy to draw fresh buckets of water from the well.

'We have to ask about what happened to your daughter, because it concerns Hywel ap Rhodri, who is dead by violence.'

'He frightened her, frightened her so bad she says no word since.' The wheelwright's chest seemed full of a deep rumble of wrath. 'Wanted to kill him myself I did, when I saw her, but . . .'

'Why didn't you?' Catchpoll asked, reasonably.

Tovi looked at him blankly.

'It is a good question, Master Wheelwright. If this man . . . harmed your daughter so, what father would not feel as you did, nor act upon that feeling?'

'He was my lord's guest, a guest in this manor. Guest right is—'

'Guest right? You did not want to break guest right? But the man broke it himself by his act, so there was nothing to prevent you taking action, nothing at all.' Bradecote was amazed. Tovi looked at the ground, sullen, and peculiarly defeated.

'I did not kill him.' There was genuine regret in the voice.

'Do you say this for fear of the penalty? Tovi?' The wheelwright did not look up.

'Answer the lord Undersheriff,' commanded Catchpoll, feeling that he needed reminding of the rank of the man addressing him.

'I did not kill him,' repeated the big man, with great emphasis. 'My Milburga is but a girl still, a little girl, not a woman. She had no strength to fend him off, no more than a lamb before a wolf. You think it does not torment me, seeing her as she is, broken in spirit, timid even with me and her brother? She flinches at sudden movement, stares at me with big, empty eyes, and makes little sounds in her dreams, whimpering wordless sounds. I would have killed him, broken him with my bare hands, and broken him slow, but it was not for me to do.' The man's face was a conflicting mask of pain and anger.

'You stood back? I cannot see how you did that.' Walkelin looked wonderingly at the wheelwright.

'It was not for me to do,' repeated the man slowly, regretfully, and Bradecote had the feeling they were words he said as often as did Father Dunstan the offices of the day.

'Then who did? Whose right was greater than yours, Tovi?' Catchpoll was trying to comprehend, and failing.

The wheelwright just stared at him, and the serjeant thought he might as well be asking questions of one of the great oaks. Bradecote was as confused. This man was ravaged by what he faced every time he looked at his daughter, guilty that at one vital moment he had not been there to protect her, and had not thereafter taken action on her behalf, gutted by the way it had taken her from him and left a trembling wraith. The first might have been beyond his power, but the second . . . Only something very important could have prevented a father taking rightful retribution for such an act upon a child.

'Tovi, in the end we must know, must know all that happened. If you did not kill him, then you must know who did, and that name we will have, now or later.' Inevitability seemed better than threat, for how could one threaten a man to whom the worst must have already seemed to have happened?

He stood immobile, not even blinking, and there was a limit to how long they could stand staring back.

'This is not the end of it,' said Bradecote, heavily, and turned to leave. Catchpoll and Walkelin followed, and for several minutes none of them spoke.

'He knows and will not tell, and he did want to kill Hywel ap Rhodri, wanted it bad.' Walkelin shook his head.

'Cannot have been easy to stop him, either,' mused Bradecote, 'which must mean more than physical strength involved, unless you had four strong men, and kept the wheelwright chained for the rest of the Welshman's stay.'

'Which means power, my lord, and that means the FitzRogers. If they promised—'

'If they promised, Serjeant, why did they do nothing for another whole day and then kill him?' Walkelin asked, with calm reason. 'They did not even imprison him, for he was at liberty that second morning to be with the lady Avelina and attack the maid Winfraeth. It is madness.'

'We are missing something, something important.' Bradecote shook his head. 'And we have nothing in proof but victims who tell us little or nothing.'

'We really need that horse,' sighed Walkelin, 'then we can face them with being involved, all of them. One will break rank in this shield wall of silence.'

'Then that is your duty for the morrow, Walkelin. Follow Corbin, since it was more likely him than some man-at-arms that moved the beast, so he knows where it is concealed. Find the horse, and Serjeant Catchpoll and I will try and untangle the FitzRogers.'

'I knows which task I would prefer,' growled Catchpoll, as they entered the courtyard.

The sheriff's men ate in the manor, but scarcely 'with' it. In the hall, Bradecote felt as welcome as a chilblain, and conversation between the family veered between stilted and unnatural and wildly insulting, all conducted in angry whispers. The altercation between the two ladies had become a mixture of haughty silences and barbed comments, and Thorold FitzRoger siding with his mother had won him surprisingly little support from that dame.

'Oh, do not grovel at my feet, Thorold. It is your fault she is here, in this hall, in my place,' the lady Matilda glanced venomously at Bradecote, as if he too were to blame for this. 'I warned you, but would you listen? There was nothing wrong with the widow of Payn of Martley.'

The lady Avelina nearly choked, which would have pleased her mother-in-law.

'Golde! She is three of you, my lord, and that just in size. Had you taken her to the marriage bed she would have squashed you like a grain of wheat in the quern.'

'At least she was fertile,' snapped the lady Matilda.

'And as big as a field. Ploughing her would have taken a man like an ox team, not my loving Thorold.' Wife curled lip at husband, and Hugh Bradecote wished he could have eaten among the servants and men-at-arms, who looked as though eating were the most strenuous exercise they undertook from one month's end to the next.

'Are you wed?' asked FitzRoger, with obvious desperation.

'Yes.' Bradecote was not going to help the man. It left FitzRoger stuck, since he could scarcely ask after the lady Bradecote's looks, demeanour or, in view of what had just passed, whether she was the mother of a hopeful brood. Bradecote let him flounder, and found himself under the scrutiny of the lady Matilda, whose expression showed that she knew exactly what he was doing. She smiled, wryly.

'Clever fools are dangerous,' she murmured, 'but foolish "clever" men are worse. Give me a man of sense and I would be content.'

'Just give me a man,' purred the lady Avelina, in a voice so deep it nearly rumbled, and won a look of revulsion from the senior lady and enraged embarrassment from her husband. However, since she accompanied the comment with a lengthy gaze under her lashes at Bradecote that made it quite clear that she counted him in that category, he could not be said to enjoy the exchange.

'Do you think that my lord Bradecote is not enjoying his dinner?' whispered Walkelin to Serjeant Catchpoll, with a suppressed grin.

'I don't get ideas, not about them as sits up that end, not unless I want to see 'em before the Justices,' responded Catchpoll, repressively. 'And you ought to hope as he does enjoy his dinner, since an undersheriff with an underfilled belly is likely to take it out upon lowly things like serjeants' apprentices, and you are the only one hereabouts.'

'Sorry, Serjeant.' Walkelin looked suitably chastened, and Catchpoll relented. In truth he was wishing himself in his own home, with a beaker of ale, and an evening of ease. He was, he hated to admit it, getting too long in the tooth for riding day after day without a decent rest, and his back ached and his knees ached, and several muscles he had long ago forgotten he possessed ached. As a result he was jealous of Walkelin's youth and ability to just keep going without a sign of fatigue. It was not the lad's fault, though.

'Never you mind, young Walkelin. If you learns, and keeps yourself from getting killed, one day you won't be an apprentice any longer, and then you can be not getting ideas, just like me.' Catchpoll gave his death's head smile, and a man-at-arms opposite dropped his spoon of hot pottage into his lap and his eyes watered.

Aldith was serving, and still looked as approachable as a hedge-pig, rolled up. Her eyes sparkled with a dislike of anything male, and it was clear that the men-at-arms had long ago learnt that Aldith was not a maid to try and flirt with, at least when not in the mood for it. She was not in the mood.

'They never look happy,' observed a man-at-arms with a double chin, 'even though they gets meat more often than I could ever imagine.'

'But you imagine it every day, anyway,' sneered Aldith, as she passed behind him.

'They had pigeon last week, that the lord Durand got with my lord Thorold's falcon. Four of them there were.'

Catchpoll pricked up his ears.

'So he was up and about was he, back then?' It was a casually put question.

'Well, he was out but for an hour or two, and I doubt he rode far. I heard him say he would go mad if cooped up indoors much longer, but two days later he was back in his bed, and groaning, so I hear, same as the week before. He ought to have taken things steady, I say.'

'And there speaks the physician.' Aldith banged him on the head with her ladle. 'The only thing you do not take steady is your food, and that you take like a swine among beechmast.'

The man-at-arms reddened, and opened his mouth, but then closed it, as Brictmer glared along the table at him. The men-at-arms were not all manor born, and not 'family'. Aldith was, and Brictmer, who, like the priest, rather thought that one day she and Corbin would be plighted, was not going to let a fat man-at-arms insult her. She was prickly, and at present he understood why, but she also had a head on her shoulders, and good common sense. He liked the girl, though she had been orphaned young and had no dower.

'But they should be happy. They sleeps in comfort, eats well and fear not empty plates, and they do nothing,' whined the man-at-arms.

'Much like you, then.' Aldith would have the last word, every time.

There was laughter about the table, of the nervous sort. Aldith had a sharp tongue and wit, but the man-at-arms was big, and if he did bestir himself in anger among his fellows, could hurt.

'You are a needle-wench, Aldith, needle-witted and needle-worded, and I pity the fool—'

'Enough.' Brictmer spoke sharply and banged the flat of his hand upon the table. 'Aldith, the platters are full. Go to the kitchen,' he commanded, but without anger, more a weariness, like a mother who parts squabbling children.

She gave him a glare, but did not defy him, and stalked out as proud as the ladies at the high table.

'Mark him,' muttered Catchpoll to Walkelin, without looking up from his plate. His lips barely moved. 'Find out.'

Walkelin said nothing, but his hand tapped the table twice, as if without meaning, and the serjeant knew his apprentice understood.

Chapter Ten

Hugh Bradecote slept badly, and it was not just pondering upon the puzzle before them. Like it or not, and he liked it not at all, this murder was entwined with rape, which he abhorred. He had always done so, but, having married a woman who had suffered the unwanted attentions of a husband who wanted nothing more or less, he was filled with such an anger in his chest it almost burst out of him. It was so alien, to want to hurt a woman like that, that it set such men in his mind apart from the human. He was no innocent to think no man in drink ever went too far, or that some maids in their foolishness did not know that goading a swain too much made it difficult for him to contain himself. Such things were wrong, and the penalties existed, though in most cases the girl's father would sort the matter with a fist and then a betrothal. He did not condone the act in overexcited hot blood, but that a man should take a woman by force from premeditated choice . . . It made him angry, and these days it made him sick to the stomach. He had seen what it did to a woman, not in her body but her heart and soul. Perhaps Winfræth would be able to place that one deed in a casket of memory to bury, and wed Ketel, and, in time, forget enough that it would not cloud her life. He prayed it would be so, and then his thoughts went to his own Christina, lying now in their bed at Bradecote. He thought her life 'unclouded' now, and knew her to be happy and content, though of late she had sometimes seemed a little thoughtful and distant. She was not dwelling on the past, though, he was sure of that, but rather anxious, hoping that her prayers to the Blessed Edith at Polesworth would be answered, and they had been married six months. He smiled to himself. Six months of marriage felt as though but a week in so many ways. He settled his hands behind his head and let his thoughts stray, and the smile lengthened into a satisfied grin. After a while he shook his head. Such thoughts were not conducive to sleep, and there would be time enough for the thought and the act when all this was over, not before. The trouble was that the problem before them was a knot, and the more he picked at it, the more the strands bit into each other. He sighed, and tried to empty his head. The hall was silent, but for Catchpoll's blessedly moderated snores, and the scrabbling of rat or mouse in the corner. They were background sounds, insufficient to disturb the blanket of quiet. Voices were not.

They came, unexpectedly, from within the solar, and were 'shouting in whispers', agitated, insistent. Bradecote rose from his bed and blanket and trod softly to set his ear to the door, wishing the planks were thinner. One voice was deeper, the cadences those of command, instruction. The other was pleading, or rather insisting without expecting to persuade. He thought for a moment it was a woman's voice, but then realised it was merely young, and must be Corbin. Corbin had gone into the solar before everyone bedded down, no doubt as a strong arm if needed for the sick man in the night. The ladies may even have decided that he could stay awake and on watch and only rouse them if Durand worsened. Playing the ministering angel sounded good and noble, but was exhausting over a long period, and the man had been ill, off and on, for the best part of a month.

Corbin was in quite heated conversation with a man, which meant Thorold or Durand FitzRoger. Damn the door. Bradecote pressed his ear so hard to the wood that the grain left red marks upon his flesh. The only words that he thought he made out were 'I swear it, my lord', in a desperate undertone. There were five people in the chamber, or at least in that room and up the steep wooden stair to the chamber above. Bradecote visualised the chamber. He had not taken much notice of its arrangements, but there was another cot upon the far side, curtained off. It made sense that the lady Matilda slept there, since the son would not care to be bedding, or not bedding, his wife within feet of his mother, and the stair was steep enough to deter a woman of her age and size from ascending it nightly. The truckle upon which Durand had lain must normally be for any guest and could have been set up in the hall at need, if the guest merited it.

Were the others soundly asleep? Might they also hear, and why risk that they might do so? Whatever was being said was very private, and very important. Durand seemed the more likely other man, if Corbin was there to care for him. So what had Corbin need to swear to, and why was Durand so agitated?

The voices ceased. Bradecote moved quietly back to his own rough bed, and all thoughts of wife and comfort were thrust firmly aside. He wanted to sleep, because there was nothing he could do in the middle of the night, his suspects could not leave without him knowing, and a bleary eye and befuddled brain would do him no good when daylight came. It did not mean sleep came the quicker.

He awoke without enthusiasm, feeling jaded, and rubbed his eyes to clear them of sleep, then yawned, and shook himself, stretching muscle and sinew. It was a moment before he recalled what he had heard in the hours of darkness. He pulled on his boots and stood up, then nudged Catchpoll with one foot. The serjeant awoke with a muttered grumble.

'Can't sleep on floors like I used to,' he mumbled.

'Really? I thought you did a very good impression of a man who sleeps well anywhere.' Bradecote gave a lopsided smile. 'We need to speak,' he jerked his head to the far end of the hall, away from the solar, 'and you can wake our "slumbering infant".' He looked down at Walkelin, curled into a near foetal position. Catchpoll's boot was not as gentle as Bradecote's, and Walkelin woke with an 'ow'.

A few minutes later the trio had their heads together.

'Could it be something else, something not connected to Hywel ap Rhodri's death? I think we need to consider that, just in case the man is really ailing and perhaps agitated without cause. We look, or rather I look, very heavy-handed if that is the case.' Bradecote wanted to be sure, and there was just a grain of doubt in his mind.

'If he was rambling, my lord, it might be anything, from whether Corbin was swearing he had not left the bedside to swearing he was not . . .' Walkelin tried to conjure up a most unlikely image, 'a bear about to eat him.'

'Nasty dreams you must get, young Walkelin,' murmured Catchpoll, with mock sympathy.

'What I heard was four words among many, and somehow I do not think it was swearing for such a reason.'

'Then go with gut instinct, my lord, that is what I says.' Catchpoll thought the undersheriff could still overthink things. 'If we speaks with Corbin first and he says, straight off, something along those lines, I am thinking that might be the truth, because he is not a lad used to lying to his elders and betters beyond denying it was him as pushed another lad into the pond. Boy's lies, my lord, we would see through easy.'

'Agreed, Catchpoll. So we look to Corbin first and then approach our ailing Durand FitzRoger, if needful.'

'And should I speak with Aldith's feeble opponent of last night, my lord, who talked about when the lord Durand was feeling better?'

'Yes, and then, when we have finished with Corbin, you watch him, because he is our most obvious mover of Hywel ap Rhodri's horse, and we have to hope that is the beast, and not some animal borrowed for an odd reason from elsewhere.'

'You are making doubts where we need none, my lord,' Catchpoll said, soothingly. 'Young Walkelin has the right of it with the horse, I am sure.'

Walkelin blushed.

'If I finds the horse, do I confront Corbin with it, or leave it, or bring it back to the manor?' Walkelin wanted to do the right thing.

'Well, if you brought it back alone, they would say as it was just a lost horse, now, wouldn't they?'

'Er, yes, Serjeant.'

'And we wants to confront the manor to make 'em worry that we know the killing was done here, yes?'

'Yes, Serjeant.'

'Hmm, mayhap your brain does not work without breaking your fast, because that leaves us with . . . ?'

'I will bring Corbin in with the horse, Serjeant.' Walkelin sounded apologetic. 'Mind you, breaking our fast would be good, if I am to trail after Corbin all day.'

Corbin emerged from the solar bearing a bucket with a cloth over it. Upon being addressed by the lord Undersheriff, he stopped in his tracks, looking distinctly uncomfortable, not least because standing before someone that important whilst holding a bucket that was heading directly to the midden felt disrespectful, and he feared being cuffed about the ears for it. He put the bucket down, carefully. He looked wary.

'You're not in trouble, lad,' Catchpoll reassured him, and then added the caveat, 'at least not as long as you answers the lord Undersheriff good and true.'

Corbin looked even more worried.

'What upset the lord Durand in the night, Corbin?'

'Upset, my lord?' Corbin blinked at him. 'He never sicked

up anything last night, which pleased the lady Matilda.'

'Not upset his stomach, upset his head. You and he had heated words in the dark hours.'

Corbin looked blank, but not confused blank. It was the look of one who was trying to keep his face immobile.

'No, my lord.' He then tried too hard. 'The lord Durand slept through the night without stir.'

'Then you spoke with the lord Thorold? About what at that hour that could not wait until daylight?'

'I did not speak with him, my lord.'

'You spoke with someone, and it was not a woman.' Bradecote did not raise his voice, but it was firm.

'I . . . You must be mistaken, my lord. I . . . I says things in my sleep, so my father says. Mayhap that was it, aye, and so I would not know what it was nor why.' Corbin looked cheered, as though he had just found the ideal answer, but that lasted barely a moment. Catchpoll growled at him.

'Don't you tell lies to the lord Undersheriff, or he will lose his temper, and so shall I.'

'I . . . I did not speak with the lord Thorold. He sleeps above with' – Corbin blushed even mentioning her name in association with a bed – 'the lady Avelina. They had retired to the upper chamber when I entered the solar.'

'Which takes us back to my first question. What did the lord Durand become agitated about?'

'Nothing, my lord.' Corbin looked like a cornered animal now. 'He . . . it was nothing.'

'Then tell us, and let us decide if it was nothing.' Bradecote persisted, but did not show any sign of losing his temper.

'Well, my lord, being ill, as he has, makes some things confused in his head. He . . . he opened his eyes, the once in the night, and mumbled, which awoke me on my stool. He looked at me and accused me of trying to kill him with poisons. I told him I had done no such, but he was not convinced. I may well have said, "I swear" when trying to persuade him.'

'And he believed you? That was enough for him? Your word?'

'I think he half-believed, but was so tired he slipped back into sleep, my lord.'

'So why did you first tell me he did not waken?' Bradecote frowned at the lad.

'Because . . . because with all you investigating a death as murder, I wanted no idea that I was poisoning the lord Durand.'

'You are a very poor liar, Corbin son of Brictmer.' Catchpoll looked grim.

Corbin looked at the floor, but said nothing more.

'You see, if you lie, we wonder why you lie. What is it that you are covering up, Corbin?' Bradecote kept up the pressure.

The youth did not raise his head, but shook it.

'So we have to ask the lord Durand himself?'

Corbin looked up then, and he was uncertain.

'He will not recall, might say something different, my lord.'

'That at least we can believe. Not easy is it, when you have not had the chance to decide what to say,' Catchpoll let his lip curl in derision, and Corbin looked beseechingly at the lord Undersheriff.

'It is not that, my lord, I swear.'

'You are doing a lot of "swearing". I seek only the truth, and if it is nothing to do with Hywel ap Rhodri's death, it is of no interest.'

Corbin just stared. He looked to Bradecote to be in a situation he could not win, fearing betrayal of Durand FitzRoger, and the shrieval power.

'I am sorry, my lord, I can tell you nothing you need to know.'

Catchpoll looked at Bradecote, who shrugged.

'Then be about your task, and hurry not back. The midden is about where you are, right now.' Catchpoll dismissed the scared youth.

'Not exactly no help at all, but leaves much to be found out,' sighed Bradecote. 'I do not relish prodding Durand FitzRoger for more.'

At which point Walkelin peered around the door.

'My lord, there is things you ought to know.'

Walkelin revealed his discoveries. Dismissed to his duties, he had pondered as to how he might find the large man-at-arms alone, but was fortunate to have seen him with a hunk of bread in one fist, about to ascend to the small upper chamber to the left of the gate. Walkelin wondered if he was sent there upon guard duty, and if so, against what did he think he was guarding? Thinking quickly, Walkelin darted into the kitchen, beamed at the cook, and pleaded very politely for two beakers of small beer for his serjeant and the lord Undersheriff, whose title alone guaranteed a positive answer. Armed with two beakers, he followed where the man-at-arms had gone, though he found climbing the ladder stair to the upper storey awkward whilst balancing both filled beakers. He emerged into the chamber like a rabbit from a burrow.

'Good morrow. I thought as you might have a thi—' He stopped. The man-at-arms was stretched out on the floor, on a rough palliasse, arms folded and clearly settling himself for a nice snooze. 'Oh!'

'Kind of you to bring the beer, mind,' grinned the big man. 'Work you hard in the employ of the lord Sheriff, I have no doubt. See, here it is different. The lord Thorold, he keeps us "just in case", you might say, but who threatens us? Nobody. It is all show. So why bust your guts on a hot summer's day when one can take one's ease, or so I say. The lord Thorold will not come up here, for sure.' He laughed at Walkelin's shocked face. 'Now you see how life could be, eh? Poor you. Best you sits here, and has the other beaker, unless you brought them both for me.'

Walkelin thrust a beaker towards him, still rather stunned, and took up the offer of a seat upon a heap of sacking.

'Is it really this quiet here?' he asked, quite genuinely.

'Oh yes. In the old days, before the lord Durand left, there was shooting in the butts, and even quarterstaff work, according to Will, who was born here. Before my time, glad to say. The lord Durand took things a bit seriously, so I am sure everyone was glad when he went off to serve with the lord Gilbert de Clare. Big military household, so I hear, which would suit an active sort of man.' He took a draught of his beer, and wiped a hand across his mouth. 'The trouble is – younger sons. What do you do with them? If you are a lord, that is. The lord Thorold would not want him here, in the way, and hoping somehow his brother might just break his neck one day. Oh, you look askance, but there is no love lost there, I promise you, and even less these days.' The man settled himself as one about to impart good gossip. 'The lord Thorold went and wed, didn't he, and a pretty piece, though not my place to say. Nobody is quite sure why he did so, since he has never shown interest in anything in a kirtle. Sort of bloodless, he is. Anyway, when the lord Durand came to see his lady mother, the real "lord of Doddenham" even now, he found his brother with this lovely wife. Made him jealous it did. He went back and had his eye on some tidy little heiress, but got short shrift, because he is a Lackland, and will not have anything unless he wins it in deeds for his lord. So the lusty lord Durand has been thwarted, and what is more' – the man-at-arms leered and gave a knowing wink – 'he would gladly provide the lady FitzRoger with what she's not getting from his brother. Not as I am saying they have, mind, just that they would if they could, and mayhap they have. Who is to say, eh?'

'What about while he has been sick? They say as she and the lady Matilda tended him.' Walkelin, interested in this background but keen to know when Durand was in his better condition, made the suggestion eagerly.

'Hmm, well not when he got here, that is for sure. He was in a poor way, and that's no lie. I helped carry him in from the litter and he was dead weight and raving in fever.'

'But isn't it one of them fevers that goes up and down?'

'Seems it is. He arrived at death's door, I would say, and had the lady Avelina, the lady FitzRoger, wringing her hands and a-weeping over him. The lady Matilda, now, she is a tough one, she just said he would not die. Methinks she simply would not permit him to die. It was she who made the things he took for the fever, and the younger lady just dabbing his brow like, according to young Corbin. He got better, then a bit worse, then a lot better after about ten days. He even got up and on his horse, though I would think if it shied he would have been

170

off it in a trice. Went hawking, like I said last night. What I did not say was as I also saw him from up here, walking slow, but walking, and he went to the hazel coppice.'

'He did?' Walkelin played surprised and confused.

'Aye, and guess who went to the same place not all alone, but a bit later?'

'Not *her*?' Walkelin invested the word with all the awe the big man could have wanted.

'Yes, the lady Avelina, and whatever she was going for it was not to see how the cobnuts are progressing. Came back looking "occupied" I would say,' he guffawed lewdly, 'but the lord Durand nigh on staggered back. Something, or someone, took a lot out of him in that there coppice, but I am not sure the lady was . . . satisfied.'

'Was that before the Welshmen came?'

'Couple of days. The lord Durand looked a bit pale and stayed within the hall after that, and was laid upon his bed last day they were here. Not been up since.' He grinned. 'Which might have been his problem among the cobnuts.'

Walkelin tried not to blush. The man handed him the now empty beaker.

'If there is any more, in an hour or so, do not be afraid to wake me, friend.'

'So that is what I have, my lord,' Walkelin concluded his report, a little flustered of cheek.

'Which implies that Durand and the lady Avelina have been disappointing Father Dunstan, or at least trying to,' Bradecote said, quietly.

'And if what that idle bastard says is true, Durand has been disappointing the lady since he was ill. If he failed her, how much more likely that she was open to Hywel ap Rhodri's silver tongue, to put it mildly.' Catchpoll could do a leer that cast that of the man-at-arms into the shade.

'What is also important is that Durand was not writhing in his bed when Hywel ap Rhodri arrived, so it is logical that the Welshman told him about his brother's "illegitimacy" so that he could stand back and watch him smoulder like kindling, and maybe even do something.'

'He looked ill, though, after the er, coppice,' Walkelin reminded his superior.

'Hywel might not have known or thought of that at first,' replied Bradecote. 'What is also clear is that if the lady Avelina was thinking Durand a . . . spent force, shall we say, and fluttered her eyelashes at Hywel ap Rhodri, Durand would be a very unhappy man.'

'So you are saying as either he fell sick, and had Corbin kill the man for "insulting the lady Avelina", or he faked being as poorly as he claimed, and did it himself that second night.' Catchpoll sucked his teeth. 'Though he must have had an accomplice to get rid of the body, and that would be Corbin, most like.'

'Er, the problem of Rhydian arises, though, Serjeant.'

'Pox on the man. Could Durand have bought him off?'

'Not only do I have my doubts over that, but also whether Corbin would have killed to silence him.' Bradecote rubbed the back of his neck. 'You said yourself, Catchpoll, he is not one who has killed, just a peaceable lad from a manor.'

'So could the lord Durand have killed Hywel, and it was in the back so no struggle, and then killed Rhydian and persuaded Corbin that he had to in self-defence, having saved the lady Avelina's honour?' Walkelin's offering was put with caution.

'Possible, but not highly likely. However, it would account for Corbin's swearing his oath in the night.'

'Wait a moment, my lord, this gets more clever, on Durand FitzRoger's part.' Catchpoll pulled a face like a man with toothache. 'How about he does as Walkelin says, but tells Corbin that Rhydian threatened to tell everyone about his master and the lady, besmirch her name. If he has not done for him himself, in that case he could set Corbin off as the noble saviour of his lady's honour, and what with Rhydian being a scrawny chap, I doubt not Corbin could best him and kill "with right at his shoulder" in his own misguided eyes. He would then arrange for the disappearances of master and man and the manor would keep very quiet about it all, for Corbin's sake more than the lord Durand's.'

'I wish you were jesting, Catchpoll, but I can see you are not, and it makes a sort of sense. Holy Virgin, this gets more difficult the deeper we delve. So, I have to confront Durand FitzRoger with adultery with his brother's wife,' Bradecote ticked off his fingers, 'murdering Hywel ap Rhodri, and Rhydian the servant, or Hywel ap Rhodri and instructing another to kill the servant, or even killing neither but instigating the deaths. He will like that, and as for his lady mother . . . I am not sure I will get out of that solar alive if she gets nasty.'

'Which means, my lord, we have to get you in, while the others are out, lord and two ladies both.'

'I almost forgot Thorold. Mind you, if he suspects his wife with Hywel, I bet he has done the same with his brother, and would be quite happy to see said brother carted off before the Justices for murder. Loving family, this one.'

'Well, nobody has emerged from the solar since Corbin left, and they have not broken fast.'

'Ah, so I go without my own sustenance to get in and confront Durand. If I faint with hunger later . . .'

Catchpoll chortled, and Bradecote feigned looking hurt, which made Walkelin clutch his sides. It was upon this scene that Thorold FitzRoger came as he left his chambers. He stared at them.

'Is murder not serious to you?' he asked, coldly.

'Very. But a long face does not solve a crime any the faster,' replied Bradecote, much to Catchpoll's delight.

'The faster you solve it, the sooner you leave.'

'We leave when ready, trusting to your hospitality until then, FitzRoger.'

Thorold FitzRoger looked sullen and went to the hall door, where he yelled for a servant and food. Catchpoll grinned at Bradecote, but by the time the lord of Doddenham stomped back to seat himself in his lordly seat, the wily old serjeant's face was a mask of respectable impassivity.

Chapter Eleven

In fact, Hugh Bradecote was able to break his fast, because not only did the two ladies emerge from the solar, but also Durand FitzRoger, leaning upon his mother's good strong arm whilst the lady Avelina fluttered at his other side like a moth about a flame. Her husband sneered. Bradecote was initially taken aback. The younger FitzRoger was whey-faced, and his steps that of an old man, but the latter could be easily faked, especially if his mother was complicit. He stared at Bradecote as if trying to remember where he had met him before, and that was the giveaway. He remembered the interview of the day before, Bradecote was certain of it. The fragility had been an act, an act to see what was known whilst giving little or nothing away. The only thing that jangled in Bradecote's mind was that Durand had been described by Brictmer the Steward as impetuous, and this was showing more thought. Then it hit him. The only person

Durand attended was his mother. No doubt it was she who was pulling the strings, to make sure Durand did nothing 'foolish'.

He ate with suitable languor and lack of interest, which had the lady Avelina pressing things upon him with worried looks. Cynically, Bradecote wondered if she had come round to the idea that Durand would recover, in all aspects, and that feeding him up was a good thing. The lady Matilda treated it as her own table, and made discourse with her elder son, which sounded like instruction, and then turned to the undersheriff.

'I wonder that you remain, my lord, when the servant to the Welshman is gone.'

'Had he gone when his master was murdered, my lady, he would be in Wales long since, where our jurisdiction is non-existent. We have as yet no proof that he killed his master, nor that he was not himself killed.'

'That would be rich, one killing the other! What do you think we did, look on and cheer and then eat the horses?' Thorold snorted, not unlike a horse.

'Do you know, I had never considered that method of removing evidence.' Bradecote smiled, but it was not the sort of smile that won one in response.

'This is ridiculous.' The lady Matilda tapped her palm upon the board and nearly overset a jug.

'No, my lady, it is murder, and that is many things, oftentimes, but not ridiculous.' He looked at Durand. 'I would have words in private with you, when you have finished eating.'

'When he has finished eating, he will return to his bed,' declared the lady Matilda, bristling.

'In the which case, I shall escort him, and we will conduct

the interview, in private, at the bedside. I doubt he would like it in public.'

'I will not—'

'Quiet, Mother.' Thorold FitzRoger did not shout. His voice was almost silky, but his eyes were hard, and his words carried weight. She stared at him, taken aback by his temerity, and her mouth opened and then closed at what she saw, or thought she saw, behind those eyes.

'I care not,' sighed Durand FitzRoger, weakly. 'Ask what you will of me, I am sure I can aid you not at all.' He emptied his goblet, which contained, from the smell of it, mead with herbs in it, no doubt of his mother's concocting. A trickle ran down the side of his mouth to his chin, and he wiped it away with a shaking hand, a hand that shook just a fraction too much, in Bradecote's view. He pushed back his seat and rose, leaning forward upon the table a little. 'Let it be now.'

Bradecote did not offer his arm, but did walk at the man's side close enough to catch him if he fell. The sheriff's man wondered if he might try that, but then thought that it was too much, and a feigned fall would be felt as he caught him. They entered the solar, with one tall shutter opened to let the morning light into the chamber. Durand took uncertain steps to his bed, and sat upon it heavily, letting his head droop and his shoulders hunch.

'Be of good cheer, FitzRoger, your lady mother is confident that you will not die, of this disease at the least.' Bradecote sounded brisk.

Durand looked up at that.

'She does not know everything.'

177

'About illnesses or you? Does she know you have been mounting your brother's wife, or just guess?' Durand said nothing. 'She knows Hywel ap Rhodri told you your brother was a bastard and you are the rightful lord of Doddenham, and she told you that was a lie. Do you believe her?'

'She would not lie over that. If I had the right, she would have seen it made so, long ago.' The voice was low, but stronger than before.

'So you are happy to have nothing and your brother all?'

'Of course not. Who would be? Thorold is what the people here, in their language, would call a "nithing" which is—'

'I know what that means.' Bradecote spoke sharply. He felt vaguely offended that this man saw the people of the manor as 'them' and different from the 'us' of the lordly class, though logically, in the hall of a great baron such as Gilbert de Clare, little English would be spoken. It occurred to Bradecote that in so many ways he felt closer to Catchpoll, and even Walkelin, than this man upon the bed's edge.

'Well, it describes him aptly, I will say that. He is lord in name, husband in name, but he is lacking, always lacking.'

Bradecote noted he was no longer talking in short phrases.

'So you would take his place, in the latter, if not the former?'

'It may be a sin, but you cannot hang me for it. What point do you make, sheriff's man?' He shrugged.

'Well, if your illness left you, shall we say, more like your brother, you would not care for the Welshman – whom we know liked to get his hands on women – getting his hands on the lady Avelina. A motive for murder, I would call that.'

'Hah! Not liking is one thing, but, even if it were so, I was lying in this sickbed. I could no more kill him than fly like the birds.'

'You need not be the hand, just the head behind it. Young Corbin has aided you in your frailty. He could aid you as the "hand". What did you demand his oath upon last night?' He dropped the question suddenly into the conversation like a stone into a pool, and watched the ripple seen in the expressions on Durand FitzRoger's pallid face. Surprise was followed by annoyance, then a cloak of pretence.

'Nothing, nothing I recall.'

'Ah no, do not play the "sick man's memory fails me" any more, FitzRoger.' Bradecote shook his head. 'I heard, heard the strength of his avowal. It was important, to the both of you.'

'Ask him, then.' Durand shut his eyes, shutting out the questions and the questioner together.

'And expect an answer? Come. If it does not concern Hywel ap Rhodri, we will leave you to be sickly in peace.'

'For which you think I should thank you?'

'Not at all. The truth is more use than thanks.' He pressed, without easing, wearing down the will shaken by fevers.

'I did not kill the man, nor have him killed.'

'Then why did you need assurance?'

'Because I needed to know that . . . my brother did not know something, not for sure.' Durand sighed.

'Thorold? About you and his wife? Why would you care, if he is a "nithing"? And besides, Corbin would not be the person to involve, since he sets his lady upon a height in the adoration of youth.'

'He does? But he is a peasant.'

'I have news for you, FitzRoger. Peasants are not beasts of

179

the field, but the same creatures as lords and even kings, and if you ignore that your life may end sooner than you think.'

'Of course they have feelings, but to admire a woman so far above him . . .'

'Is undoubtedly half the attraction. Adoring the unattainable is part of growing up, for most. Perhaps you were one of the few to whom that did not apply. However, it does not change the point that Corbin would not have concealed knowledge of her falling from grace and still been in the throes of calf-love. So, try another answer, one I can believe.' Bradecote sounded almost bored.

'I did not want Avelina to know about . . . well, about another woman, one I mentioned when lost in fever. Corbin asked me, impertinent boy, who was the lady I mumbled for in my dreams, and I said she was nobody, but if he mentioned the name "Isabelle", then it would betray me. Avelina would know it was not some tumble with a field wench, something she could forgive when I was elsewhere so long.'

'If you "mumbled" it before him, who is to say you did not do so also when the lady Avelina tended you?'

'Because her manner has not altered, of course. Do you understand women so little? You cannot be wed.' Bradecote said nothing. 'If a woman is jealous there are no bounds to what they will do. If Avelina thought I played her false, she might make it seem I had killed the Welshman as her revenge upon me.'

'So much for love, then.'

'Love? Love is for boys and for gullible fools, and women, which last two are often one and the same thing.' Durand sounded very cynical. 'What a man needs is a comely woman who supplies his needs, obeys his commands, and gives him sons. It is simple enough. Love is a complication I can do without.' There was a trace of bitterness, and Bradecote thought, for all the coldness, Durand had at least been besotted with a fair face once, and been supplanted, or excluded. Perhaps even this 'Isabelle' had inspired more than ardour in his loins, and it was she whose hand had been refused him. For one moment Bradecote knew pity for the man, not because of the lost 'love' but because he saw no advantage to the emotion. Well, Hugh Bradecote had experienced a marriage based upon no more than tolerance and mild affection on his own part, and it paled like a winter dawn compared to midsummer noon when set against the marriage he had now. Then pity shattered like ice on a puddle at Durand's next words.

'The Welshman was more like me, I suppose, and certainly more like me than my brother. He was, however, lacking discretion. Avelina said dallying with him was sport, and I think she did it to spur me on, but she later admitted it was poor taste to play seduction with the wife of one's host.'

Durand was not looking at the undersheriff. Had he done so, Bradecote's expression would have made him edge away. There was silence, and Bradecote could feel his own pulse throbbing in his neck. Durand FitzRoger almost admired Hywel ap Rhodri, and, had the depths of the bastard's crimes been revealed, Bradecote sensed he would have 'condemned' them for the risk the man ran, not for what he had done to innocent women. Hugh Bradecote could do nothing to Hywel ap Rhodri, whose punishment lay with God, but knew a desire to throttle this callous lover as his proxy. He controlled himself, slowed the heavy beat of blood in his veins, and when he spoke again sounded cold, and calm.

'I have no more to say to you, or to ask, unless I find falsehood in your truth. Keep to your bed if you wish, I am unlikely to drag you from it.' Bradecote turned away, and strode out, the door reverberating as he slammed it behind him. It was that which made Durand FitzRoger wonder.

Catchpoll was not in the hall, but out in the bailey, chatting 'idly' to a man-at-arms who, unlike his fat and somnolent comrade, was at least standing upright, and was in fact holding a heavily built horse by the halter stall. Catchpoll, observing not just the beast, but the man's manner with it, saw an opportunity, and was discussing horseflesh as though Catchpoll loved the beasts more than he did his wife, which was not the case.

'Good strong back there. Bet she pulls a goodly load when asked. Myself, I prefer the wagon beasts to the fancy ones that are ridden as much for show as good purpose. The constable in Worcester, he has a chestnut, very pretty to look upon, but no depth of chest and a narrow back. He is always sour after a long day in the saddle, and I can tell why. Of course, it had white stockings and I never trusts a horse with more than a pale fetlock.'

'Oh, I do not know. That Welshman's horse, he has a white stocking and moves sweetly.'

Catchpoll nearly crowed like a cock, but maintained his casual expression. The man-at-arms must have realised his mistake, though, and muttered about best being about his duty and taking the mare to hobble at the pease field borders for an hour or so of grazing. Catchpoll let him go, and turned, with twitching lips, at the sound of the undersheriff's long stride. The humour died. Bradecote looked like thunder, and it took a lot to anger the man.

'His reason was good, my lord?' He fell into step beside him, and the pair of them walked through the gateway. Bradecote turned to the left and halted where there was a little shade close by the palisade. He ran a hand through his hair.

'I can see no clear fault in it, though whether it is true or false is not decided, not yet.' Bradecote paused, forced down his natural anger, and gave the explanation, and the man's attitude. Catchpoll made a good guess. As he saw it, the lord Bradecote coped very ill with the mistreatment of women, which was praiseworthy, except he took it to heart and let it show. Catchpoll assumed that lay with having been burdened with the thought that the lady Christina had faced the very real threat of mistreatment and dishonour at the hands of a mad bastard, and it was too close to home. It was as near the truth as even Catchpoll might sniff.

'It fits, there's the trouble with it, my lord, and thinking of women in the same light as a horse or a good sword comes as natural to some men. Wrong that may be, but not unlawful of itself, unless it leads to worse, and the Hywel ap Rhodris of the world are few, heaven be praised.'

'Amen to that, Catchpoll. Durand steps back a pace from our line of suspects. However, and I say this with caution, I still wonder if it is the real reason.'

'Why so, my lord?'

183

'For one thing, he feigns greater weakness and sickness than afflicts him at the present, though the reality of his past fever I do not doubt. Why does he play the invalid while we are here? Secondly, I doubt him because if he cried for this woman Isabelle in his fever, we are being asked to believe he not only did not mention her before the lady Avelina, but also the lady Matilda, and if she had a name like that to play with, can you imagine what use she would put it to, taunting her daughter-in-law?'

'True enough, my lord. It would be a sharp bodkin to prick her with, and the dame would enjoy every dig. That means the lady Matilda would be looking secretly smug, and the lady Avelina betrayed and afflicted, and neither of those things have we seen. It is a good point. Make that half a step back from our line of suspects, then?'

'That line is swiftly reducing to one man, Catchpoll.'

'It is that.'

'So what was his motive, and what did he do with Rhydian and the grey pony?' Bradecote folded his arms and leant against a sun-warmed wooden wall.

'Man and pony I can say nothing about, my lord, but surely the motive must be his wife.'

'The wife he already suspects, unless he is a fool, of playing him false with his brother. Yet he has not killed the brother, and I would guess there have been short times when the ailing Durand was unattended and would have been easy to stifle. None would have questioned if he had stopped breathing in the midst of such sickness.'

'Then let me try your thoughts upon him, my lord. You said he was one to watch rather than do for himself, yes?'

'I did.'

'Then he kills Hywel, knowing he has been sniffing far too close to her skirts at the least, and waits.'

'For what?'

'Well, the sensible thing to do if you kill a man is bury him, good and deep.'

'Which Thorold FitzRoger would not do for himself, even if his life did depend upon it.'

'No, but he could get Brictmer and his son to do so if he hinted that Hywel went too far and insulted their lady as he had the maidservants.'

'Go on.' Bradecote was interested.

'He therefore does not bury the man, but gets one of those two, Corbin at my guess, to take the body into the next Hundred and just hide it, except Corbin goes too far and ends up back in the same Hundred, but there. He then waits for it to be found, and investigation made.'

'Easy to see after the fact, Catchpoll, but at the time? It needs the corpse to be found, not just buried by some nervous villagers – and I would guess that happens on occasion and no word said – and for us to work back to this manor. As we said ourselves when we found the body, even getting a name was unlikely then. Stripping the body was a mistake. Leaving something distinctive, preferably Welsh, upon it, would have helped.'

'Er, what might he have that marked him as Welsh, my lord?' Catchpoll looked genuinely puzzled.

'No idea, but it would make sense. Anyway, my concern is it is leaving much to chance.'

'If nothing comes of it, he got rid of a man whom he did not like, and whose secret death makes him feel clever. He is the sort to like to feel clever.'

'I agree with that, Catchpoll.'

'And if we turn up, he makes it hard enough so that the finger does not point too clearly, and then makes sure his brother Durand looks guilty as sin, my lord. Thus, he gets rid of the cuckolding brother, and mother's favourite, and watches every move of it.'

'By using the excuse of the man being jealous or . . . Catchpoll, he stressed the loyalty of Gilbert de Clare at the first interview, without belabouring the point. He could use "Durand the loyal King's man" if the "jealous lover" failed.'

'That bucket holds not water, my lord, alas, since we are on the King's business, and killing a man involved in treason would be more likely to be applauded in some quarters. He was not to know which way it would fall.'

'You say that, Catchpoll, but it must be common enough knowledge that William de Beauchamp is of the Empress's faction, at a personal level, however well he collects King Stephen's taxes.'

'I still think "angry, impetuous lover" sounds the more likely, my lord.'

'True. Now we come to the final problem.'

'Which is?'

'He has not actually pushed us towards suspecting his brother. In fact, it was Durand who tried to hint at the opposite.'

Catchpoll said several very rude things.

* * *

186

In the solar of the hall, Thorold FitzRoger dismissed his wife.

'Upstairs with you. This is not your concern.' He glared at her, and she pouted, and flounced to the stair, where steepness precluded anything other than a practical ascent. He stood, hands behind his back, and stared at his brother. 'You are better again. I want you gone, tomorrow, before you have this family and manor shamed.'

'He cannot go, Thorold. His fever . . .' the lady Matilda intervened.

'He will go. This is my manor and I say it. He can take the spare horse, which is better out of here as soon as possible, and Corbin can ride with him in case of fainting. If he ails again, well he might find even better care among Holy Brothers. All that he will do here is stagger towards a noose. Why did you do it?'

'You do not seriously think that I killed the man? Sweet Jesu, I was not fit to—'

'Not fit to bed my wife, no, but killing a man takes but a moment of stamina.'

'Thorold!'

'Come, Mother, we are not children. Durand has been usurping my position when he can, but upon this visit . . . I think not.' He looked at his brother in thinly disguised dislike. 'That is all you will usurp. I do not know why you took against the Welshman, but—'

'I did not kill him.'

'Your denials do not interest me very much. Under the wing of de Clare you have some protection, at least as long as he remains upon the side of King Stephen, but I cannot, and indeed, will not, put myself out for you in this shire.'

'He is your brother, Thorold.'

'And I cannot ever forget it. You will not let me forget it, so precious is he to you. I am as much your son.' He threw the words at her.

'If he said he did not kill the man, he did not kill him.' The lady Matilda could be infuriatingly calm.

'Then if you believe him, why have you been aiding this . . . mummery, of him being weak and incapable?'

'The fever waxes and wanes, but it is difficult to make such a thing seem real. It is better for him to remain "sick", for you saw how exertion when Hywel ap Rhodri was here set him back. That way he will get better faster, and also be less tormented by the impertinence of de Beauchamp's undersheriff.'

'Which is the point. He was well enough when our unlamented cousin was here, and suddenly ill when he disappeared. I find that . . . odd.'

'But I did not kill him, so it is I who ask, who did? Was it you, Thorold? It hardly seems possible of course, you actually doing anything but . . .'

'Me? Why? It seems your mind does wander into fantasy, after all. You might be right, Mother, he is a sick man still, brain-sick.'

'Stop this, the both of you. You bicker like spoilt children, and this matter is not childish. Throwing accusations at each other is both dangerous and madness, and I will not have it.'

'Then help him pack.' Thorold FitzRoger shrugged, and turned away.

'You will attend to me, Thorold.' Her voice commanded.

'Do you know, I do not think I shall. I have let you delude yourself, even submitted to you, for the sake of a little peace, but it ends now. This is not your manor, but mine. You will remember that or find solace in a house of nuns.'

There came a slightly hysterical laugh from up above, where the lady Avelina was knelt at the top of the stair, listening. Thorold looked up, and his lip curled in derision.

'And a nunnery would be the best place for you, my lady wife, to learn to curb your lustful appetites. I hear some are quite strict.'

Outside, beneath the still open shutter, Walkelin did not laugh, but he smiled, and just for once that smile had echoes of Serjeant Catchpoll's.

Chapter Twelve

The smile was still on Walkelin's face when he came up to his superiors.

'I was coming from the stables, where I think I have worked something out, and passed the solar. Not a happy family in this manor, I will say. Brother is against brother, and son against mother.'

'You listened. Good lad.' Catchpoll praised him.

'The lord Thorold has told his brother he wants him out of the manor tomorrow. He does not think his brother at death's door any more than we do, and repeatedly asked him why he had killed Hywel ap Rhodri.'

'He did?' Bradecote looked at Catchpoll, and then back at Walkelin, who was a little disappointed at the reception to his news.

'Yes, my lord. He wants him gone to prevent shame upon the manor. He is also very aware that the lady Avelina and his brother have . . .' Walkelin blushed, 'been sinning in the past.

Adultery is a sin, but with a brother's wife it must be even worse.'

'Leave morality to priests, lad, and carry on. What else?'

'The lord Durand kept denying it – the murder not the adultery, that is. The lady Matilda tried to intervene, to say the lord Durand could not leave yet, but the lord Thorold would have none of it. He even threatened her with a nunnery, and said he would no longer let her pretend she controlled the manor. He was very firm.'

'Well, that throws our latest thinking back in our faces.'

'My lord?'

'What the lord Bradecote means is that we had just decided that Thorold FitzRoger is the one most likely to have killed Hywel ap Rhodri.'

'Ah.'

'I could think of other things to say,' sighed Bradecote.

'But I may cheer you with what I have discovered about the horse, my lord.'

'You have found it?' Bradecote brightened.

'Er, no, not yet, but in the stable the straw had been disturbed in that empty stall. I . . .' Walkelin looked a little sheepish, 'looked carefully. It was pretty good and clean yesterday, bar one heap of fresh, and it had not been mucked out by today. My guess is what with haymaking and us about, it had been forgot. Today that old muck had been trampled into the straw and there was more. To my thinking, you would not leave the horse out, alone and tethered, not at night. The risk that it would become panicked and either break the tether or get twisted up in it is too great, so the horse was brought in last night, which keeps it safe, and removed after dawn. Once they know we are in that hall for the night, there is little risk. Therefore, at the very worst, we find the horse here, late this evening.'

'Good work, Walkelin, and good reasoning,' Bradecote commended. 'But I would like that horse found earlier, if possible. There must be a limited number of places within the manor's bounds where it might be.'

'And it cannot be Corbin as took the animal this morning, my lord,' added Catchpoll. 'He was in the solar until everyone stirred. My guess is it was Brictmer, but he is simply the most likely.'

'So do I watch, or do I search, Serjeant?'

'Better off searching. As the lord Bradecote says, it will be within the manor, hobbled behind a thicket, or some building. The ground is hard, which aids you not at all, but the only horse I know out within the manor right now is a big mare taken to the pease field border. If you find fresh heaps of "evidence" elsewhere, it may be the sign you wants.'

'I thought as the life of a serjeant's apprentice would be hunting lawbreakers, not horse dung.' Walkelin shook his red head sadly, but his eyes danced.

'The advantage with horse dung is it does not move, and it does not try and kill you, so be glad it is that you hunt. Get on with you.' Catchpoll clapped him on the back, and, as he set off out of the bailey, his serjeant watched approvingly. 'Did the right thing there, my lord. I'll make a serjeant of him yet. He has the ferreting brain, but what he needs to do now is learn how to act the serjeant, look the serjeant, and feel the serjeant. Doing things on his own helps that.'

'So why do you keep him feeling "the apprentice" when with you, Catchpoll?'

'Because, my lord, he must not think he has mastered his craft too easily or too early.' The wily serjeant paused, and then surprised Bradecote with a confession. 'I nearly got myself killed about his stage, walking into a situation I thought I could handle, when cool sense would have told me to hang back and wait.'

'It is hard to imagine, Catchpoll.'

'What, my lord, me making a mistake, or me being young?'

'Both. Now, from what Walkelin overheard, do we put Durand back alongside his brother as a suspect?'

'Cannot but do so, my lord. There was three of them arguing, and setting up such a thing in order to be overheard sounds most difficult and unlikely. Thorold FitzRoger cannot have known young Walkelin would be under that shutter. It sounds as if it happened natural, so why would the man accuse his brother if the brother knows himself innocent? What does it achieve?'

'Would it persuade the lady Matilda?'

'Well, if he thought it might at the start, he did not by the time he threatened her with the cloister.'

'So we return to Durand being much better than he looks, or rather better two weeks past, and killing Hywel ap Rhodri himself, or getting Corbin to do it, and using the lad to clear up afterwards. So where are Rhydian and the grey?'

Catchpoll's face contorted into an expression of total mystification.

Walkelin liked working independently, although a fear of disappointing his mentor, and the lord Undersheriff, still clouded his blue sky of contentment. He had a task, and one which was both simple, yet not necessarily easy. He had seen Corbin about the bailey, emptying the midden bucket, giving Aldith a hand with water from the well, which she accepted whilst indicating she was perfectly strong enough to do the task herself. She was a good-looking girl in her way, but not the sort to catch his fancy. He liked a girl to think him the one who would protect her, and Aldith was not only the sort who protected herself, she even looked as if she would stand before her man in any risky situation, with a household implement to hand, and threaten violence, thus robbing him of any chance to look heroic. His own Eluned would be more the shrinking sort, giving full rein to his masculinity. If she had not given 'full rein to his masculinity' in other departments it was because she was a decent maid, who thought wooing was not a wink and a few sweet words. He sighed, and concentrated upon the task in hand.

He began outside the palisade, and did a quick circuit of the perimeter, in case it had been thought clever to leave the manor buildings by other than the track between the simple hovels of the village. For a moment he wondered if the horse might even have been put inside one of these dwellings, since livestock and family often shared one space, but rarely anything that big. The steward could not have it, since it was possible they, the sheriff's men, might go to him there, and the church and priest's house were not to be considered. Most other homes were low and small. The wheelwright's workshop was too noisy and had too much of a smell of burning. A horse would be in a sweat of nerves if left there. He looked at all the other buildings. No, there would be no horse within, and he had soon been about the outsides.

He went next to the fields. The draught mare was cropping the grass by the pease field, and Walkelin had an idea. He was quite observant, but a horse would sense another horse before he did, and if he was really lucky, one would whinny to the other. It did occur to him for one moment that if the man-at-arms returned there would be a panic over a stolen horse, but he told himself this was in the way of him doing his duty as best possible, so went to the mare, who blew through her velvety nose at him and shook flies from her haunches. A bulky horse could not go everywhere, but then if the brown was concealed, it had to be where it could forage, and not be unable to move. He untethered the mare, clicked his tongue encouragingly, and led her, slowly, along the field boundary to an area of scrubby trees and bramble thickets, keeping one eye upon her ears and nostrils, and one on the lookout for himself.

The odd pairing wandered, a little aimlessly, until Walkelin was certain that this area of the manor contained no hidden horse, and then passed along the edge of the wheat field, showing signs of summer ripening. Here, between the grain and the meadow that was cut for hay, stood the hazel coppice where Winfraeth had suffered under Hywel ap Rhodri. Walkelin chastised himself. If Corbin was helping with the hay, then it was most sensible to have left the horse here, so that he might check upon it during the day without wasting too much time, and without drawing attention to himself. He advanced, keeping back from the border nearer the haymakers. The mare blew down her nose, and her head came up. At the same time Walkelin heard a voice, a gentle, male voice, soothing. He let all but the end of the halter rope loose and edged forward, but the mare followed him anyway, and stealth was not her strong point. He stepped into a small clearing as Corbin turned, his face showing alarm that was instantly replaced with a question.

'What are you doing with Claefre?'

'And what are you doing with Hywel ap Rhodri's white-stockinged brown? Has it too got a name now?'

Corbin stood very still. Walkelin could almost hear his thoughts.

'Well, saying "what horse?" is foolish, and so is thinking either that you can drop me, or run away. Oh, and if you think of galloping off bareback, best to remember the horse is still hobbled. You can loosen those now, though, because we are going back to the manor to see what the lord Bradecote has to say. He will be pleased with me, but I am not at all sure that he will be pleased with you.' Walkelin sounded very calm and reasonable, hiding the excitement he felt at success. 'I do not need to draw my sword now, do I?'

Walkelin walked into the courtyard with barely a hint of swagger, which he knew would have Serjeant Catchpoll cuffing him about the ear for being cocky. The girl Milburga was carrying washing out to the drying ground, her feet bare and wet from trampling the washing in the butt, but did not look up as they passed her. For a moment the serjeant's apprentice was worried that both Serjeant Catchpoll and the lord Bradecote were elsewhere, and he would be facing an angry lord of the manor without support. However, he called the serjeant's name but once and the man himself appeared from the kitchen, where he had been making the cook feel important.

'What do we have here, then, young Walkelin?' asked Catchpoll, grinning.

'Hywel ap Rhodri's horse, Serjeant,' declared Walkelin with a little pride.

'Then best you leave that mare in the stable and go and run to the church, where I think the lord Undersheriff has gone to speak with Father Dunstan.'

Walkelin obeyed eagerly, leaving Corbin, looking rather forlorn, and holding the brown horse in the middle of the courtyard. Walkelin returned, or rather followed the long legs of the undersheriff, who came only just short of running. Bradecote, who had failed to find the priest, looked jubilant.

'The hidden horse. At last. Well done, Walkelin. Now, I want everyone from the field, however much they grumble about the hay.'

'Yes, my lord.' Walkelin departed, almost at the double.

'Catchpoll, all within the manor walls, and remember the sleeping man-at-arms. There can be none who do not see, do not face us now.' Bradecote sounded formal, hard. Catchpoll knew the terse command was not aimed at him, but for the consumption of those that heard it.

'Immediately, my lord.' He could play that game.

Bradecote was left standing in the courtyard, with Corbin holding the horse, which looked the only thing present at ease. It lipped at his sleeve, and the big eyes were almost soulful. The few already in the bailey shuffled their feet. Those within the manor buildings emerged into the sunshine, blinking, the cook with her hands floured, the maidservants with sleeves rolled from washing day. Father Dunstan had been with the haymakers, and his habit was tucked up so that skinny white calves contrasted with the dark cloth of his habit. Thorold FitzRoger came, looking angry, his mother regal, his brother sick and his wife worried. Brictmer the Steward came at the head of those from the haymaking, his brow furrowed. They gathered in silence, not born of respect, or even fear, just blankness.

'This,' Bradecote pointed at the horse, melodramatically, 'is the horse of Hywel ap Rhodri, the murdered envoy of the Prince of Powys. It gives the lie to the man having left here with his servant and meeting his death thereafter. You all of you know the Welshman died here, and at least a good proportion know how his body was disposed of. Your silence is a lie.' He spoke in English.

'He was a lecher,' cried Aldith, her head high in defiance.

'He was Welsh,' came a voice from among the villagers.

'Neither of which is a reason for murder,' growled Catchpoll, surveying the assembly like a wolf selecting the weakest in a flock. Bradecote thought it ironic that it was Catchpoll who denied the man's blood as a reason for killing, after all his grumbles and patent dislike.

'You cannot persist in saying "it is nothing to do with us". The proof stands upon four legs before you.' Bradecote's voice was 'Authority'.

'All right, stop this show. You may sound big to your men, but you do not to us.' Thorold FitzRoger was white-lipped. 'The horse was left in payment.' In contrast to Bradecote, he spoke in Norman-French.

'You are saying Hywel ap Rhodri walked from this manor?' Bradecote's disbelief was patent. Unconsciously, he changed his language.

'No, he rode the pony. The servant walked.' FitzRoger sighed. 'He came to me, and he agreed his behaviour was an offence against me and this manor. He said as the horse would be in payment and he would buy another in Worcester.'

'If his duty was to take the Prince of Powys's message to Earl Robert of Gloucester, why did he not say he would buy a beast in Worcester as he returned, and hand over one of the two as he passed on his way back?' This time Bradecote reverted to what all might understand, though it did not alter FitzRoger's words.

'Because I did not give him the option. I said I did not trust him, trust his word, and if his "duty" meant so much, why did he remain here two whole days when he might have travelled after a night of rest?'

'But he made no denial of the maids?'

'No. He said . . .' Thorold looked directly at Aldith, who stared back, as if daring him to speak. The question meant she knew what he must speak about, but his response was in a tongue alien to her. 'He said women were unimportant, and the fault lay within them. He agreed it breached my hospitality, and ultimately that the horse would remain.'

'He agreed to that? Why?'

'Because I said he would not leave at all if he tried to keep it. I said I would let them have him.' He pointed, accusingly, at the folk of his manor, who looked back sullenly, with no idea of what he said.

'Them? What happened to "us" of a moment back?'

'"Us" is . . .' Thorold waved his hand vaguely behind him, where mother, wife and brother stood. The lady Matilda looked at her son as if he was mad.

'They are not "us" but "ours", as the land is ours. They are not just "them".' Her voice reprimanded.

Bradecote did not think it much of an improvement, because it sounded too possessive. He held Bradecote, which was 'his land' that he would defend to the death, and the people were 'his' people, but he was 'their' lord. There was an impossible to define mutuality to it that was lacking here.

'And the people here,' Bradecote avoided 'your', 'know why the horse is here still?'

'Yes.'

'And why the lies? Why all the pretending? The man was dangerous with women. Why not say how he was, tell us yesterday?'

'It was our business. It has no connection with the death. There is none here.'

'No, that I do not believe, FitzRoger. The manner of man that he was is relevant to his death, I am certain of it.' Bradecote swung round to face the crowd, a crowd trying to work out the answers from the questions only. 'The law does not say you can act upon your own when it has been broken. Your lord says that this horse was left by Hywel ap Rhodri, who left upon his servant's pony, with the servant walking. Neither reached Worcester and we have one body only. There is more here, and we will find it out. We will. You can aid us, or obstruct us. It is your choice, but the law does not take well to obstruction.'

'The law is only here, my lord, because the man who died was a prince's man, important. The law – your law – is not interested in us.' Aldith spoke up.

'No. When we went to see the body that was discovered, we knew nothing of who it was. We do not say "this person looks unimportant, so just bury them and forget".' He countered her, but did not berate her for daring to speak. He looked at her, looked into her, and saw a young woman taut as a bowstring, full of anger and also of fear. The man who might have harmed her was dead, so what did she fear? His instinct said her fear was for Corbin, the companion of childhood, the youth becoming man who tested his unfurling emotions on the unattainable. She was perhaps not even as old in years, but she was more mature. Unconsciously, she was waiting.

The other villagers kept their eyes lowered. They probably agreed with her, but were not so bold, or foolhardy. Then Bradecote glanced at Corbin. His eyes were not lowered. He looked as if he had been hit so hard his wits had flown, as though she was someone he was seeing for the first time. Bradecote suddenly felt a wave of revulsion for his duty. If Corbin had obeyed someone he dare not disobey, and had committed murder, he would hang, yet the person who commanded him might escape that fate, and the simple and everyday wooing of steward's son and village maid that might make two souls happy would not happen. Catchpoll would say that it was not their 'fault', being the law in person, but that it was the ripples of crime that affected far more than just culprit and victim. Actually, thought Bradecote, giving himself a mental shake, Catchpoll would just tell him not to be a fool, but in more polite terms than he would use to Walkelin.

There was a very uncomfortable silence. What happened next? Should they just drift away and return to the important tasks of their day? Catchpoll stepped forward.

'What the lord Undersheriff says is true. Be about your

business, but know we do not leave until the truth is before us.'

It was the dismissal they sought, and there was a relieved sigh, as if the community exhaled as one. The courtyard was empty in a couple of minutes except for the sheriff's men, and Corbin, holding the brown horse with the white stocking, a horse that fidgeted now, ears twitching, no longer relaxed.

'So, Corbin, son of Brictmer, what have you to say to the lord Undersheriff?' Catchpoll did not shout, but then he did not need to shout.

'Sorry, my lord.' His head was bowed, and he sounded like the child caught in misdemeanour by an adult. Catchpoll rolled his eyes.

'I do not need an apology, Corbin, I need honesty.'

'My lord, I—'

'I have told you what happened. You have no cause to put pressure upon one of my servants who has simply obeyed my commands. What can he tell you except that he has done what he has been told, and taken the animal to pasture in the day?' Thorold FitzRoger stood in the doorway of his hall, and this time he spoke in English, though he looked at Bradecote, and ignored Corbin as much as he did the horse.

'We have your words only, FitzRoger.' Bradecote did not disguise the fact that he doubted them.

'Then ask him, and see if I care.' FitzRoger leant against the doorway.

Bradecote knew it was pointless, but he had to continue.

'Corbin, tell us about this horse.'

'It is the horse of the Welshman, the lordly one, and was left here by intent. My lord told me to care for it, because I

202

am good with horses and take charge of the stable. When you came, my lord, I was told to take him out of the way, and that I have done, not out of disrespect to you, my lord, but because it was what I was told to do.' There was a peculiar confidence to Corbin's response, and, as Catchpoll had said, he was not a good liar. Perhaps he had been told the horse was meant to stay and had no more thought than he had offended the undersheriff, and upset his lord by being found with the horse. If Corbin had killed, Bradecote thought it would show, in fear or even a defiance, but there was nothing other than embarrassment. Yet in the case of both Durand and Thorold, for different reasons, Bradecote would have said another was more likely to have done the killing. Had they got it wrong? Was the 'other' Brictmer? Surely it was not one of the men-at-arms, who, despite being soldiers, looked about as fit for killing as a choir of novice nuns, and would be unlikely to be as trustworthy as old retainers.

Thorold FitzRoger went back into his hall.

'I find it in me to be angry with you, Corbin, for a fool if naught else,' growled Catchpoll, but Bradecote half-raised a hand and stopped him going further.

'Corbin, the last man we brought into Worcester upon a charge of wilful killing was a man more powerful than the lord Thorold. Rank does not mean the law ignores you. Aldith was wrong in that.' Bradecote knew that for a half-truth. There were certainly many things that never reached the ears of the law, and had they done so would be considered too unimportant to spend time upon. A substratum of justice, and injustice, existed for 'small' crimes, or 'small' people who discounted the law as Aldith did.

Corbin continued to look downtrodden.

'I would say "get out of my sight", but I will be watching you, steward's son.' There was nothing avuncular in Catchpoll's manner now. 'Take that horse away. Walkelin, you can take that mare back to the pease field, lest she get hungry, and then watch the haymakers.'

Walkelin nodded and went to the stable.

'I sounded confident, Catchpoll, but are we any closer to unravelling this?'

'Of course we are, my lord, and I liked the way you made sure the folk knew what was going on, as best you could. Thing is, people who commits crimes gives less away when they feels safe and secure that their crime will stay in the dark. Now it is known that the crime will see the light, so to say, the cracks will appear. The guilty will get flustered, and then they will make a mistake. It was never going to be "Here is the horse, so hands up who killed Hywel ap Rhodri? Good, come with us".'

'Put that way it does not sound so bad, Catchpoll, except how do we watch for these cracks without looking as lazy as FitzRoger's men-at-arms?'

'By appearing everywhere, when least expected, and least wanted, my lord. That flusters them good and proper. It is one of the best parts of the job.'

Chapter Thirteen

Catchpoll might enjoy getting on people's nerves, but Bradecote found it less amusing. It felt to him more that he was wandering about, looking an idiot who did not know what to do. It was agreed that Catchpoll would cover the manor staff, and that he would be in the way of the 'family', which was about as comfortable as sitting on teasels. It also had the issue of access, for demanding that they accept his presence in the solar was intrusive, and sitting in lonely isolation in the hall rather ridiculous.

It was therefore almost with a sense of relief that he found Thorold FitzRoger sat in his lord's seat, which was pushed back so that he could rest his booted feet upon the table before him. Bradecote had a secret suspicion he was doing this because he knew his mother would disapprove. He had a goblet of wine in his hand, and an unpleasant expression upon his face, sour and discontented.

'I am trying to think which is the worse, having you here or the Welsh bastard.'

'Well, it must be a difficult decision, since I do not molest women but am going to be here a lot longer, at least until we find the answer to Hywel ap Rhodri's death and his servant's disappearance.' Bradecote did not sound in the least annoyed.

'I can throw you out of my hall any time I please.'

'You can try. I am not sure those men-at-arms of yours are particularly offensive, and . . . just how many men have you killed, FitzRoger?'

'I have . . .' the man began with vehemence, and then paused, 'too much wit to answer that one.' He gave a grim smile. 'If I say none, you will call me feeble, and if I say I have killed, we will be back to the nonsense over the Welshman.' He sneered at Bradecote. 'I also do not feel the need to prove my manhood by killing people. A sword is not another version of a man's "prowess".'

'From what is said, then, you are unacquainted with action in either sense.' Bradecote suddenly wanted to annoy.

'You ought not to talk to whores.' FitzRoger tried to sound merely bored.

'I need not talk to anyone, just listen. It is common knowledge.' This was met by silence. 'I have to admit, the puzzle at present is what happened to Rhydian, and even more baffling, that grey pony.'

'I told you, the Welshman rode the grey and his servant walked beside it.'

'No.' Bradecote shook his head. 'That is a foolish lie, because when a man leaves, he will later arrive, and Hywel arrived as a stabbed and naked corpse, and the pony and servant have not been seen in Worcester or upon that road. They have not arrived anywhere.'

'Well, since he would not be delivering the message to Robert of Gloucester, why would the servant go to Worcester at all? He would head back to Wales, where they would understand his tongue.'

'An interesting point, I agree. Would that be because the message is, or was, still here? I assume it was in Latin, since Madog ap Maredudd could not expect there to be a Welsh-speaking scribe in Earl Robert's hall. Though unless you learnt reading, I doubt you have the meaning of it. Asking Father Dunstan would be too great a risk, and he looks the sort of parish priest whose Latin is now pretty well confined to the Offices. Whose side are you on, FitzRoger?'

At this Thorold FitzRoger laughed, and slapped his hand upon the arm of his seat.

'Ha, you think I would kill to gain credit with one or other? I am too small to be remembered in more than the tax accounts and nothing I might say would change that. I have never dreamt of that sort of power. I care not if King or Empress rules if they leave me to my own life. If you want partisan, then ask my brother. Gilbert de Clare is not consistent, but he sides with the King at the present. Ask Durand about any message.'

'But Durand was ailing then.' Bradecote kept his knowledge to himself.

'An undulant fever is a very useful illness,' said FitzRoger, smoothly. 'I do not deny he arrived here sick, but he has been well enough at times, even to take out one of my hawks for pigeon, and while the Welshman was here, he was not plucking at his sheets and raving.'

'So now it is not that Hywel ap Rhodri left upon a grey pony, at least not upright, and the possibility that your brother killed him. We progress.'

FitzRoger lost his calm.

'I did not mean—you twist words, set traps with words. Words can lie.' He looked flustered, and his fingers gripped the chair. 'You progress not at all.'

'Words are certainly difficult to take back, like opening a cage and letting out a bird. It is nigh on impossible to recapture.'

'I have a bird that leaves and returns.' Thorold FitzRoger stood up. 'You cannot confine me to my own home. I am taking my goshawk, and my man, and shall return when I wish, not upon your command.'

'I have no lure to swing for you, FitzRoger? No, probably not. Go then, because I do not fear you will not return, unless you pile your horse with raiment and treasures, and we would notice that.'

The lord of Doddenham stormed out, and Bradecote contemplated the door to the solar.

What Corbin wanted was sympathy, and he had no idea where he might find it. He had been put in an impossible position, and thought that he was likely as not going to get a whipping when the sheriff's men left. It was very unfair. The lord Thorold would blame him, because it was always someone lower down that was blamed. He had hidden the horse because he was told to do it, and keeping it hidden was not easy, for a horse was not like a trinket that could be concealed, buried. The only thing that had surprised him was that his lord had not simply shrugged, decided that telling the lord Undersheriff that his steward's son must be the murderer was the quickest way to get the man out of his manor, and offered shackles. He put the brown horse in the stable, where it gazed at him in soft reproach, and headed for the drying grounds, where the linens were spread upon the bushes.

From the small chamber where the fat man-at-arms had spent the morning, Catchpoll watched him walking, hunched, defeated.

Aldith was spreading a large cloth. The illness of the lord Durand had meant much more laundry work, and she and Milburga had spent the morning rubbing until their knuckles were sore. She looked up as Corbin approached, but did not smile at him. Part of her resented his presence. If he wanted solace, go to the lady, that part thought, although she knew that was outside of imagining. He was such a fool, but underneath she was the greater fool, for she had a tenderness for him that threatened her prickly exterior.

'Why does it have to happen to me?' bemoaned Corbin.

'Why should it not? Especially if you act like an idiot.' She sounded exasperated, then mellowed a little. 'When will you grow up, Corbin, and see that life is not a game?'

'I am grown up, fully grown up.' His avowal made him sound even younger. She shook her head and laughed. He threw himself down upon some close-cropped grass, and sat, knees raised, hands clasped about them. She paused a moment, and then sat down beside him.

'Because I was born here, I am treated as I was when a boy.' He sighed. 'There are men my age who have fought battles.'

'And far too many of them are in the earth. A sword does not make a man.'

'What does, then?'

'Why ask me? I am a woman. Ask your father.'

'He will laugh and say "time".'

'It is not a bad answer, Corbin.'

There was silence for a minute or so, though not an uncomfortable one.

'Sometimes I think I will leave Doddenham,' he said, impulsively.

'But you are the son of the steward. This is your manor.'

'It is the lord Thorold FitzRoger's manor, and you see how little he values me,' he grumbled.

'No, Corbin, it is yours, as it is your father's and was his and his before that. This,' she rubbed her palm across the grass, 'is more yours, more mine even, than theirs. They do not truly care for it, just what it shows them to be. It is a badge of rank, like their foreign tongue and their fancy clothes. You are not just Corbin, but Corbin son of Brictmer, son of Ulf, son of Wilfred, son of Agar, son of Eadbald. That means something, something more than looking grand.'

He stared at her, much as he had stared at her in the courtyard. The lady Avelina was the most beautiful woman he had ever seen, but deep down, beneath the dreaming, he knew she meant as little to him as he to her, which was nothing. Aldith did not have the curves, the bow of a mouth with soft, red lips, but there was a reality to her, and a raw vital courage that now seemed to shine from her. She was brave, and she was clever, not in learning, but in thinking. She thought important things; she saw important things. Her profile was strong, and also, he realised, with a lump in his throat, pretty.

'Will you give me a reason to stay, Aldith?' he managed, in a broken whisper. His hand moved to cover hers upon the warm green blades. For a moment he wondered if she would hit him, as she had the Welsh bastard.

'You ask such stupid questions,' she replied, softly, and turned to face him. 'Very, very stupid questions.' Her other hand reached up and she ran a finger down the cheek where a man's stubble was cautiously replacing the fluff of adolescence, and her eyes smiled.

Catchpoll shook his head, and went down the ladder. There was watching, and there was peeping, and there was learning too. They might be learning, but they would not be teaching him anything he did not know, had not known for decades, and peeping was grubby. He headed for the kitchen and the hope of a beaker of cider.

Walkclin felt guilty watching the others working, bending aching back and tired arm. He was not, as he had admitted to Winfraeth, a man of the land, but perhaps the earth called long, even through town living, and he felt an urge to offer what help he could. Also, he reasoned, he would be a less resented presence, and he could still keep an eye on who went where and what was discussed.

He approached Brictmer.

'Master Steward, I have no skill, but two arms and two legs. This work does not look as though it takes much experience, for there are infants here with the milk scarce dried upon their lips, doing their part. Will you accept my labour, to direct as you will this afternoon?' He spoke with an honest sincerity, and Brictmer, whose face had been solemn, softened.

'See how a soft Worcester lad takes to farming, eh? Well, the arms and legs will be useful, and if you should manage to get it wrong, the joke will lighten the day. I would not have you build a rick, but you may assist upon the one where Father Dunstan is working, to the left.'

Father Dunstan, with hay in his circle of hair, and rather ruddy of face, was indeed helping in the creation of a hayrick, and the advantage was that he was rather better at describing what needed to be achieved, and how. Walkelin commenced cautiously, fearing to look the fool, but soon found himself part of a team and fully involved, sweating with the rest.

Having stared at the door without getting anything useful from it, Bradecote sighed, and opened it. He felt it was like walking into a cage of wild beasts, liable to snap at him or each other. Durand was no longer in the bed, but sat upon a seat against the far wall, clothed, but with a cloak about him, wrapped tight. The two women were apart, as though they were the corners of some invisible triangle. The lady Avelina had some stitchery in her lap, but she was not plying her needle. The lady Matilda had her hands upon her knees, in a rather more masculine pose, and she was frowning, even before she looked at Bradecote.

'So, you are feeling better than this morning, FitzRoger. The pretence of fragility had gone on rather too long, so I think you are wise to abandon it.'

Durand scowled at him.

'Your tongue is sharp, but your wits are dull, lord Undersheriff,' the lady Matilda snapped, 'or you would not still be here else. You will not find your missing Welshman under our beds, or in hers,' she glared at her daughter-in-law, 'though he would be one of the few not to have been there.'

The lady Avelina threw her sewing onto the floor, but that just made the lady Matilda laugh. Bradecote did not want another round of fighting between the two women, and looked directly at Durand.

'What reward do you think Gilbert de Clare would give to the man who brought him a secret communication to Earl Robert of Gloucester? Would he give treasure, or a bride? Would he even make the name known to the King for preferment?'

'I have never considered it.'

'Not even when a messenger to the Empress's chief supporter slept within this hall? Come. Your lady mother knows, and your brother knows, so do not tell me you were never aware that Hywel ap Rhodri carried a message from Madog ap Maredudd to the Earl Robert. Why would they hide such information from you, even if you did not hear it from the man himself.' Bradecote turned to the lady Avelina. 'Did he tell you to impress you, lady?'

'He did not impress me.'

'Then why were you so upset to hear of his death? And if he did not impress you, why did you stand in his embrace in the hazel coppice?'

The eyes of the other two people present became fixed on the lady Avelina. Her fingers intertwined, and moved, nervously.

'I did not.'

'You were seen.'

At that she looked up, and her face grew very pale.

'Do not look so shocked, Durand. What she would do with you, she would do with anyone.' The lady Matilda sneered at them both from across the chamber.

'He must have been quite persuasive, after the maid made her complaint.' Bradecote's voice was almost admiring. 'You said that you "forgave" him. What a clever idea, to tell husband and . . . brother, that he had admitted his sin and you were shocked, and then slip away with him. Is that when you also revealed to Durand that he was an envoy?'

'She never told me that. My mother did,' cried Durand.

'At last we hear some word of truth.' Bradecote turned back to Durand FitzRoger. 'You did know he was going to Earl Robert. That takes me back to my first question. What would getting your hands on that message win you?'

'I never saw a message, nor did I kill him. How many times must I tell you?'

'Many, and with reasons.'

'A sick man—' the lady Matilda began, but was interrupted.

'A sick man, or a woman, need only employ someone else to use the knife, a person malleable enough to their will through habit, devotion, call it what you will. Undoubtedly, whoever killed Hywel ap Rhodri had help afterwards, in moving bodies and horses. I think it is Rhydian's death that rankles with me, you know. After all, his only crime was to be the servant of a murdering rapist.'

'Murdering . . . ?' the lady Avelina breathed.

'Yes, he was. It appears he was known to the women of the court in Mathrafal as a man who seduced, but also forced. However, coming over the border he ceased to worry about concealment. At Bromyard he murdered and raped, in that order, a decent woman who fought for her honour. Since then he has attacked at least three women, if you can count the child Milburga as a woman. Aldith got off lightly, and probably lives because he was so reckless as to assault her within the manor buildings.'

'Holy Mary,' the lady Avelina crossed herself, and then stood, shakily, went to the door, and was heard running through the hall.

'May he rot like his father.' The lady Matilda crossed herself also. Bradecote was watching Durand, who looked shocked, but more in surprise than revulsion, and, thought Bradecote, grimly, more at the revelation about the lady Avelina and her meeting with Hywel ap Rhodri.

'Rhydian, a man who spoke almost no English, and was described as "faithful unto death", had no part in all that. He did not deserve to die, but then, so many victims of murder do not deserve to die.'

'You would punish a man for ridding the world of one whom you would have hanged?' The lady Matilda was still thinking of master not servant.

'Well, since the murderer did not know what we know, yes. They killed him for what he carried, or out of jealousy, but not because of his crimes, and besides, have you ever watched what happens to a man convicted of rape and of murder? A quick death by the knife was better than he deserved.'

She actually nodded in agreement at that, and said no more.

'For all that you say, I deny it still. I did not kill, nor have killed, either Welshman.' Durand spoke slowly, pressing home his innocence.

'We will find out if that is true, or not, for ourselves.' Bradecote walked out, and at the door of the hall, passed the lady of the manor retching.

* * *

Catchpoll was out of the sun, though it was warm in the kitchen, and the cook, who eventually divulged her name as Hild, had beads of sweat upon her brow as she sliced onions into the pottage that would be the evening meal for the majority. Milburga, returned from washing duties, was turning the spit on which three fowls were in the early stages of roasting. She had spared Catchpoll one swift glance as he entered, and shrunk closer to the hearth fire as if cold. To begin with Catchpoll ignored her, as she undoubtedly wished. At least, he seemed to ignore her, quietly drawing the cook from cool wariness into an exchange of cooking tips that he would forget long before Mistress Catchpoll would have him at her hearth, in fact probably as soon as he left the kitchen. However, by dint of recalling some trick his beloved wife had with the herbs in a fish stew, he wormed his way into Hild the Cook's good graces, and was accounted worthy to hear her views upon everything from bran poultices to the massed failings of the male of the species who numbered less than two score years.

'No wonder the lady Matilda treats them both as if they were having their noses wiped for them. They squabble like five-year-olds, and,' she dropped her voice to a dark whisper, 'I would swear the lord Durand makes eyes at the lady Avelina just to spite his elder brother. Neither could abide the other to have a thing they did not possess also, and many is the time the lady Matilda took from the both of them, and took a birch twig to their backsides. Not,' she added, with a blush, 'that she uses that particular punishment now they are meant to be men grown.'

'Ah, but men do not appreciate their mothers fussing over them.' Catchpoll shook his head as if that were a failing too. 'I hardly think the lord Durand has enjoyed being tied to his bed with his mother standing over him with potions and commands to drink this, and inhale that.'

'She has a good head for remedies, has the lady, I will give her that, but no, I doubt he has. Always on the move he was, when young, and hardly better now. She told him, she did, to take things slow, but the moment the fever left him he was up and about and trying to do too much, and lo, he was back and moaning something wicked within three days. Glad I am he is on the mend proper now, though. His appetite is like a man starved, and I have been sending bowls refilled I know not how often this week. I only wonder he has not looked so strong when up and about, but mayhap he is taking the care he failed to do before, eh?'

'Attending his mother, aye, having learnt the hard way.' Catchpoll glanced quite openly at Milburga. 'I've a granddaughter her age, and a useful girl about her mother's kitchen too. Fine chance we would have to see her roasting three birds on a spit, unless it was sparrows out the eaves!' He nodded at the spit. 'For the high table, I suppose?' He kept the run of the chatter culinary, but had brought the girl in.

'Of course. What would we be a-doing with fowl roasting and this not a high feast day? Lucky we are then to have the bones for soup and a sliver each with our meal. Mind you, I cooks the livers and adds them to our pottage, and the high table do not even think of what there is besides the meat upon the bones. Milburga here is learning, for there is an art to spit cooking, though you would not think it. Turning too fast is common, and turning too slow so as it burns is too obvious afterwards, when them in the hall sends complaint. She is a good girl, my niece, a good girl.' At which the cook seemed suddenly overcome, and dabbed at her eyes with the corner of her apron.

'Does it make you hungry, the smell of roasting fowl?' Catchpoll finally addressed the girl.

She did not look at him, but, after a moment, nodded. Deep down, Catchpoll felt the anger that had filled Walkelin. Catchpoll's granddaughter was laughing and lively, not a wan ghost like Milburga.

Aldith came into the kitchen. Catchpoll noticed the slight flush to her skin, the brightness of her eyes, and the way she veiled them with her lids.

'Washing'll be dry within another half-hour – that first tubbing, at least,' she said, casually.

'And what kept you so long? I was going to get you to fetch me some wild garlic from the edge of Small Wood to rub on them birds, and they is too far cooked to add it now.'

Aldith, the Aldith who slapped the faces of lecherous lords, who spoke up before the undersheriff, mumbled something inarticulate, and coloured.

'Well, I could make a sauce with mushrooms, if you go off now and get some from where you found them three days past. Not the big ones, mind, nice and small and flavoursome is what I want. Off with you, now.'

Aldith went without demur, and Hild the Cook watched her with a sapient eye.

'Hmm.' She might have said more, but for the lord Thorold's hawker entering with a drake in his hand.

'Here, mistress, she brought down this bird for you, she did.' He spoke of the hawk as if a friend.

'Not for my lord?' Hild smiled at him.

'Not for him. He likes to watch, and feel he has command of her, but she has her own mind, and it is her skill. And you have the skill with the duck when it is for the table, so I reckons as you, ladies both, are in league.'

'Flatterer.' Hild blushed and clucked, hen-like, then took the bird from his grasp. 'Pity there is but the one, but a fine bird.'

'Strael brought down the mallard when we had hardly started, really, but then the lord Thorold lost interest, and sent me back with it. He has other things upon his mind, I suppose, and rode off upon a loose rein, frowning.'

The sunlight was dappled among the trees, and Aldith hummed to herself as she picked the mushrooms. It was not a task that took thought, and she had much better things to think about just at the moment. Her reverie lasted until her little basket was full, and then she began to retrace her steps. She wondered if any of the spread-out washing was dry, and diverted her path. Corbin was still there, lying asleep on his side. She pursed her lips. She had to get back to her work, but Corbin felt he could lie in the sun. She relaxed into a smile. At least he had something better to dwell on than being put upon by his lord, but if he lingered, he would be berated for his absence. She walked towards him, the basket of mushrooms on her hip.

They fell to the ground as she screamed.

Chapter Fourteen

Catchpoll nearly knocked over the cooking pot as he turned to the door, moving surprisingly fast for a man of his age. The cook stood open-mouthed, and her spoon fell upon the floor.

Bradecote had been in the gatehouse, whence he had gone to think quietly, and was both younger and longer of leg. The source of the screams was not difficult to locate, although they had changed from terror to cries for assistance. He saw Aldith, on her knees, and beside a body. Only when he reached her did he see who it was.

'Help him,' she cried, rocking to and fro.

Bradecote was not sure that he could. Corbin looked as good as dead, and there was a bleeding wound to the head.

'Grab that washing and bring it here.' It would get the girl out of the way for a moment while he decided whether they needed a bandage or a shroud. He rolled Corbin gently onto his back and placed his hand upon his chest. Was it still moving? He leant so that his ear pressed to it. He thought he heard the beat of a heart, but was it his own thumping?

'Be alive, Corbin,' he commanded, more in hope than expectation.

'Is . . . he . . . dead?' Catchpoll managed to gasp as he leant, hands upon knees and head down, struggling to get enough air into his own lungs.

'I do not know.' Bradecote raised his head. 'There is a lot of blood.'

'Head wounds always bleed as if forever, my lord. You have seen such.'

'Yes, but he neither moves nor groans.'

'Depends how long ago he was hit. Mayhap his brains are addled by the blow. Here, let me try.' Catchpoll knelt with a groan of his own, and placed his hands either side of the neck.

'You think his neck is broken?'

'No, but when you're dead the blood does not move. A dead body does not bleed like a living one, the bleeding stops, otherwise all the blood in the body would leak out of the hole of the wound. Physicians know about blood, and what it does. I just knows without it you die, and I think when you are alive it trembles in the vessels, which must be so it does not thicken and congeal, which it does when it comes outside. When you die it thickens, and grows heavy and sinks towards the ground, from which we come and to where we return. Once it does that it does not move again, which is why we sees the darker patches on bodies that have been in one position some time. Blood must tremble in the vessels, and if there is a wound and it leaks out, then more blood comes to fill the empty part. I can feel it with my fingers, like a heartbeat in his neck, and the bleeding is not quite stopped, neither. He is with us yet, but ask me not how long.'

Aldith, sobbing, returned with arms full of washing. Without a thought, Bradecote ripped a length from a cloth, tearing it with teeth and then strong hands, folded part into a pad and wound the rest about the head.

'We will carry him on the largest cloth. Lay it beside him, Aldith.'

She obeyed, bosom heaving, hands trembling. The two men lifted Corbin's inert form onto the linen.

'Now go to the fields and fetch Brictmer, and the priest also.'

'The—he is dying?'

'I do not know. We will take him to the steward's house. Run, girl.'

She ran. Bradecote and Catchpoll looked at each other, and lifted their bleeding burden.

'What was he doing here, with drying washing?' wondered Bradecote.

'It was not the washing but the washer, that attracted him,' Catchpoll said, jerking his head after Aldith.

'She was here, here when . . . ?' Bradecote was confused.

'She was here a while back, laying out the washing. He came to her, not by design I would say from the language of body. He was hunched, miserable. I would guess he sought a bit of comfort, and someone to talk to.' He grinned, despite all. 'Words wasn't needed when I stopped watching. There's some things we need not see.' The smile faded. 'She came into the kitchen about an hour since, a little bright of eye, and was sent to find mushrooms by the cook. There's mushrooms scattered about, so we know she found them.'

'And she is distraught, really distraught, so she could not have . . . No, that would be madness.'

'What happened between those two was willing on both parts, unplanned but willing. She was a bit dazed, but happy, when I saw her the last. She's a girl who would fight for her honour if any tried to take it, but she gave it, and no doubt left him lying in bliss.'

'So who hit him, and hit him to kill him?'

'Someone who was afraid, my lord, afraid he would get as we wanted – flustered – and crack.'

'But I was in the solar, with Durand and the two women, for much of the last hour, and only went to the gatehouse, which was empty, to think, and but a few minutes before the scream.'

'It would take but a few minutes to be out here, and back again.'

'For a man who has been ailing? Perhaps. Thorold I let go hawking, so . . .'

'He sent hawk and man back, with a duck, and went riding, preoccupied, if the hawker is to be believed, and I see no reason he should not be.'

Bradecote's eyes narrowed.

'Preoccupied with what, I wonder?'

'My thoughts too, though we cannot exclude the others just yet.'

They reached Brictmer's door, and Bradecote fumbled the cloth into one hand to nudge up the latch. The chamber was dark, a little stale, and, for all the little that it contained, lacking in neatness. A broom stood in one corner, but the ground was strewn with bits of hay stalk and a thin vestige of having had rushes upon it. At one end was the bed, a wide, low wooden cot with a lumpy palliasse upon it, and a rough blanket. They laid Corbin upon it, as Brictmer and Aldith arrived, with Walkelin, and followed, breathless, by Father Dunstan.

'My boy,' cried Brictmer, in anguish, and came forward, hands outstretched.

'What do we do?' Aldith had a voice now, and a desperate calm. Her eyes were wide, and her fingers trembled, but she could function.

'We clean the wound and bind it better than I could do at the first.' Bradecote also thought if the skull were broken they might see, and guess the outcome, but did not say it before father and love.

'And yarrow,' muttered Brictmer, to himself. 'My wife always used yarrow on wounds, for healing.'

Catchpoll thought that rather hopeful, but agreed.

'I will fetch the water,' announced Walkelin, seeing no other task he could perform.

Father Dunstan knelt at the foot of the bed, to pray.

'Wait, Walkelin, before you bring the pail, see what horses are in the stable.' Bradecote threw him a meaningful glance.

'Yes, my lord.'

Brictmer, looking down at his only remaining son's pale face, reached for the hand of Aldith beside him.

'Surely it is not a judgement?' he mumbled, and Catchpoll wondered.

Bradecote began to unwind the bandage, but was almost shoved out of the way by Aldith.

'Let me . . . my lord.' Her fingers were the more deft, though he wondered how she would react to the wound. There was a sharp intake of breath for sure, but she neither swooned nor wept. With her initial shock over, Aldith would not weep, not unless, or until, the worst happened. She dabbed at the blood that had spread into his hair.

Bradecote, peering as best he could in the poor light, saw no whiteness of bone, which he thought a good sign, nor did the wound sag inward at her touch. Walkelin returned with water, and a nod of having done as he was told, and the wound was bathed. What was clear was a gash, straight but not blade narrow, not a splitting of skin.

'Something with weight, but not a stone. Something that has an edge to it, but not steel. A sword would have cloven the skull, and the cut is broader than a knife. That is my guess.' Catchpoll declared.

'Bind the wound, keep him warm, for his skin is cool, and sit by. There is nothing more we can do,' Bradecote commanded.

'And pray,' added the priest.

'Yes, assuredly, pray hard,' Bradecote agreed.

'But it was not murder,' muttered Brictmer to himself, Bradecote took him by the sleeve.

'Tell us now, and tell us all, because we need to find out who did this and why.'

Brictmer just stared at him, and Bradecote realised that, for the moment, the man's mind held only the thought that his son would die.

'Catchpoll, Walkelin.' Both followed him out of the cottage.

'The lord Thorold's horse is gone.' Walkelin had, understandably, been thinking the culprit might have ridden away.

'More that it has not come back, Walkelin.' Bradecote explained what had happened.

Catchpoll turned towards the manor entrance at the sound of a horse arriving at a brisk trot.

The horse that entered under the gateway was sweating, and so was its rider, but he was smiling also. Walkelin's jaw dropped.

'How in the name of all the saints did you get here, now?' Catchpoll stared at the smiling face of Rhys ap Iorwerth.

'Pleased to see me, are you? The Earl Robert was at Tewkesbury, see, and the road was good. I managed to get back to Worcester last eve. The castle cook has a fine Welsh wife who bakes the—'

'Yes, we know about Nesta, Drogo's Welsh wife. But you were not rushing back to her cakes.' Catchpoll did not want a tale of cooking.

'No, no. I wanted to be by here, as I promised. Would have been here sooner had the horse not cast a shoe.'

'To make sure we do things right.' Catchpoll did not look pleased, and Rhys raised a placating hand.

'To do my prince's bidding. I have seen nothing, nothing I tell you, that I would say to Madog ap Maredudd shows lack of care over finding out who killed his man.'

'Yes, well best you get off that poor beast before it collapses under you, and come with us. We need to speak.' Bradecote caught the eye of a man-at-arms honing a blade in a desultory fashion. 'You. Take the Prince of Powys's envoy's horse, and see it rubbed down and watered.' He commanded and was obeyed.

'There's grand,' murmured Rhys the Interpreter, as he handed the reins to the man, who bowed his head, just in case the Welshman was really as important as the undersheriff described him. Rhys grinned at Bradecote, but got no smile in response, and his face clouded. 'Oh dear. I am not going to like what I hear, am I.' It was a statement.

'No.' Catchpoll's answer was bald.

'That bad?'

'Yes.'

'*Duw!* He has not killed again?' There was no smile left on Rhys ap Iorwerth's face.

'No, but nearly as bad, so come where we can tell you.' Bradecote was not displeased to see the Welshman, but he did not want to discuss events in the manor bailey.

They went to the shadows cast beyond the gate, and before the end of the tale, Rhys was on his knees.

'It seems impossible to believe a man could . . . and yet I know it to be true. It is ashamed I am, ashamed, for I sat at table with this man, laughed with him, and beneath it all . . . Are you sure he . . . I mean . . .'

'He took the village girl by force, in revenge for her seeing him with the lady Avelina. The child Milburga has not spoken, we have been told, since she was "frightened" by Hywel ap Rhodri. She is like a ghost haunted by another ghost. A girl is not struck dumb by a man stealing a kiss, and knowing how Hywel had behaved those last few days, no, we are sure. The only miracle is that she was not strangled, but mayhap he thought a missing girl would cause too much of a stir, and if she was scared and ashamed enough, she would be silent. How silent he could not guess.' Bradecote felt no need to spare the details. Rhys needed to know everything about the man his prince had commended.

Rhys ap Iorwerth looked crushed.

'Did you know Rhodri ap Arwel?' Catchpoll asked, and had to repeat the question, for the Welshman was muttering to himself in his native language.

'Not well. I was at court only a year or so before he died, and he was not a young man then. His wife was dead many years. He was likely to leer at a pretty face, but leer was all he did, for he was closer to three score years than fifty by his death, and he had aching bones such that he walked slowly, and with a stick. Disliked the damp, he did.'

'In Wales?' Catchpoll scoffed. 'Damp is part of the country.'

'We are well watered, but the grass is green and lush, so there are benefits, and the wells are always full.' Rhys ap Iorwerth did not rise to the bait.

'Well, his son Hywel came here and told Durand FitzRoger, the younger son, that his older brother was a bastard.' Bradecote saw little would be gained on Rhodri ap Arwel.

'That would upset him. Was it true?'

'You do not get the point. Here, in England, only a legitimate son may inherit. If it were as in Wales, where a bastard acknowledged by his sire may do so, well, Earl Robert of Gloucester could have had the crown of England long since, and he has never claimed it, only fought for his legitimate sister's right.'

'Ah, yes, it is a different rule. So he was sowing great discord.'

'You might say that. He also confronted the lady Matilda, mother to both sons.'

'Nasty, though she would know the truth.'

'Dangerous you would say, once you met the woman,' said Catchpoll.

'Then was he a fool, or else why did he tell her? And did she kill him?'

'I think telling her, telling Durand, was a revenge on his mother's behalf,' declared Walkelin. 'It makes no difference to him in many ways, whether Doddenham is at peace or no. He could not gain land or power. If the sisters parted at such odds they never spoke again, and his mother told him often of her sister's perfidy . . .'

'What perfidy?' Rhys ap Iorwerth looked from one to the other of the sheriff's men.

'We return to Rhodri ap Arwel,' said Bradecote. 'It seems he wooed both sisters before taking the younger to wife. There is a high chance he took the elder another way first, and he revealed that to the younger when the girl married him.'

'So the bastardy is true?'

'The lady has sworn not, though she has not sworn she was a maid at marriage. The elder son here was an early brat, but not impossibly early, and she says the wedding to Roger FitzGilbert was three months after her sister went into Wales. She also regrets that the first son, whom she sees as weak, inherited, yet she declares his right. I think she speaks true. If her sister hated the thought of her, then Hywel either believed her, or wanted to revenge himself upon the sister his mother thought betrayed her.'

'But if this lady knows the accusation false . . .'

'It is still shaming, and casts doubts. He may even have threatened to tell Durand if she did not pay him with something of value.'

'You think Hywel ap Rhodri a blackmailer, my lord?'

'I put nothing past the man, and in comparison with his other crimes it is pale.'

'So the mother had cause to wish Hywel ap Rhodri dead? Could she have done it, or commanded it to be done?'

'Possible but not most likely, and—'

'My lord, hoof beats,' Walkelin broke in, and looked along the track that bisected the cluster of cottages. Thorold FitzRoger, straight-backed and proud, was cantering towards his own gate. He pulled up as the sheriff's men barred the way. He looked at the new face.

'Who is this?' FitzRoger frowned. 'You need more men here?'

'This is Rhys ap Iorwerth, sent as messenger to the Earl Robert of Gloucester by his prince, and also to report on what we find about the death of Hywel ap Rhodri.'

Thorold FitzRoger stared at Rhys ap Iorwerth.

'He is not the lord Sheriff's man,' he said, placing him in the third person, and at a distance. 'The Welsh have caused enough grief and anger in this manor. I will not have him within my walls. If stay he must, then let the priest, in charity, keep him. I shall not.'

Before Bradecote could say anything, the Welshman bowed, lower than needful.

'It is your manor, my lord, and I shall comply with your wishes.' He sounded not in the least put out, which infuriated FitzRoger, just as he intended.

'Where have you been, FitzRoger?'

'Hawking, as you well know.'

'Your hawk, and its prey, came home nigh on an hour since.'

'So? I rode. I do not have to have someone with me at all times.'

'Better for you if you had. Corbin the steward's son has been attacked.'

'He is dead?'

'Not yet, so does that count as failure?' Bradecote goaded him.

'You bastard!' FitzRoger flung himself down from his horse, and his hand went to the hilt of his sword.

'Do not be an even greater fool, FitzRoger.' Bradecote stared him down, as Walkelin stood, prepared to pounce upon the man.

'This is my manor, and these are my peasants. I want to know who did this as much as you do. Was it some jealous brawl over a girl?'

'The villagers, your "peasants", were in the hayfield, and so was Walkelin.'

Walkelin did not want to admit that at the time in question he could only vouch for those engaged upon his rick of hay, or that he had been enjoying himself immensely, and thought his superiors would also prefer the confession to be in private.

'Then who?'

'We are finding that out.'

'Yet you have been here two days and not found out who killed Hywel ap Rhodri.' FitzRoger could goad also, but to less effect.

'That is what you think.' Catchpoll did not add 'my lord'.

'I am going within my own bailey, sending my horse to my own stable, and then going to my own hall. Have you grounds for preventing me?' He glared at Bradecote.

'Not just yet.' Bradecote stood aside, and the lord of Doddenham strode angrily into his manor.

'You know, I do not think that I like him very much,' remarked Rhys ap Iorwerth, in a conversational tone.

'You are not the only one,' said Bradecote, watching the man.

'Will he have my horse thrown out?'

'I doubt he will even know it is there.' Catchpoll spat into the dirt. 'Now what, my lord?'

'Now, I think we return to Brictmer, and if his mind is not quite so numb, we find out what happened to Hywel ap Rhodri.'

'Should I come?' Rhys ap Iorwerth looked uncertain.

'I think not this time.'

'Then I will go to the church, and pray, pray for this Corbin that he does not die, and pray you find the truth, my lord.' He made a little odd bow, and walked away towards the church.

'That will be some weighty praying,' observed Catchpoll.

The trio returned to Brictmer the Steward's cottage. The door was open, letting in more light. Father Dunstan was still praying. Aldith sat upon the bed, stroking Corbin's face and murmuring gentle, if desperate, words of encouragement to waken. Brictmer was crouched upon the floor, like a thing broken.

'Brictmer.' Bradecote repeated the name before the man moved a muscle, and then he looked up, his eyes deep pits of misery.

'He is all I have of sons to follow me,' he whispered.

'Yes. You said, "It was not murder", Brictmer. You must tell us how you know this, and what really happened. You

232

must do this.' Bradecote spoke softly, compelling and yet not commanding. The man nodded.

'What my lad did was right, right I say, and shall say before any Justice.' His voice wavered with emotion. 'He saw him, the Welsh bastard, and what he was doing to poor Milburga, his cousin. She is just a child, a child not even a woman grown and yet . . . No wonder she has said not a word since. He saw the man, and he killed him in the act, and that cannot be murder, can it?'

'No, but what else, what happened to the servant, Rhydian?'

'He left. He was shocked, because he was there, after it happened, even before I got there, I think. He might not have the English, but he could see the girl and what his master had done. There was no doubt to it. He was upset, confused. We told him, by sign more than word, to get on the pony and leave, go home. It was not his fault his master was dead, but nor should that death be avenged, because it was just. He looked quite lost, and would not even ride the pony. He took the chattels and trappings the Welshman had with him, and walked away.' Brictmer looked at the priest. 'Murder is a sin most foul, Father, but he was defending his cousin, a little girl. God will pardon him?' He broke down.

'The sin was in the act upon her, not the saving, my son.'

'Then how is this a judgement upon him?'

'It is no more a judgement upon him than the offence upon little Milburga was a judgement on her. We may be afflicted for our sins, but crimes cannot be judgements else criminals would be doing the work of the Almighty, and such crimes as we have heard of and seen here are an abomination unto God.' Father

Dunstan spoke with a certainty, a confidence, which gave hope to the already grieving father.

'What I do not understand,' said Brictmer, 'is why anyone would harm my son. His act has been not just accepted but approved within our community, and he and Aldith . . .' He looked at the back of the young woman tending his boy. 'There is no rival. Never has been. You hear of such jealousy leading to deaths, but none festers here.'

'If God spares him,' murmured Aldith, 'plight us, Father.' It was as solemn as a vow.

'You can be assured that I shall, and gladly, my daughter.'

She turned her head, and looked at the sheriff's men.

'Can you tell me he does not lie here because of you?'

'Aldith.' Brictmer frowned.

'Can you, my lord?'

'No Aldith, I cannot, because when crimes are looked into, the criminals may act to protect themselves, and there seems little other reason to harm Corbin outside of him being connected to the death of Hywel ap Rhodri.'

'My lord, could not the servant have returned, and thought to take revenge?' The priest had not yet returned to prayer.

'What say you, Brictmer?' Catchpoll looked at the man, who concentrated, brows furrowed, lips compressed.

'Truly, I say no. Had you seen him, that night, no, he would not have sought revenge.'

'Ah then, no. But what if he got back to Wales, wondered how he would explain to his prince?'

'Still I say, no, Serjeant. To return here, to strike a blow upon a man not expecting it, without challenge, if you will, cannot have been the path of the man I saw, and nothing, not even a prince's disapproval, could make what his master did acceptable, in whatever realm. Whoever did this, it was not the Welsh servant, and when they are found . . .' His hands formed into tight fists.

'No, revenge is not defending the innocent, Brictmer.' Father Dunstan laid a hand upon the taut muscled arm. 'The law will see right done. Leave it to the law, and to these sheriff's men.' His voice calmed.

'The good Father is right, Brictmer. There are few who could possibly be involved in this, and we will find out who it was.' Bradecote looked at him.

Brictmer nodded.

'Then best we be about it,' murmured Catchpoll, and it signalled their departure. They ducked out of the doorway.

'I spouted fine and honestly spoken words, but something does not make sense in all this.'

'But the answer lies in that hall, my lord, of that we can be sure.'

'Yes, Catchpoll, but it is like a nest of adders and finding out which one it was, that "bit" will not be easy.'

They set off back to the bailey. Milburga passed them without looking at them. She was carrying a basket and heading to collect whatever was left of the washing.

'My lord, what if it was the lord Thorold, and the weapon was with him upon his horse? Might he have cast it away when he "disappeared" after hitting Corbin, and was biding his time before returning?' Walkelin liked all ends tidy.

'He might, though it would be good to have that weapon,

whatever it was. If he did not throw it away, mayhap it was concealed in the folds of his garb. We might check the stables, and the straw, for a start. Come.'

Walkelin did not actually think the lord Bradecote would be the one grovelling among the straw and horse dung.

Rhys ap Iorwerth left the church. He was thinking, thinking how he would even begin to explain to Madog ap Maredudd. He saw a child, a girl, walking slowly towards the gatehouse, so weighed down with washing she was almost obscured. He shook his head, and quickened his step.

'Here, little maid, may I take some of your burden from you?'

Chapter Fifteen

Milburga turned, and from lips that had been silent came a high-pitched scream, one that seemed without end. She dropped the basket and backed against the palisade, gripping the timber as if to hold her up. Everyone who heard came running. Brictmer got there first, and, for a man who did not look belligerent, was remarkably aggressive. He saw Rhys ap Iowerth standing, transfixed, his eyes wide and staring, and hit him full in the face. The Welshman fell, and Brictmer reached down and grabbed him by the cotte, pulling him to his feet and yelling obscenities the man could not even comprehend.

The three sheriff's men arrived to see Rhys being shaken like a rat, and with blood streaming from his nose.

'I did not touch her,' he was yelling, as best he could for lack of breath and blood in his mouth, and Milburga was screaming still, as if she would do so until her lungs burst.

'Let him be, Brictmer,' cried Bradecote.

'The Welsh bastard . . . All the same.' Brictmer was not a man of temper, but once lost it was lost completely.

'Never touched her,' repeated Rhys, whimpering now.

'Let him be, I tell you. He did not touch the child, I will vouch for him.'

'Then why does she scream?' Brictmer still held the limp figure of the interpreter, but looked at Bradecote.

'Because, no doubt, she heard him speak, heard the Welsh accent. He did not need to touch her to scare her witless. Leave the man be and see to your niece.' Bradecote stepped forward, and Brictmer blinked, and obeyed, simply dropping Rhys ap Iorwerth to the ground, where he lay, moaning. Catchpoll picked him up, and he sagged against the wall where Catchpoll thrust him.

'I swear, my lord, I touched her not,' he gasped.

'What happened, exactly?'

'I came out . . . out of the church. I saw the girl with a great armful of washing. I could scarce even see her face, she carried so great a pile. I am no servant, but . . . I offered to carry it for her, and she dropped the lot and screamed as if her life were about to end.' He sounded mystified, and aggrieved.

'The girl is Milburga, the wheelwright's daughter,' growled Catchpoll, quietly. It was explanation enough.

'Oh.' Rhys said no more, but held his nose to try and stem the bleeding.

Hugh Bradecote approached the hysterical girl. Brictmer was trying to calm her, and the screams had ceased, but she shook as if with the ague, and her eyes stared wide, like a panicked doe. She came no higher than Bradecote's lowest rib. A child, that was all she was, he thought, the age of his Christina when she had suffered. He crouched upon his heels, so that he looked up at her, not down upon her.

'This man meant no harm, Milburga. The man who hurt you is dead, you know he is dead. He is no ghost. Look at him. He is a different man.' Milburga kept her eyes on Bradecote. 'Look at him, child,' he repeated, gently but firmly, and she raised her gaze and glanced at the bloodied face of Rhys ap Iorwerth. 'That is not the man.'

She shook her head, slowly, her thin chest heaving. It was not words, but it was a response, and Bradecote wondered if he would learn anything else from her, and whether prompting was wrong.

'The man who harmed you. Was he killed when he was . . . with you?'

'You should not—' Brictmer began angrily, but was silenced by Bradecote's look and raised hand. The undersheriff looked back into the face of the girl. Had Christina looked that frightened, overwhelmed? It made his guts churn. He thrust the thought from his mind with difficulty. Perhaps what Milburga saw on his face, an almost broken-hearted pity and sympathy, made her respond. She nodded.

'Listen to me, Milburga. If someone killed the Welshman because of what he was doing, right then, they were defending you, and do not face hanging, or a wergild they cannot pay. Nobody has to stand by whilst a crime is committed, and what happened to you was a crime, not your fault, not your fault one little bit. Do you understand me?'

She nodded, more strongly.

'Did Corbin save you?'

There was a pause, and then she shook her head. Brictmer gasped, opened his mouth and then shut it again. Bradecote looked puzzled.

'Then . . .'

Milburga raised a shaking hand, but pointed her finger, very definitely, at Rhys ap Iorwerth.

'But he was not—' Brictmer cried, and the girl flinched.

'You mean,' Bradecote smiled at the girl, 'the other Welshman, the servant, saved you?'

She nodded, kept nodding, and tears began to fall upon her cheeks.

'Rhydian,' breathed Rhys, in a voice of awe.

'Rhydian was "faithful unto death" according to the lady Susanna ferch Gruffydd.' Bradecote's face was solemn. 'Well, I think he was. He must have looked the other way so often, tried to persuade himself that it was not Hywel ap Rhodri's fault, but what was happening in England could not be ignored.'

'It makes no sense though, my lord,' Walkelin interrupted. 'If Rhydian killed his master in the act of . . . trying to . . .' he paused, blushed, and carried on, 'and had argued with him over the forcing of attentions on Aldith, why had he remained with him after the murder and rape in Bromfield. If he did not know, he would not think the man a danger particular like, not more so than "at home" in Powys, and if he did, why did he not kill him on the road to Ludlow next morning?'

'What occurred in Bromfield, I think he knew no more of that than his master had been having his fun with another woman, but when he was here he heard Aldith in all her

240

righteous wrath, and warned Hywel, which was why they were heard to argue, and why the lady Avelina thought him like a nursemaid, watching closely.'

'He killed a woman in Bromfield?' Brictmer crossed himself, thinking what would have happened to his niece. The sheriff's men ignored him, focussing on the details.

'And the second day Rhydian was given much to do, which meant he could not follow out to—'

'See what he might be about,' interjected Walkelin, loudly, before Bradecote could say more. He was reminded that he had promised not to reveal Winfraeth's ordeal to any within the manor. Catchpoll looked sharply at him, but then nodded.

'Aye, making plans no doubt.' It was a meaningless phrase but Catchpoll knew it would suffice the manor folk present to hear it, and there were those enough about them now.

'And come the evening, by chance he came across you, Milburga, going to your father?' Bradecote still spoke softly. It was a guess, but it could not have been within the bailey for that would have risked all.

She nodded, and a sob escaped her.

'Then I think at that time he was being watched. Rhydian watched him, worrying, and then he saw what could not be denied, not made out as willing compliance.'

'But he was loyal,' whispered Rhys ap Iorwerth.

'He was, but even loyalty could not be complicit with that, and I think that Rhydian understood, at that moment, just what Hywel ap Rhodri was – had been for a long time – and knew both that it had to end, and that if he were caught, there would be great dishonour, to him, and to Mathrafal.' Bradecote paused for a moment, and then continued. 'He did the one thing that would save Hywel ap Rhodri from the fate he actually deserved, and he probably saved Milburga from death also. He stabbed him in the back, once, cleanly. Hywel may never even have known who did it.'

Milburga was listening, as if to a story. She held out her hand, touched Bradecote's arm as lightly as a feather to attract his attention back to her, and shook her head. Her mouth opened.

'*Et in hora mortis nostrae*,' she whispered, like a dying breath. Hild the Cook, who had come out and was hovering close, gasped and covered her face, weeping, to hear the voice at last.

'So, Hywel did know, for Rhydian spoke. "Pray for us sinners, now and in the hour of our death". Hywel ap Rhodri was assuredly a great sinner, and it was indeed the hour of his death.'

'But my Corbin . . . He did it, he told me the man was dead, and . . .' Brictmer was still confused by the truth that was not quite truth.

'Did Corbin come? Did he see?' Bradecote looked at Milburga, who reverted to her nod. 'Then I think he saw Rhydian do what he, as kin, would have done, and saw also not wrong but right in the deed. What happened thereafter, Brictmer?'

'He came to me,' the man's shoulders sagged again. 'He said as how the Welshman was dead because . . . He said the servant knew, and it was wrong to blame him. I saw the man. He looked almost as dead as his master, white of face, staring of eye. He wept too. I wish he had had the English. As I said before, we pressed him to go, got his pony, his master's horse. He thrust the reins of the horse back at us and said something, a word.'

'*Galanas*,' offered Rhys ap Iowerth, solemnly.

'Aye, very like.' Brictmer nodded.

'That means he was offering it as the wergild, as best he could, for what had happened. The horse, by right, should be Milburga's, and if it is sold, hers is the coin for it,' Bradecote explained.

'There now, we wondered so why he did that.' Brictmer shook his head, sadly. 'He left, with the trappings and the pony, but he took off his shoes and would not ride the beast, but led it, off into the night. I have no idea where he went, or if he lives still or is dead. That I swear.'

'And we did not ask what happened after he left, did we?' murmured Bradecote, to himself.

'Corbin took the body away?' Catchpoll asked.

'He did, and hid it, beyond the Hundred.'

'Actually, so far away he was back in the Hundred, but since the death was of a Welshman by a Welshman, I doubt the Hundred will have to pay for that mistake.' Bradecote gave a small, wry smile.

'But, my lord, who has killed my son? And why?'

'He is not dead yet, Brictmer. Prayers may still avail.'

'I dare not hope, my lord, dare not.' The man shook his head.

The death was solved as not a crime, but overlaid by a crime, a crime without doubt, and that remained. Bradecote was about to get up, for, after all, it was not a commanding position for an undersheriff, but before he did so he addressed Milburga once more.

'What happened is done. Treat it as you would a death, for deaths are remembered always, but do not stop us living. Time will aid you, and you have kin and friends here. The money for the horse is dower for the day, and the day will come when you are woman grown, that a man you can respect will care for you as a husband. You will not forget, but you will live, and you will know happiness.' His tone asserted, though in his heart it was more of a hope and prayer. He stood up.

'Rhys ap Iorwerth, you will not charge this man, Brictmer the Steward, with assault.'

'No, my lord, I will not.' Rhys was solemn, still taking in all that what he had heard meant.

'Good. Then the death of Hywel ap Rhodri is declared by me no crime, for he was killed in the acting of a crime most foul.'

'But the hiding of the body, my lord?' Catchpoll raised the unpleasant fact of law.

'Bodies of dead men are often moved over Hundred boundaries. Someone in this Hundred moved it, thinking it was into the next. Such crimes rarely have culprits found.' Bradecote looked straight at Catchpoll, but was making his decision known to the manor.

'Very true, my lord, very true.' Catchpoll nodded. Law and justice were not always the same thing, and if a little justice might prevail in this, all to the good.

'And my son?' Brictmer moaned.

'That is a crime for which a man will answer. Wrap the girl warmly, for she has been shocked, and give her spiced ale, a little. Have a care to her.' Bradecote half-turned, and nodded at the cook, who dipped in a curtsey of obedience to the command, and gathered Milburga into her motherly embrace, and led her away to the kitchen. 'We know much more now, Brictmer, and from that we will find out who attacked your son. If we know why, the who follows. Serjeant. Walkelin.'

244

He jerked his head towards the church. 'We will speak.' It sounded very formal, but that was what the inhabitants of Doddenham needed, some certainty.

'And me, my lord?' Rhys ap Iorwerth was still a little nervous in the company of the massed English, with a reason to hate the Welsh, and thought of the sheriff's men as his 'sanctuary'.

'If you wish.'

The four men walked away, and Walkelin gave a great sigh as if a burden were lifted.

'So we have completely solved a murder that was not a murder and are faced with what may well become a murder as a consequence.' Bradecote shook his head. 'We sit by the priest's house, and think, think hard.'

'Me too?' asked Rhys ap Iorwerth.

'Just do not think in Welsh,' mumbled Catchpoll, but a muscle at the side of his mouth twitched, 'and stop bleeding.'

They sat, a few minutes later, propped each elbows upon knees, in the hay-bleached grass beside Father Dunstan's little dwelling.

'It makes no sense, that is the trouble,' bemoaned Walkelin.

'If it did, then it would be obvious, lad.' Catchpoll sniffed. 'It has to be to do with the killing of Hywel ap Rhodri. It cannot be chance. The lord Bradecote is right, and we are going to end up back in that hall.'

'Then we go back through that first, for we have been led astray at times, and must have the clear path now. Since it is to do with Hywel, then we start with his arrival. He came late in the evening. He made himself known to the lord of

Doddenham as kin, and was accepted. Presumably he slept, being too weary to have managed more than a lewd suggestion to a village maid.' Bradecote raised two fingers, almost like a priest giving benediction. 'He was here thereafter two days only, and left dead.'

'That first day he must have found time to speak with the lady Avelina, and ply her with his charms, since Durand FitzRoger was up from his sickbed.' Catchpoll stared at a ladybird climbing a stalk of grass, but was thinking.

'That I do not understand, Serjeant. If she thought the lord Durand was getting better, why listen to Hywel ap Rhodri?'

'I can answer you that, Walkelin bach.' Rhys looked grim. 'She did so because when he wanted, Hywel ap Rhodri had a tongue like a bard. If a woman responded to flattery she would be eating out of his hand in the twinkling of an eye, if doing nothing more.'

'Yet you doubted us at the beginning,' complained Walkelin.

'Oh, he was ever silver-tongued, but . . . The lady Susanna would not speak false, and her words were clear. I thought him a seducer then. It is not a thing of which a man should be proud, but some are. There is a huge difference between a man who gets what he wants with words, and one who gets it by strength of body, and against the will, let alone who would kill. Were it not that I think the lady Susanna will support what I say, I would dread revealing the truth to my prince, lest he cut out my tongue.'

'So Hywel ap Rhodri seduces the lady Avelina, even under the noses of her husband and possible lover. Daring, or foolhardy.'

'Which gives both a reason to want him dead if they saw,'

Walkelin was frowning, concentrating, 'but neither killed him.'

'What else does he do that first day? He lays hands on Aldith, a young woman of spirit, who gives him a slapped face in response. I am guessing Rhydian heard both the girl's complaints in the kitchen, and he would not need English to get her meaning, and Hywel sounding hard done by because she resisted. That leads to Rhydian warning Hywel about how he behaves in the manor.' Bradecote rubbed his chin. 'None of which involves young Corbin.'

'Except he would support Aldith, and if he saw anything of Hywel wheedling his way into the lady Avelina's arms, he would blame the man not the woman. And that is no reason to hit Corbin over the head, either.' Walkelin looked glum.

'But it makes him more likely to do another's bidding,' growled Catchpoll. 'I said as he could be used, and that, my lord, is where I am sure our connection lies.'

'But he did not kill Hywel ap Rhodri, so even if he was doing another's bidding, there was no call to silence him, since he did not do the deed.' Rhys was keeping up in a second language, and struggling, so he sounded a little desperate.

'Holy Virgin, that is it!' Bradecote sat upright, so suddenly his head spun.

'My lord?' Rhys blinked.

'His attacker assumed, as everyone in Doddenham assumed, that Corbin had killed Hywel ap Rhodri. He did not kill the man, but even his own father thought that he had, defending Milburga. The person who hit him believed he was the killer, and had obeyed their command, using the attack as valid cover. It is unlikely Corbin would have gone on about the honour of his cousin, and perhaps more likely told of her being "frightened" the way we were told. I doubt the inhabitants of the hall see Milburga very often and would not speak to her, so they would never consider what that really meant.'

'What about Rhydian, and the horse that was left, my lord?' Walkelin chewed his lip, thoughtfully.

'Rhydian was just a servant, and how much loyalty do they inspire in their own servants? Would any be "loyal unto death"? That seems impossible to me. So they assumed Rhydian saw the sense of not remaining, and may have thought he left the horse because leaving with the pony was all he was offered, in addition to his master's clothes and baggage. So they have feared that under our increasing pressure, Corbin would implicate them, and therefore wanted his silence.'

'And my guess is the lad thought throughout it mattered little in the fact, and if the manor thought he had done it, well he would be something of a hero, even to his lady Avelina, if he believed her offended also by the man. The foolishness of youth might cause his death.' Catchpoll shook his head. 'And for what, a boast, or what must account as one, even if he did not say outright "I killed the bastard".' Catchpoll looked at Rhys, wondering if he would object to the epithet, but the Welshman did not bat an eyelid.

'So we are saying Corbin followed Hywel, but more cautiously, and waited as he began to deflower his cousin? I doubt that.' Walkelin was sceptical.

'Agreed, if that were so, Walkelin. But what if Corbin was steeling himself to do the deed as ordered?' Bradecote had the sequence in his head. 'He has never killed a man, and remember that most men never see more bloodshed than an accident with a farming implement. Killing like he was going to do would need building himself up to it, getting himself mad and angry enough to do it in hot blood. So he is not following, but somewhere in the village, and near enough to hear a cry from Milburga. He investigates, but a single cry is hard to place, and so unlike Rhydian, he arrives late, and in time to see the blow delivered only. Rhydian becomes distressed, Milburga is distressed. My guess is he gets both into Tovi's home, and runs for his father, because he is his father and also the steward. By the time he tells the tale, who delivered the blow is not important, and he does not want whoever set him up to kill to be disappointed in him. He takes the "honour" since Rhydian clearly does not want it, and earns it by dealing with the aftermath.'

'I would say that has a ring of truth to it, my lord. So often truth is dipped in chance.' Catchpoll nodded, wisely. 'So now we see the why, we just needs the who.'

'That can only be one of three.' Walkelin sounded more hopeful.

'Four.' Bradecote corrected. 'All along we have discounted the lady Avelina, for sound reasons. But, and it has to be considered, what if what was seen by . . . the girl in the field on the second morning, did not develop as she assumed? What if Hywel got nasty, forceful, and the lady Avelina decided she was not prepared to go beyond fondling in the shrubbery?'

'Nobody mentioned her looking upset.' Catchpoll pulled a face.

'I agree, but it is possible she gave in without a fight, but without wanting to. If that were so, she would be one very, very angry lady, and if she suggested to Corbin even a fraction of what happened . . .'

'No, my lord, he would have been a young hothead and gone straight out with his eating knife and done for him in full view.' Catchpoll saw the flaw.

'By nature, yes, but she would not want it common knowledge. She would have pleaded with him to do her this service quietly, and she would be forever indebted.'

'You mean till he asked something of her, and then she would revert to "my lady" and look down her nose at him,' scoffed Catchpoll.

'Without a doubt.'

'Then there is four as has reason, but I cannot see the lady Avelina hitting Corbin over the head, and so hard as to knock the wits, if not the life, from him.'

'I agree, Walkelin, but it had to be looked at to be discounted. So, of the three, who is next?'

'The three?' Rhys ap Iorwerth looked at each in turn.

'Thorold FitzRoger, Durand FitzRoger, and their mother, Matilda FitzGilbert.' Bradecote ticked them off on his fingers. 'And either man might just have done it if the lady Avelina had played the duped female, betrayed by a wicked seducer, and then blackmailed by a foolish boy.'

'Oh no, please let us not have her back in,' cried Rhys, and Catchpoll actually laughed.

'Is Durand fit enough to have got from the hall to the drying ground, hit Corbin hard enough, and got back, and not been remarked upon, having been scarce outdoors in a month?' Walkelin asked.

'Good point, young Walkelin.' Catchpoll nodded his approval.

'It makes him less likely, for sure. He is certainly not as weak as he or his mother have made him out to be, which still makes me wonder why, but he would have to have been lucky not to have been seen. What about the lady Matilda?' Bradecote looked at the others.

'Strong enough . . . Corbin is a tall lad, and she is quite short, but if he was lying down, daydreaming, or scrambling to his feet, it is perfectly possible.' Catchpoll folded his arms. 'But with what? What could a woman carry and explain if seen, and cause that wound?'

'Which leaves us . . . you, with the lord Thorold.' Rhys ap Iorwerth announced.

'It does. So we needs to know how he did it, and find some way to prove it, because the man is as slippery as an eel and will deny every word.' Catchpoll grimaced, which was a long-winded process that fascinated the Welshman.

'Corbin was struck down sometime after Aldith left him, and before she went back to him, perhaps an hour later,' Bradecote frowned. 'That gives little margin for anyone wanting to do the deed, and Thorold FitzRoger was not in the company of his goshawk and man for the half of it.'

'My lord, may I ask a question?' Walkelin looked suddenly as if not asking would make him burst.

'Yes, of course.'

'If you were in Bradecote, at your ease, and went hawking . . . if you have a hawk that is, and . . .' Walkelin's tongue tied itself in a knot.

'Get on with it, lad,' Catchpoll prodded him.

'Well, if you did, would you wear your sword?'

'Er, no, I suppose not. I do not wear it at my hip every hour of the day.'

'Then why did the lord Thorold wear it to go hawking?'

'Did . . . yes, of course he did, because he wanted to draw it upon me when I angered him! Well done, Walkelin. But he stormed out of his hall without retiring to his chamber, so he was wearing it before he decided to go out.'

'Or he was going to go out and you speaking with him merely delayed it, my lord. At which point we ask, does he always wear a sword, to make him feel more the man and lord, or was it just today?' Catchpoll shut his eyes to think back.

'I was out in the bailey when he went out a little after we arrived, my lord. You and Serjeant Catchpoll went into the hall, but I did not. I saw him call for his horse again, and mount up. I would swear he wore no sword then.' Walkelin's voice had risen a tone.

'So today he had his sword. But going out and finding Corbin somewhere and slicing him in two would be making himself the most obvious suspect. Who else wears a sword and is out and about?'

'But he told his brother to leave tomorrow. If he could put enough suspicion upon him so that he feared us and left early, it would look clear that it was the lord Durand as did it.'

'You know, young Walkelin, once you rid yourself of this habit of looking as if you might pop like a soapwort bubble in a washtub, you are going to be an asset,' said Catchpoll, with a smile of approval.

'So, Thorold FitzRoger plans to do away with Corbin, and if another method had presented itself, I am sure the sword would not have been first choice.' Bradecote was too focussed to be lauding Catchpoll's apprentice. 'He is on horseback, so sees him at the drying ground with Aldith. He thinks that opportunity gone because she is there and it is too close to home for blood and whatever fatal wound he planned, but might hope Corbin would linger afterwards. His hawk strikes first time, so he sends it back, and returns to see what has happened. Aldith has either gone or leaves. He dismounts not too close, and instead of sword he uses the sword in the scabbard. That would work for the wound, yes, Catchpoll?'

'It would, my lord.'

'But why,' asked Rhys ap Iorwerth, 'was this lord with his horse able to ride up to the youth and strike him without a murmur?'

'Because I doubt the lad was thinking of anything other than what had gone on between him and his girl, Aldith, so recent he would still feel as if upon a cloud.' Catchpoll winked.

'You mean they . . . ?'

'They did, I would almost swear to it. I saw the maid, though she no longer had that title, afterwards. You could have trotted a troop of cavalry past him and he would not have opened an eyelid.'

'At which point we have FitzRoger taking the opportunity to strike Corbin a sharp blow to the head, and leave him unconscious and bleeding. What is the bet that it is the first time Thorold has ever wielded a sword, even scabbarded, at a real live man. He does not know what killing feels like, or even looks like, so blood and a swoon seem more than adequate, and I will grant the lad looked like death when we found him. He jumps back on his horse, trots away for a suitable time and then comes back long enough after for everyone to be in a panic over the attack, and him as calm as if he has done nothing more than exercise his steed. He can also feign righteous indignation at our failing to prevent the deed.' Bradecote hit the ground with the flat of his hand. 'It all works.'

'It works, my lord, but could you prove even one part of it? Let alone have the man confess. I do not know your law, but it sounds doubtful, though I am sure what you say is what happened.' Rhys ap Iorwerth sounded apologetic.

Bradecote ran his long fingers like claws through his hair and muttered a fluid line of obscenity. The Welshman grinned, despite all.

'There, now that sounded so poetic it might almost have been Welsh.'

Brictmer the Steward appeared suddenly from around the corner of the building, chest heaving.

'My lord, my lord, come quick.'

'What has happened now?'

'My son has woken, Corbin lives!'

Chapter Sixteen

Nothing had changed within the single room, and yet everything. The deathbed was now a place of recovery. Aldith had one of Corbin's hands in hers and was gazing at him as if she might never look away. Father Dunstan was on his knees still, but hands upraised and chanting a psalm. Corbin lay very pale, but his eyes were open.

'See, my lord, our prayers are answered. It is a miracle, so it is!'

'Glad to see you alive, lad,' Catchpoll sounded once more the kindly uncle. 'You just tell us what happened.'

'When?' The voice was threadlike. Everyone stared at him. Father Dunstan stopped mid sentence. Corbin looked back at them, a small frown between his brows. 'When?' The question was more insistent.

'Corbin, you know me?' Aldith whispered, with fear in her voice.

'Yes . . . Aldith . . . Grew up together.' He looked muddled, and vaguely annoyed at the silly question.

'And today?' She squeezed his hand. 'On the drying ground?' He looked more puzzled, and her face fell. 'Do you not remember?'

He still looked confused, and she leant and whispered very softly in his ear. His eyes widened.

'No!' he cried. She pulled back, affronted, shamed. 'Would 'member that. Would 'member, please say would 'member?' There was an edge of panic to his voice, and it actually eased her.

'You will, Corbin. I will help you remember,' she soothed.

'All of which means you do not know who hit you.' Catchpoll heaved a heavy sigh.

'Head hurts.' He closed his eyes.

'Do people get their memory back, after such things?' Bradecote whispered to Catchpoll.

'Bits, I think, but it seems more luck, what returns, my lord.'

'How far back will he have forgotten?'

'I am no physician. If he has forgot something as important in his young life as . . .' Catchpoll raised an eyebrow and looked at Aldith's back as she murmured to the lover who could not recall the act of love, 'then perhaps not since this morning, or yesterday, or weeks, for all that I know. There was a mason, fell from the scaffolding on the priory once, far enough to break bones, but not yet die, and he forgot even how to speak. The only thing he knew was stone. If you placed a mallet and a chisel in his hand, and sat him before stone, he would work it.'

Hugh Bradecote pondered, and came to a decision. He addressed the injured youth.

'Corbin, I am Hugh Bradecote, Undersheriff of this shire. I know your head hurts, but I must ask you one question.' He waited, and then continued. 'Do you know why the Welshman Hywel ap Rhodri was killed by his servant?'

The gloomy chamber was heavy with the absence of words. After what seemed an age, Corbin's voice, weary now, gave a word.

'Milburga.'

'Thank you.' He looked at Brictmer, and Catchpoll. 'If he recalls that, then he will know who sent him to kill the man also.' Brictmer opened his mouth, but Bradecote raised a hand. 'Whoever tried to get him to kill Hywel, and we will find that the reason given would have seemed good, that person tried to kill your son today. Walkelin, you do not let anyone in other than the people you see now, not until we have the answer.' Bradecote kept his eyes on the steward.

'Yes, my lord.'

'God be praised your son will recover. We will not press him now, for his mind is as sore as his skull, and cannot think much, but tomorrow, we will ask more questions, the important questions, because answers must come before long. You understand?'

'I do, my lord. Will he have to answer for . . .'

'For not doing something? If every man who has dreamt of ending the life of another, if every man who has considered it, were arraigned, the Justices would never sleep, nor eat.'

'Then the man who set him upon the Welshman cannot be taken up for it either.'

'No. But you see, today they really did commit a crime for which we will take them. Keep Aldith here tonight, for her safety as well as Corbin's comfort of mind.'

'I will, my lord.'

Bradecote nodded, at him, and at Walkelin, then he, Catchpoll, and Rhys ap Iorwerth went out into the sunshine.

'Do you wish me to leave now, my lord, now I can tell my prince who killed Hywel ap Rhodri, and why?'

'I suppose you could reach Leominster before sunset, but I am reasonably sure that if you wait until the morrow, you will be able to give him the fuller story.'

'Why did you not ask him now who set him to kill Hywel ap Rhodri, my lord?'

'I wondered that also,' added Catchpoll.

'Because . . . I do not understand minds, but his answers were childlike in simplicity.'

'Then surely the simple, but most vital, question was the one to ask. The answer would have been but a name.' Rhys frowned.

'Perhaps, but if his answers were a child's answers, I feared his reaction to the question which put him in trouble would be like a child's. If you confront a small child with a misdeed, how often do they deny it, even if it is undeniable? If he is left, and his head aches the less by dawn, his father and his strong-willed young woman will be telling him how important it is for him to reveal that name, and he will not have to lie there and say "Yesterday I told you false".'

'I mislike the wait, but see there is sense, my lord,' Catchpoll gave a grudging approval.

'And when he gives the name, the name of his lord Thorold, will it be enough, the word of a steward's son, against a lord? You said this Thorold was clever, and he looked it. Nasty but clever.'

'Well, I have not thought the Justices fools often, thus far, and I agree with the lord Sheriff, who said that Thorold FitzRoger was clever, but not as clever as he thinks he is. The planning of the death he can deny as reason for the assault upon Corbin, but I think the attack ought to stand.'

'And after? There will be a price to pay in coin for breaking the lad's head, true enough, but what of steward and son after that? Will not the lord dismiss both and send them from the manor? Will he not then have won, and they lost?'

It was a good question, and Bradecote had no good answer. It was in a very sober mood that the three of them went back under the arch of the gatehouse.

'Do we confront FitzRoger now, my lord, as if we had the sworn word of Corbin?' Catchpoll wanted an end, and this lingering rankled.

'I am tempted, Catchpoll, sorely. I think . . . yes, first we will ask to see his sword, and I think he will smile, because he knows it bears no mark upon it. But you will study that scabbard, and study it closely for the smallest trace of blood or hair. If that gives us what we want, then we definitely press with what we are likely to have as if it were ours already.'

'Where is my brother?' Thorold FitzRoger did not ask with any trace of affection in his voice. He stood in the solar, looking at the two women in his life, and realising he wished neither were part of it, and tossed his gauntlets onto the table.

'He has, against my advice, gone to look at his horse, and the brown that Brictmer's boy will ride.' The lady Matilda regarded her son, stonily.

'Corbin will not now be accompanying him.'

'Why?'

'He has suffered an . . . accident. His head is broken. He will likely be dead before morning.' He sounded unconcerned.

The lady Avelina, who had been working upon her stitchery for real under the baleful glare of the older woman, let her knife slip as she cut a thread, and exclaimed as it made a tiny cut in her finger. She dropped the knife onto the table, and sucked the injured digit as the red blood welled up.

'Did he fall? Was he up a tree?' The lady Matilda was understandably surprised.

'The sheriff's unwelcome brood say he was hit about the head, but they only want to make trouble.' He expected her agreement.

'Who hit him?'

'Does it matter?' Thorold sounded irritated.

'If someone hit him, then why? Is not everyone in danger?' The lady Avelina ceased sucking her finger.

'No. It will be some peasant's squabble.'

'Why are you so sure of that?' The lady Matilda did not let go of a subject easily. 'And what says the undersheriff?'

'I do not know and nor do I care. I thought you believed the undersheriff a fool, anyway.' Thorold paused. 'My hawk brought down a duck, so . . .'

'Thorold! This is important. Corbin is the son of our steward, and to follow him.'

'I never thought he would make much of the position. I will select another.'

'But his family have been stewards of Doddenham for generations.'

'Then the line breaks now. It is not important, not to me. The boy is no loss. All he has done is trot about the solar like an ever-faithful hound, with great eyes only for "my lady" and doing whatever she may snap her fingers at.'

'He was of good use when Durand was very ill.' The lady Matilda could be fair when she chose.

'More, then, the pity.'

'You speak as if you wished Durand had died.' The lady Avelina looked reproachfully at her husband.

'We wish each other dead. That seems fair to me.'

'But he is your brother, my lord.' She was shocked. 'You may dislike him, but you cannot wish him dead. He is your blood.'

'Is he? Or is he but half my blood, Mother?' Thorold turned suddenly upon his mother. 'Was it true what that Welsh weasel told me? Am I Thorold FitzRoger or Thorold, bastard of some Welshman? Because Durand would oust me if he could, doubt it not. Will you help him, since he has always been favoured?'

'You must have been drinking. This is the madness of wine talking.' The lady Matilda glowered at her firstborn. 'Do you think, if I indeed prefer Durand, that I would have had you take his father's estate, if you were indeed the son of Rhodri ap Arwel? Do you? No. It makes no sense, as you make no sense.

261

Just because I despise you does not mean I would supplant you with an usurper.'

'You "despise" me?'

'Of course I do. You are too like unto your father, that is the irony. I despised him too. Roger FitzGilbert was indecisive, weak of will, though at least strong enough in body when younger. You arrived small, and small you have remained, in body, in courage, in mind. You have pretended, worn the mantle of a lord, but your shoulders are not even broad enough to wear that of Roger FitzGilbert.' The woman was angry, angry not for the moment, but for a lifetime of disappointment, and her words spilt out in a bitter torrent. 'You have replaced strength with guile, and puffed yourself up in the delusion that a little cleverness among the ignorant is as good as being a strong man, a real man. At every turn you have been weak, mistaking the taking of any decision for taking a good decision. When you said you would wed, I warned you about her.' She pointed at the lady Avelina, who was staring at her, open-mouthed. 'What did you think, if you thought at all? That her beauty would fire you out of disinterest, out of impotence? What that Welsh serpent did, molesting our servants, was disgusting, but do you know, just for one small moment when I had heard that the girl Aldith had slapped his face for his temerity, I wished it had been you. Never, even in the first flush of manhood, did your father have to berate you for stealing a kiss from some peasant girl, or appease an angry father whose daughter you had seduced with sweet words. You were simply not interested, as though women were trees. Yet you pick a woman that has men slavering after her just by drooping her lashes at them. She is little better than a common whore, but you have made her so, by ignoring your duty. You did not have to enjoy it. Heaven knows we women rarely do so, but we do our duty, aye, and the greater duty since we have to carry and bear. Did you try? Did you consult a wise woman, or a physician to help your ardour? No. You just pretend to be a man when everyone knows you are without desire.' Her voice slowed, and became resigned. 'There are men who cannot sire heirs, but they can still be lords, puissant in their shire. You sit here, without ambition, without an aim but to sit here, and you watch, watch life and the world pass Doddenham by. It may suffice the peasants who seek only stability, but you are not a peasant, and it ought not to suffice you. "FitzRoger the Watcher" is how you will be remembered for a time, and then forgotten as if you had never been. My sire said once that he had been told that in the old, old days when our ancestors were heathen in Normandy, they said immortality was being remembered in the halls, as a warrior, as a "giver of treasure". While men spoke of you, you lived on. You, Thorold, will be "dead" within a hand of years after your body lies in the earth.'

'How little you know me. You say I watch, and do nothing, but it is just that you do not see all I do, all I achieve. Hywel ap Rhodri, your sister's son, came here and made trouble, trouble by his words and by his deeds. What would your strong lord have done? Shouted at him, thrown him out? That is nothing. I achieved far more, for I achieved his death,' Thorold said it proudly, 'and without even getting as much blood upon my hands as that finger of yours, wife.'

The lady Avelina put her hands to her cheeks, and gave a low moan.

'You killed him? Why?'

'For several good reasons. The first was that I did not want him telling all that I was a Welshman's bastard. The second was that I disliked him taking liberties with my servants in my manor. And the third was that I really objected to him tupping my wife among my own hazels.'

'You saw? No, someone else must have—'

'I saw. I "watched", and some watching gives no pleasure. However I use you, or not, you are my wife, mine. He had no right. So you see, Mother, I can act, and far better my way than ranting and roaring and flashing my sword at him. I had him killed, and it was easy, and very satisfying.'

'If you did that, then . . . Has Durand fallen back into illness because of poison?' The lady Avelina was white-faced, excepting a smear of blood upon her left cheek.

'Now there is an idea.' Thorold laughed.

'Fool. I have seen such fevers as Durand's, and his is natural, not the effect of poison.' The lady Matilda was watching her son, and, having despised him for years, was aware of a blossoming flower of fear within her.

'Agreed. But it is still a nice idea. I had hoped, of course, that he might just die. It seemed such a likely thing for a while, but he disappointed me. If you want to know why I have not dealt with him as with the Welshman, it is simple. I could do nothing to pay back Hywel ap Rhodri except take his life. With Durand I take hope. As long as I live, he is a landless sword in the pay of Gilbert de Clare. He has no power, no woman, no "heirs of his body". He has a living death of failure. Why end the pleasure of seeing that?'

'And if I bore his child?' The lady Avelina spat the question.

'Alas, it would not survive . . . And maternity is such a risk, isn't it? I would grieve, of course, but . . .' Her eyes widened in horror.

The lady Matilda was horrified too, by the lack of emotion. She could understand a man killing a deceiving wife in anger, but the idea of him watching and waiting, pretending to be pleased at her swelling form, and all the while planning her death, two deaths, was more than she could take. And then it hit her, with a cold certainty.

'You said you had Hywel ap Rhodri killed.'

'Yes, I did, Mother.'

'Was it by Corbin?'

'Yes.'

'Jesu, it was you who hit him, then.'

'He would make things awkward with the sheriff's men, now the horse is found.'

'You sent a boy to do a man's job.' It was her first thought, that even in this her son had not been 'the man', and the disgust made Thorold snap. He strode the two steps towards her and hit her across the face, hard, with the back of his hand. It took her completely by surprise, and she fell. Her head caught the table edge and then, as she hit the floor, there was a peculiar, distinct sound. It was the sound of a snap. Matilda FitzGilbert stared up at her son, and her gaze did not reproach, because it was sightless.

Thorold looked down at her, caught between horror, disbelief, and a strange sense of release.

His wife gave a strangled cry that broke the silence, and he heard heavy footsteps in the hall. Not clever, was he? He grabbed the knife that lay discarded upon the table and plunged it into the dead woman's chest. The lady Avelina stood, frozen, and he rose, grabbed her by the arm, and flung her round that he might pinion her before him. Then he yelled.

'Murderess! She has killed her, killed my mother!'

The door burst open, and undersheriff and serjeant almost fell into the chamber. They saw the woman on the floor, the knife protruding, the wild-eyed man with the equally wild-eyed woman in his firm grasp.

'She killed her,' he cried again, and caught his breath on a sob.

Avelina FitzRoger just stared.

'Why?' Catchpoll barked the question.

'They were arguing, not shouting, the usual clawing with words. My mother called her a whore, and then . . . My mother!' The word became a wail.

'No,' whispered his prisoner. 'He did it.'

'But it is her knife, and look, she is not used to wielding it to such a purpose, for she cut herself where finger grasped blade. He prised open her hand, where the cut still showed a red line.'

'The knife slipped as I cut a thread.' Her voice was small.

'She got blood on her face when she put her hands to it, seeing what she had done. It was a moment of madness, but she killed my mother.' Thorold pushed his wife towards Bradecote and fell upon his knees by the body.

Bradecote looked at Catchpoll, and Catchpoll looked back. It sounded simple at first glance, but nothing was right. Bradecote took the woman's left hand and looked at the cut. It was tiny, and upon the tip. If the knife was held to stab, and grasped too low, the finger would be cut in the closest part to the hand. He wondered also at the fact the injured finger was upon the left hand. Some people preferred the left, but it was not as common as using the right. Catchpoll came to the other side of the corpse, and reached, gently, to close the sightless eyes. FitzRoger did not expect his hand to move next to the neck. The other hand helped lift the head, even as Thorold sat back upon his heels.

'Now there is a thing,' remarked Catchpoll, without haste. 'Why should the lady stab a woman whose neck is broke?'

'She fell when the blade went in,' sniffed FitzRoger.

Catchpoll looked at the knife hilt, sticking from the chest. The angle of the blade was slightly upwards.

'Done a lot of killing, have you, my lady?' Catchpoll enquired.

'No, I —'

'You see, I have seen many knife wounds, and many who have wounded with a knife. A woman can kill with one, yes, but they are actually very bad at it. You see, a woman does not learn to use a knife, and she will stab down,' Catchpoll made a fist about an imagined blade and matched action to words, 'but a man, he knows the best way, the sure way, is to stab upwards, like so.' He performed the action. 'This knife went in on an upward stroke.'

'What are you saying?' FitzRoger scrambled to his feet.

'I think what Serjeant Catchpoll is saying is fairly clear, FitzRoger. It was not your wife who killed your mother.' Bradecote had set the lady Avelina to one side, and she stood, trembling.

'She killed her, I tell you, stabbed her and she fell and—'

'Pick up your sewing, my lady.' Bradecote had to repeat the command. She blinked at him, but did so.

'The lady is right-handed, yet you say she stabbed with the left because the blade cut her. Most . . . unusual. And Catchpoll here has seen more corpses than you have eaten roasted heron, I would think. You killed her.'

'He hit her, and she fell.' The lady Avelina found her voice. 'Her neck broke then. He took my knife from the table and stabbed her after . . . when he heard you coming.'

'Now that,' said Catchpoll, with satisfaction, 'is a much better explanation of what we see here.'

'No!' The exclamation came not from Thorold FitzRoger, but his brother, steadying himself against the door frame. His recent pallor was increased. He stared at the scene before him, and then launched himself towards his brother, though unsteadily. Thorold was on his feet before Durand reached him, and began to draw blade from scabbard. He had forgotten Catchpoll, and forgetting Catchpoll was always a mistake. The serjeant simply linked his hands and struck a blow, as if a two-handed sword swipe without the sword, catching FitzRoger behind the knees and sending him to the floor. Bradecote grabbed Durand, as he half fell and half threw himself upon his brother.

'No, let the law have him, Durand. He has even more than this to answer for, and he will answer.'

The man struggled for a moment, and then gave up. Catchpoll had pinioned Thorold FitzRoger, and Bradecote, leaving the crumpled Durand, stepped to unbuckle the man's sword.

'You will need good light to inspect this, Serjeant,' he said. 'Leave the prisoner with me. Oh, and best you fetch the priest and tell Walkelin his watch is stood down.'

'Yes, my lord.' Catchpoll took the sword belt and the sword in its scabbard. Bradecote looked at the people in the chamber. Catchpoll said you should not get involved, with victim or culprit, but sometimes that was hard, even impossible. Yet here he felt he was standing back, observing from a distance. He had felt more concern over the youth Corbin, hoping he would live, and not just to provide the answers to questions. These four, three living and one dead, were the people of this hall, this solar, and none cared deeply for any of the others. The wife might have cuckolded husband with brother, but there was no love between them, just need. She offered no comfort to him now, but sat upon the floor as if dazed. Both sons had been in awe of the mother, and held her in feared respect mixed at times with dislike, though Durand wept for her now. The two brothers hated each other, and the two women likewise. It bore no more relation to his own hall than starlight to mud. There was silence but for the sound of Durand's emotion.

'My mother was right, she was always right, though I hated her for it. I ought to have done things myself.' Thorold spoke almost dreamily.

Walkelin arrived, for the second time in a few hours followed by a breathless priest. Father Durand shook his head, crossed himself, and went to the side of the body of the lady Matilda. He began prayers for the dead. Walkelin had a length of rope with him.

'I thought this might be useful, my lord.'

Bradecote just nodded.

Chapter Seventeen

By dusk, everything was quiet and arranged. Thorold FitzRoger was tied securely in the stable, and the body of the lady Matilda laid out upon a trestled board before the altar of the little church. Durand FitzRoger kept to the bed in which he had slept since his return, somehow not wishing to take the bed in the chamber above just yet, though it might have been from the exertion required to get up and down, and the lady Avelina slept in that bed alone, yet no more alone than she had throughout her marriage.

The sheriff's men slept in the hall, and Rhys ap Iorwerth joined them.

'The good Father has more to deal with, what with the injured and the dead, a burial and soon a wedding, to want to look to me,' he explained, 'and besides, I would like the whole tale, that I can get it quite straight in my head to prepare for my prince.'

'I do not know about a straight "tale". It goes round more like a dog chasing its "tail",' complained Walkelin. 'There was Thorold FitzRoger and his mother both saying as the servant Rhydian did it, thinking it a lie to cover Thorold's involvement, and Brictmer saying the same to cover Corbin's, so all of them was lying, but yet telling us the truth!' He shook his head. 'And since we find out lies, we could not see the truthful lie, or was it the lying truth. I give up.'

'Never give up, lad, just take time to reconsider. It always sounds better,' advised Catchpoll, wisely, picking his teeth.

'It is still going to sound as "moon madness" to the lord Sheriff, though.' Bradecote accepted the fact.

'Ah, but the lord Sheriff, for all his scowls, has been lord Sheriff long enough to know that sometimes "moon madness" is all there is.' Catchpoll appeared philosophical.

'Could we have untangled it without other deaths, other near deaths too, I wonder?' Bradecote rubbed the back of his head.

'We had the attacks upon the girls in the wrong order, my lord, and that complicated things. It was easily done. We took them in the order we heard of them, and there was no clue that was not the way of it. Thus we had it the bastard went so far that the girl Milburga was struck into silence by what happened to her, that he then tried his luck with the older and more womanly Aldith, who was caught in a public enough place that she could fight back and mayhap threaten to scream, and then next day he found Wi—the village girl, whom he had eyed on arrival. She kept her mouth shut because she feared being disbelieved, and he had power.'

'Should we not have wondered why the manor men did not kill him after the first attack, if we thought that the one upon Milburga, since it was so serious?' Walkelin wondered out loud. 'We wondered about Tovi.'

'If Milburga was struck dumb, they might have got nothing from her, nor even guessed it all that first night. That was what I assumed. We could not fathom why Tovi had not killed him, certainly, but the real answer is that of course he did not know of the crime until after Hywel was already dead. That is why he said it was not for him to do. It was done. Since nobody was really talking about what happened to her, least of all herself, we did not grasp that she was attacked last of all. Should we have seen?' Bradecote tried to set things out in his own mind. 'In my head I supposed she was the quieter sort, and perhaps nobody would have thought the unthinkable that first day. They thought her young, innocent, and shocked by the sort of manhandling Aldith fought back against. That is how I saw it then. Think of it. Aldith had defended her honour and was angry enough and bold enough, and wise enough too, to make it known. Nobody, knowing her, seeing her wrath, and hearing her denounce Hywel ap Rhodri, would think he got very far, and besides, it would make him ridiculed within the manor. She had her victory, and no real harm done.' Bradecote looked grim. 'They would not think him persistent.' He paused. 'And also, Thorold FitzRoger used the plural "maidservants" from the first and at that stage I had not seen Milburga for myself. By the time we spoke with her father, Tovi, I had set the timing in stone in my mind, I suppose.'

'And the field wench,' added Catchpoll, 'was out in the village proper, and would not have heard as quick as by next morning what had happened to Aldith in the manor if the wench slept by the kitchen.'

'And Rhydian did know he was persistent,' mused Walkelin, almost to himself, taking up the word. 'That is why he argued with his master that evening, warning him to curb his desires. He did not know what really happened in Bromfield.' Walkelin shook his head. 'He closed his mind to it as much as he could. The cook gave us that at the first. She said he indicated his master was a good man but susceptible to forward women, and said he looked as if trying to get himself to believe it true.'

'We also had brother trying to place brother before us as the killer, or at least the one who ordered the killing, and without the compelling reason of seeing Milburga being attacked, we were casting about for reasons, none of which ever sat well.' Bradecote ran his hand through his hair. 'Dog chasing its tail. You are right there, Walkelin.'

'But you got to the truth, my lord, and in no longer a time than Hywel ap Rhodri was in this manor. My prince will not see that as failing.' Rhys tried to sound encouraging.

'Ah, well he is the person we have not failed, since we could not chase after Rhydian two weeks after he left.' Bradecote pulled a face. 'But you see, if we had taken Thorold earlier, Corbin would have been saved a broken head, and the lady Matilda her death.'

'Couldn't have taken Thorold FitzRoger before he hit the lad, not as it stood, my lord, not with more than suspicion as would not stand, and once we had tried to get what we could from Corbin we came. We just came a mite too late for the lady.' Catchpoll disliked Bradecote's tendency to flog himself over failings he could only see with hindsight. There was quiet for a while.

'So tell me again, why did the lad Corbin take the body all the way to the next Hundred and not just bury it in a field by here, where none would reveal what had occurred?' Rhys ap Iorwerth had had a long day.

'Ah,' Bradecote leant back against the wall, and looked less brooding. 'I think the answer lies in the fact that these people are not criminals.'

'But they committed a crime by conceal—'

'I did not say they did not commit a crime, just they are not criminals. Hear me on this. They think like ordinary people. They are afraid of the law. You did not hear what Aldith said to Walkelin, that she did not think the law would care for what happened to her because she was just a servant girl. They know the law about the proof of Englishry. If the body turns up in their Hundred, they are amerced for it if the corpse is not proven English, and they knew Hywel ap Rhodri was not. A criminal would assess the risks and see it would be better to know where the body lies, and keep it deep. These people reacted out of instinct . . . They wanted the body far away, and since they have his horse, they cannot cry foul murder upon Rhydian, because they are complicit. Corbin mistakenly took the body too far and back into his Hundred, but that was ignorance.'

'You know we were led astray from the beginning, by the lady Susanna ferch Gruffydd,' concluded Bradecote, and, as Rhys opened his mouth to speak, added, 'not by intent, no. But her words were so keenly felt. "Faithful unto death" was true, except in the end it was Hywel ap Rhodri's death. We could only see that Rhydian would have had to be killed if Hywel was killed, and were fretting over where we could find, or even look for, the body.'

'You know, Hywel ap Rhodri never knew that when he came to England, he brought a conscience with him, and that conscience smote him.' Rhys ap Iorwerth shook his head and yawned. 'I am for sleep.'

They parted from the Welsh interpreter after they had broken their fast next morning, and with some amity, even from Serjeant Catchpoll, who recommended that he was careful not to catch a chill when it began to rain upon him as he crossed the border.

'I was never proud to have English blood, not before now,' admitted Rhys. 'It has always seemed to make me a lesser man among my peers, though the knowledge of the tongue gained me position at court. I had never been here, see. Now I know I need not feel any shame, because good men are good men, and bad ones bad, and how we say our words matters little, excepting in the understanding between the two. The English are not all thieving hell-fiends.'

'That is good to know.' Walkelin grinned. 'I am not sure how to be a "hell-fiend".'

'That is because your mother brought you up properly, young Walkelin.' Catchpoll winked at him. 'You would not be much good at thieving, either.'

'Well, I took the mare from the pease field edge to help me

find the brown horse, but I took her back again afterwards, so that would certainly make me a poor thief.'

'Think how much easier our lives would be, if thieves returned everything afterwards,' sighed Catchpoll.

'Easier perhaps, Catchpoll, but if that day came you would shrivel like a leaf in frost with nothing to do.' Bradecote gave a lopsided smile.

'True enough, my lord. I wasn't quite born a serjeant, but serjeanting has been my life more years than worth counting, and I dare say I will not stop serjeanting until my final breath, which is in God's hands as to when.'

'There's morbid.' Rhys looked a bit surprised.

'Not at all. I calls it hopeful. I cannot think of a better way of things.'

'Well, I hope that lies years hence, and wish you, all three, good hunting of them as breaks the law.' Rhys looked at Bradecote. 'I will tell Madog ap Maredudd the bad things, and the good outcome, for good it was, and the only mystery will be what happened to Rhydian and that grey pony, which I think will not give him sleepless nights. I bid you farewell, my lord.' Rhys ap Iorwerth made obeisance, and mounted his horse.

'Take care upon the road home, and God speed to you,' Bradecote nodded, and the Welshman trotted away, raising a hand before he turned a corner and was lost to view.

'Rather him than me, in all that damp, wet, miserable—'

'Yes, Catchpoll, we know what you think of Wales.' Bradecote smiled, and clapped the serjeant on the back. His face became thoughtful. 'It is strange, but Doddenham may be the better for all this.'

'My lord?' Walkelin looked puzzled.

'Brictmer said Thorold FitzRoger was a good lord, because he did not act in haste, yet in the end his judgement was flawed, and he was getting no heir.'

'But that would mean his brother inherited anyway, in time.'

'Yes, but he was not able to secure a bride himself, so there was no guarantee at all he would sire sons when he did get the manor, if he lived long enough. Now he is lord and will find a wife.'

'But the lady Avelina . . . He cannot wed her,' said Walkelin.

'No, though lust rather than love joined them. I think she will be sent from here swiftly, back to her own kin, the widow to be wife again elsewhere, with looks like hers, and hopefully without a husband's mother to get in the way, and with a husband to husband her.'

'And Durand's bride will not have another woman giving the orders,' nodded Catchpoll.

'Nor will Durand. I cannot say I like the man, only that he may do better than his brother, and what I think is unimportant.'

'Unless you are me, my lord. It is pretty important to me.' Walkelin could not hide the grin.

'Thank you, Walkelin. My day is the better for the knowledge.'

Their own departure from Doddenham was a mixture of cool formality and real thanks. Durand FitzRoger had woken to the realisation that what he had always wanted was his, and without the overbearing presence of his mother, but the image of her staring, sightless, up at him, dampened his pleasure for a while. The lady Avelina was somehow less lady of the manor, and yet not yet the widow, so was trapped. She was realistic enough to see her time at Doddenham was limited, and did not much regret it. Next time, she hoped, she would be at least as fortunate as other wives. They both bid the sheriff's men farewell with formal words and little feeling.

This was not the case among the villagers. Aldith had been prised from Corbin's bedside to attend her duties in the hall, but Corbin lay looking much improved, and with a stronger colour that his father called upon all to see. He still had no memory of being hit upon the head, but was able to recall everything up until he stood in the bailey with the brown horse discovered.

Bradecote took note that the broom in the little cottage had seen use, and the place already had the look of one with a woman in it.

'Aye, and glad I will be to have her here. We might be bullied a bit about the home, for she is a strong-willed wench, but she will do Corbin no end of good, make him grow up – and as for me, ah, I learnt long years back how to give in graceful like, to the woman of the house.' Brictmer beamed at them.

Catchpoll asked about serving Durand FitzRoger.

'We shall see what we shall see, with him. It might have sobered him, and if he settles, well, we should get on well enough. I sees no use in looking for problems before they comes and finds me.'

'Very sound, very sound,' approved Catchpoll.

'And Brictmer, I said to the lord Durand that the law was clear upon the horse of Hywel ap Rhodri. By his law and ours both, the beast is to sell on Milburga's behalf, and the money kept for her as dower. He will not question that.'

'Thank you, my lord. It will take time but . . . it will take time.'

'We have discussed also how we take our prisoner to Worcester.' Giving FitzRoger title and status now seemed wrong. 'He should, by right, follow us bound, and upon foot, but we have homes and families, and do not relish delay. If you permit, we will take him, bound, but upon that brown horse. The man will not be returning, so we would see the horse sold for the best price in Worcester and send young Walkelin back with whatever it fetches, to be kept for Milburga. If you keep the horse, you have to feed it, and there is always the risk it might fall sick and die. This way the coin is secured.'

'You would get a better price in Worcester and we have much to do in these months coming, upon the land. Thank you, my lord. What you suggest seems best, and I know that the coin will come back.' The steward was both relieved and pleased.

They spoke briefly to Father Dunstan, who sent them upon their way with his blessing, and then mounted to take the Worcester road. They came a while after to the dip where the little stream marked the Hundred boundary, and glanced up to the left to the trees among which Hywel ap Rhodri's corpse had been found. It felt a long time ago.

'That, my lord,' remarked Catchpoll, 'is made the more so by him being just a victim at the start of it, and becoming as much the criminal before the end. We have, so to speak, two men.'

'Do we tell all to the priest at Cotheridge, Catchpoll?'

'It is not so far as gossip will not come through Broadwas. I think we gives him the truth, with a few details left to slip quiet into "forgotten", my lord.'

'Yes, that is the best course.'

So they diverted off the trackway to the little church, and its near blind priest, who welcomed undersheriff and serjeant cheerily, and listened to what they had to say, whilst Walkelin hung back with their prisoner.

'I will speak with my flock. I doubt they will offer any more prayers for the man buried here, but as long as they leave him to God's judgement, I will be content, and they will pray for the innocent, wherever they may be. I shall see to that. Will you also inform Father Prior in Worcester, my lord?'

'Yes, I will see that done.'

'Thank you.'

There was amicable silence among the sheriff's men, and morose silence from FitzRoger, as they descended from the ridge above the Teme. Then Bradecote asked the question to which he had wanted the answer for the better part of the time he had known the old serjeant.

'It is no use, Catchpoll. I have to ask, though you can refuse to answer. Why is it that you hate everything Welsh?' He turned his head to look at him in profile. Catchpoll sniffed, and shrugged.

'Nearest you could call it is "blood feud", my lord, though that is more personal. Come down the family it has, and it goes against the grain to do aught but follow it.' He paused, and then, as if it were a failing, mumbled, 'My oldmother, my father's dam, came out of Herefordshire.'

Bradecote looked puzzled, then his brow cleared a little.

'Ah, over on the border th—'

'South of Hereford. The Welsh burnt it, bit over ten years before yo—the Battle, and King William.' Catchpoll felt it was wrong to feel Bradecote was 'foreign', and there was English enough lineage on the distaffs. 'They burnt Hereford, and they burnt the place she lived. Mite she was, no more than seven or eight, I suppose. They killed her father, though she did not see, and she hid, hid well enough they did not find her as they did her mother and sister. She saw that well enough, and we was brought up to know . . . and promise . . . As a place, as a people, I will keep to that. As for single souls, I am not so foolish as to think all for damning. Drogo's wife, well, she has lived in England long enough to lose the taint, if not the accent at times, and that wench of Walkelin's. He may make near an Englishwoman of her yet, and they are women. Hard it went with me to be civil with Rhys the Interpreter, mighty hard, but I cannot lie. He was a fair man, and the action of Rhydian the servant we shall never see . . . I find no fault. Just do not expect me to praise their weather, their tongue, their morals, and this, this never goes further. Even the lord Sheriff knows it not.'

'It goes not further, Catchpoll. That I swear. It is known, and being so, is forgotten.'

'Thank you, my lord.'

They crossed the Severn just after noon, and led their mounts up to the castle, with Bradecote already rehearsing all that he would say to William de Beauchamp. Walkelin took FitzRoger to the cells, and his superiors went in search of the lord Sheriff. He was in a chamber, dictating to a scribe, whom he sent away with a gesture of dismissal, and looked at his men.

'Well?' There was a certain glitter to his eyes that Catchpoll found disconcerting.

Hugh Bradecote, Undersheriff, made his report.

'It sounds a tangle, my lord, and so it was, but—'

'Oh, I do not doubt you. Indeed, as of yesterday I knew it all, at least as far as the death of the Welshman went.' De Beauchamp enjoyed the look of consternation upon the faces of his men. 'The rest is new, of course, and I cannot say the loss of Thorold FitzRoger troubles me much. His brother may be useful yet, and a better man, though he will have his work cut out to make his men worth their employ.' William de Beauchamp laughed without mirth. 'Last time FitzRoger paid service I heard his overlord complained that they were the most useless heap he had ever seen.'

Bradecote was still coming to terms with the lord Sheriff's knowing about Hywel ap Rhodri.

'Know it all, my lord? How?' He sounded suitably astounded.

'Because the Prince of Powys sent word, not by a messenger upon a fleet horse, but a traveller nonetheless, who presented it to me yesterday. It seems the servant killed the master all along, but not as a murder but defending a young girl Hywel ap Rhodri was in the process of raping. He still killed his lord, his master, and so, in penance, walked barefoot to Brecon Priory, by way of Hereford, which is why you heard nothing of him to the north. He arrived, barely able to place one bleeding foot in front of the other, and half-starved, and only after two days was he fit to make his confession and request the prior send word to Madog ap Maredudd, with the pony, which was Hywel's widow's, by right, and the man's belongings. Madog said he was incredulous, but that his wife, the lady Susanna, corroborated that Hywel ap Rhodri was a danger to women, and so he has declared that Rhydian may remain with the brothers in Brecon, where he wishes to take the cowl. The prince sent to me, that you might have no further troubles.'

'Well, he will hear how we made the discovery of the full truth ourselves, when Rhys ap Iorwerth reaches Mathrafal, and know English justice is fair.'

'Fair? Is it?' William de Beauchamp looked disbelieving. 'I will say as it could be a lot worse, and that will suffice me.'

'My lord, you spoke of not taking the murdrum fine in this case. Since it was of a Welshman by a Welshman, I take it that remains true?'

'It does, Bradecote, not least because it would fall upon the Hundred in which Durand FitzRoger needs to find his fee, so to speak, and it would not help. We can forego it quite correctly.'

'Then am I free to go, my lord? I have but to report to the Prior of St Mary's about Hywel ap Rhodri, and would then be about my own business. I hope the hay is near in.'

'Yes, you may go, but do not tell me you will gallop home to see the state of your hayfield.' He grinned, lewdly, and Bradecote's cheeks reddened. 'Catchpoll, I want you to be seen about the river wharves. The hot weather has meant frayed tempers, and brawls over who puts what where, and as yet none has had more than a bloody nose, but it would be useful for your own nose to be seen parading up and down to remind everyone to keep civil.'

'Aye, my lord, I will see to it.'

'Good. You can send the scribe back in as you leave.'

* * *

Hugh Bradecote entered the cool calm of the Priory of St Mary's, and was shown to the prior's lodgings by a brother who could ask after a cousin upon Bradecote's manor. He waited, at ease, whilst the same brother hastened to find Father Prior, who came, and listened, and sighed as Bradecote knew he would.

'The greater the sinner, the greater the need for us to pray for his soul, but I confess myself that the foul deeds of the Welshman are such as try my compassion, which, unlike that of the Almighty, is not boundless. We will continue to pray for his soul, undoubtedly in torment, but in addition will pray for all those he harmed, known and unknown.'

Before he left, Bradecote also left coin and a request, blushingly made, to Father Prior for prayers of a different kind.

'Be sure, my son, I shall include them in my prayers each day for all the next month. Your lady wife is a good daughter of the Church, and kindly remembered for her aid to our brothers in distress when . . . after Christmas. That she continued her pilgrimage to Polesworth even after the events shows devotion. I am sure her prayers, and ours for her, will be answered.'

'Thank you, Father.'

Bradecote left a little lighter of pocket but also of heart and returned to the castle to collect his horse. Catchpoll and Walkelin were about to set off to the riverside, having slipped away to Mistress Catchpoll for ale and bread. Thus fortified, they felt quite up to patrolling the wharfage. Bradecote mounted his steel-grey horse and looked down at the other two.

'Do as Serjeant Catchpoll instructs you, Walkelin, and also remember, if it comes to public brawls, it is better to stand back and let them wear themselves out a bit first before you step in and take charge. Correct, Serjeant?'

'Most correct, my lord.' Catchpoll grinned, and nodded, which was all the obeisance offered or needed. 'And I hope as your hay is ricked, and your lordling thinking of taking his first steps.'

'Thank you, Catchpoll.' He wheeled his horse about and trotted out under the castle gate.

'Now, young Walkelin,' Catchpoll rubbed his hands together, 'let us remind Worcester we are back.'

SARAH HAWKSWOOD describes herself as a 'wordsmith' who is only really happy when writing. She read Modern History at Oxford and first published a non-fiction book on the Royal Marines in the First World War before moving on to mediaeval mysteries set in Worcestershire.

bradecoteandcatchpoll.com